A Tast‹

Christine Axford

A Taste of Red

Copyright © 2022 by Christine Axford

This book is a work of fiction.

Names, characters, places, and incidents either are the product of the author's imagination or are used fictiously. Any resemblance to actual persons, living or dead, or is purely coincidental.

^^CONTENT WARNING^^

This book contains mature language and explicit sex scenes.

It is not intended for readers under the age of 18.

ISBN: 978-1-7774106-4-3

CONTENTS
A TASTE OF RED

BOOKS ALSO PUBLISHED BY
CHRISTINE AXFORD

His Angel Trilogy Series

One is a Promise (His Angel – Book One)

Two is Tantalizing (His Angel – Book Two)

Three is Precarious (His Angel – Book Three)

Writing happily ever after's, one word at a time.

Happy reading and best wishes,

Christine Axford

CHAPTER ONE

Kinsley

I huff in frustration looking at the pile of clothes scattered all over the bedroom floor and on the bed. I've changed my outfit for what feels like the hundredth time, and nothing looks remotely good on me. I severely need a wardrobe makeover. I have dozens of floor length skirts, primarily in black, and old lady blouses that should likely be burned.

I glance at the clock, knowing I have to hustle or I'm going to be late. *I can't be late!* I snatch a long black skirt off the floor and select a plain white silk blouse from my closet with a matching black blazer. I dress quickly, not bothering to look at myself in the mirror. I already know I'm dressed like a nun. I leave the top two buttons of my blouse undone, showing a smidgen of cleavage. Okay, I don't have a baby's bum at all. I really need to buy some push-up bras. I swear my current bra makes me look flat-chested. *You are flat-chested, Kinsley. Ugh!*

I pull my hair back into a ponytail, twisting it into a bun, and sticking a dozen pins in to ensure a strand doesn't fall out. I then apply a coat of hairspray for good measure, giving my head a bob to ensure everything stays in place. Good enough.

I look down at my contact lens case on the bathroom counter. I don't wear them often because they give me a headache after a few hours. Not that my glasses are much better, the bridge of my nose will start to ache in no time. They're big and clunky, but I can't afford new ones, *yet*. Why couldn't I have been blessed with twenty-twenty vision and bigger boobs? I'm blind as a bat without my glasses, and put a pair of pants and a t-shirt on me, and I can definitely pass as a boy. The only thing going for me is my lengthy long legs and my very vibrant red hair. But I keep my fiery red locks in a tight bun all day, every day.

Yeah, I don't have a chance in hell in getting this job.

Everyone knows Eric Dekker only hires blonde goddesses with cantaloupe sized fake boobs as his personal assistant. Occasionally, he has strayed and will hire a brunette beauty, but either way, none of them last very long.

This is the sixth or seventh time this job has been posted that I recall in the last year and a half. He goes through his assistants as fast as people drink water. Most of them last a month or two if they're lucky, and then they suddenly disappear. Speculation has it that all the women he has hired, and then fired, are sent away. Not sure what "away" entails, but some say he fires them with a hefty severance package that also buys their silence. That rumor seems a little more reliable and logical.

But others, mostly women, say that he locks them up in a secret location and uses them as his personal sex slaves, one for each day of the week. I guess that's one way to never get bored with your food. I shiver at that thought.

I can't imagine what it would feel like to be with a man like Eric Dekker. A "God above all Gods." That's what he is according to the media. New York's most eligible and coveted bachelor, and from the photos I've seen on social media, you can see why he's so desirable. Always dressed in an immaculately designer suit that molds perfectly to his body, showcasing his muscular physique and leaving nothing to the imagination. You know exactly what lies beneath his expensive clothing, more godly perfection.

I remove my glasses and opt for my contact lenses. I'll be gone for a couple hours, tops. I pop them into my eyes, moving them around with my fingertip, and then blink a few times to get them into position.

My cell phone dings, and I snatch it up, reading the incoming text message. The cab driver is here. *Crap!* I quickly brush my teeth, grab my purse and keys, and fly out the door. I only get two feet away when I realize I'm barefoot. I curse again, bulleting back into my apartment and grabbing my black high heels off the floor.

"Bye, Mittens!" I shout, slamming the door.

The cab driver gives me a nod in greeting as I haul myself into the back seat. I give him the address of my destination, and a second later, he's pulling away. I slip my heels on and curse a dozen more times, realizing I should have probably left earlier. Traffic in New York is hell, but at least it's not the afternoon rush hour yet. I glance at the clock. I have one hour to get to the Dekker Enterprises Holdings Inc. building. It should be enough time. *I hope...*

As the cab driver nears the building, I press my cheek against the window, craning my neck to see the pristine building come into view. Apparently, there are ninety floors filled with offices, but the first two levels have multiple commercial businesses like Starbucks, a few high-end restaurants and designer shops, and a private health club.

"That will be fifty-two dollars," the driver says, and my neck whips back to look at him.

One, I didn't even realize we had stopped, and two, fifty-two dollars? *Ouch!*

I hand him my Visa card since my bank account is suffering. I'm running on fumes. I desperately need this job, and with the base salary starting at fifty thousand dollars, landing this job would be hitting the jackpot. Most personal assistants starting out make at least ten grand less. I check the time again and see I've got thirteen minutes to spare. I hop out of the cab, thanking him, then tilt my neck back, looking way up.

It's not as tall as the Empire State Building, but holy cow, the endless wall of mirrored glass panes seems to go on forever.

The building is super sleek with curved panels and round corners giving it a superior architectural design. But what makes it stand out the most, is the yacht shape entrance that juts out predominantly, showing the world it's a force to be reckoned with and proudly making a statement.

After gawking on the sidewalk for a good minute, I make my way to the front entrance and through the revolving doors. My eyes immediately dart around, looking for the reception desk. I spot it to the left and rush over, knowing I'm cutting it close. *I'll gawk later.* When I approach, the lady behind the plexiglass wall doesn't acknowledge me as she keeps tapping away on her keyboard.

"Good afternoon. My name is Kinsley Everett. I have an interview with Mr. Dekker at 3:30."

Her hands stop clicking as her eyes slowly drift upwards, giving me the once over. She then gives me a snub look with an exaggerated eye roll.

Okay, who pissed in your cornflakes this morning?

"Take the elevator on your right to the ninetieth floor. Mrs. Davis will be waiting," she clips in an irritated tone and practically throws a visitor tag at me.

I attach the tag to my blouse, thanking her, even though I should tell her to get the stick out of her ass. *Jeez, why do some women think their shit doesn't stink?* Just because you wear designer clothes and have gaudy jewelry that costs more than the average person's salary, does it make you better than everyone else? *No!* It makes you a spoiled, stuck-up, snotty bitch that severely needs to get laid! Okay, I'm not sure about that last part. I've just heard women are more upbeat if they get laid regularly.

I can see that being true, but I personally don't know myself. I had sex once, almost three years ago, and it was a complete disaster. It was enough for me to not go looking for it again. Not that I have suitors lining up at my door, I'm a bit of a hermit. Socializing and me, don't mix. I think that's what people call an introvert, which is fine. I like being alone.

After the security guard swipes his card, allowing me access into the elevator, I arrive on the ninetieth floor. As the doors open, a middle-aged lady is waiting with a big smile on her face.

"Ms. Everett?"

"Yes, that's me."

"Oh good. I was starting to worry you weren't going to show up."

"I'm very sorry. I know I'm cutting it close."

"No worries, dear. We all know traffic can be hell, and Mr. Dekker is still with another interviewee. They should be wrapping up shortly. Please, follow me."

I nod and fall in step beside her.

"I'm sorry, I just realized I forgot to introduce myself. I'm Ivy Davis. I don't work for Mr. Dekker directly, but since he is short an assistant, I'm filling in temporarily."

"Have you known Mr. Dekker for long?" I venture asking.

"Oh yes. I've known Eric since he was in diapers. Cutest baby ever, with the most adorable dimples if you ask me."

In the pictures I've seen of Eric, he is always stone-faced. I don't think I've ever seen him in a photo with a smile.

"He knows how to smile?" I blurt before I can stop myself.

Ivy stops abruptly as she cracks up laughing beside me. I feel my face burn red hot with embarrassment. *I can't believe I just said that!*

"I like you, Kinsley. I really hope Eric gives you a chance. I've viewed your credentials, you're smart and actually have a brain. I wish I could say the same for the other half twits that apply for this position, but don't tell Eric I said that."

"I won't, and I wish I could share your optimism," I say solemnly.

Everyone knows you have to have big melons to work for Mr. Dekker. I'm really not sure why I even applied.

Money, Kinsley, you need the money badly.

Ivy puts her hand on my forearm.

"I think it's time for a change around here, and I have a good feeling about you," she says with a wink.

I give her a brief smile, keeping my mouth closed. Unless Ivy has some kind of special power or heavy pull around here, it will take a miracle to land this job.

Once we reach the reception area, she tells me to make myself comfortable, she needs to grab some files for Mr. Dekker. I nod, sitting down in one of the vacant chairs, and then quickly pull out my compact mirror, making sure my hair is still all in place. I then check my teeth for good measure. *Squeaky clean.* As I put my compact away, I feel the jitters set in as I stare straight ahead, assuming the closed door twenty feet away from me is where the infamous Mr. Dekker awaits.

Of course, I've heard several rumors about him. One being he's a cut-throat businessman that doesn't care who he railroads to get what he wants.

Ruthless.

Heartless.

And a self-made billionaire.

Makes sense seeing how he owns half of New York. But then, there are other rumors from women that covet him, saying he's the Kink Master in the bedroom. He likes his whips and chains. I shiver at that thought. No offense, but who in their right mind would willingly let a man whip them? And I don't care if your name is Mr. Dekker, *a male sex God*, no one is taking a whip to me. I bruise like a damn peach!

I strain my ears, listening for voices behind Dekker's door, but I don't hear a thing. That doesn't surprise me. Most of these buildings are virtually soundproof. You probably have to plaster your eardrum to the door to hear anything, and even then, you'll hear mumbling at best.

I sigh, looking down at my blouse, wondering if I should do up the buttons or not, when suddenly his office door opens. My mouth falls open when a blonde bombshell saunters out, swaying her curvy hips side to side with an enormous grin on her face. My eyes drift down to her breasts, seeing the endless cleavage on display. *Melons. Goddamn melons.*

The blonde beauty gives me the once over and then scoffs, surveying my flat chest.

Christ, Kinsley, why didn't you stuff your bra?

My hands quickly button up the top of my blouse, and she lets out a snort-laugh. My face burns with humiliation. I have no business being here. I may have an outstanding IQ, but clearly, that's not going to land me this job.

She pulls out a tissue from her purse, dabbing the corner of her mouth, and then licks her luscious lips with an "mmm" sound. You certainly don't need to have a high IQ to tell me what she just finished doing. She gives me a condescending smile with a devilish wink, and my spirits drop further as she strolls away. I watch her hips sashay back and forth dramatically. She's the epitome of a real woman.

I'm about to put my tail between my legs, and leave when Eric appears in his doorway... fixing the waistband of his pants.

Yup, blowjob.

"Oh, Eric, good timing. I just finished copying that file you asked for," Ivy says, holding out a thick black folder.

"Thank you, Ivy," he says, taking it from her. "Could you please write up an offer letter for Ms. Stellar? I would like her—"

"Eric, you have one more interview," Ivy cuts in right away as she signals to me.

Once again, I feel my cheeks flame with heat as soon as Mr. Dekker's dark eyes connect with mine. He hadn't even noticed me sitting here, but that doesn't surprise me. I'm one of those people that blend into the background. But now, I fight the urge to squirm in my seat as he openly inspects me. His expression remains impassive, but there's no doubt, he is scrutinizing every inch of me. *Yeah, I know I look like a nun and don't have a chance in hell.* I swallow the lump at the back of my throat, along with my pride as I stand.

"It's okay, Mrs. Davis. Mr. Dekker has made his decision. No sense wasting his time. It was very nice meeting you," I approach Ivy, extending my hand to shake.

My blasted heart thumps wildly in my chest as my stomach catapults into somersaults, when I'm merely standing a few inches away from him. His masculine cologne is quick to strike, smothering my senses and embedding itself deep into my pores. I know his scent will leave a lasting effect, something I'll never forget. Rich, decadent, with a hint of sandalwood, and extremely intoxicating, like the man himself.

"Please, call me Ivy, and I'm sorry, dear," she whispers.

I shake my head, giving her a tentative smile, and not trusting my voice to speak. I would be lying if my heart didn't feel like it's being crushed. This job was my last hope, but it's not her fault I wasn't born a blonde goddess.

I guess Ms. Stellar gave Dekker a stellar performance.

I avoid looking at Eric, but somehow, I feel his eyes boring into me.

"I'll just see myself out." I bow my head to Eric out of respect. "Best of luck to you, Mr. Dekker, and your new assistant," I politely say and turn to leave.

I tell myself I won't cry until I'm alone in my bed. I press the elevator button a dozen times, begging the doors to open and swallow me whole. Another job down the tubes because no one wants to hire a woman that dresses like a nun and doesn't have a curvy figure. I never thought in a million years it would have been this hard to find another job. Finally, the elevator door dings indicating its arrival, and then slide open.

"Ms. Everett."

I freeze on the spot as goosebumps spread across my skin hearing Mr. Dekker call my name.

"Ms. Everett, I believe I owe you an apology. I jumped the gun, not realizing I had another application." I don't have to turn around to know he's standing right behind me. I can feel the heat from his body, and his delicious scent is coiling around me, smothering my senses like a deadly snake. "Please, if you will. I would like to discuss your resume and credentials. That's if you're still interested in the position?"

Part of me wants to say, " *Why bother? We both know you're going to hire blondie. You know, the one you were just straightening your pants after, I'll suck your cock all day long, if you hire me.* " But the other part, the voice that's screaming inside my head, "Y *our life depends on this job, Kinsley.* " And because of that, I can't turn down this one percent opportunity. I don't have a clue how I will be able to change his mind, but I need to try or I'm going to find myself out on the street soon.

The elevator door closes, and I take a deep breath before turning around and facing the eminent Mr. Dekker. In an instant, I feel the air shift around us, crackling with energy as we come face to face, with inches separating us. I have to physically suppress a gasp as his dark eyes dilate, growing intense. Dekker is tall, but so am I, and when you add my heels into the equation, we stand eye to eye.

I was considered a mammoth during elementary school when all the girls my age were only five-foot-one at best, but at the ripe age of thirteen, I shot up like a bad weed, towering over all at five-foot-five. I eventually settled on five-foot-ten.

His eyes slowly skim down my face until they settle on my lips momentarily, then back up to my cheeks. I bite my bottom lip out of nervousness. I don't like being scrutinized. I know I have freckles splattered across my cheekbones, I'm a redhead, it comes with the territory. At least they seem to have faded over the last couple of years. They're not as prominent as in my younger years, and the kids loved to remind me they were there. You know, the whole "hey, freckle face," I heard a million times.

I lower my lashes, considering he hasn't stopped inspecting me in the last thirty seconds. The close proximity to him is slightly nerve wracking. I've never had a man look at me this long, and I'm not sure what to make of it. I can feel the heat rolling off his body, but not only that, his posture asserts power and authority while he stands there motionless in his perfectly tailored suit. And his eyes... dear Lord, help me. They are dark, and brooding, and demand your attention.

"Yes, I am still very much interested in the position, but I don't want to waste your time, Mr. Dekker. You are a busy man, and I completely understand your decision," I finally speak up, breaking the strange tension happening between us.

"My decision is not final."

I give my head a nod, and he steps aside, holding out his arm and signaling me in the direction of his office.

"Thank you," I whisper and force my legs to move.

For a moment, I think he's going to guide me to his office with his hand on my back. It's there... almost touching, but he drops his arm a second later. *Thank God!* I'm sure if he had touched me, I would have liquefied on the spot. He gives his head a nod, and I make my way to his office as my heart rate kicks up, with the reality, I'm going to be alone with this man in a few seconds. *Oh God, I hope I don't pass out or make a fool of myself.*

CHAPTER TWO

Kinsley

Ivy's face breaks out in a wide grin as I pass by. "Good luck," she mouths.

I smile and enter Dekker's office. Why I call him Dekker, I'm not sure. It seems more fitting, and I'm also not used to voicing his first name. If I land this job by the grace of the Gods, I'll call him Mr. Dekker or Sir. It's more traditional and formal, given his stature.

As soon as I step foot into his office, I'm hit with the smell of mahogany and leather with a hint of lemon polish as I take in the extensive space. It's tastefully decorated with a wall of floor-to-ceiling windows directly in front of me, and an open view of the vibrant city to my right.

"Please, have a seat, Ms. Everett. I'll just grab your file." His voice is low, like liquid amber tumbling across my skin, and I realize I haven't moved, I've been gawking.

"Sorry," I mumble, feeling my cheeks heat a little, and I lower myself into one of the vacant high-back chairs facing the front of his desk. He disappears a second later, and I take in his large solid oak desk. I can't help that my mind goes straight to the gutter, wondering how many women he has bent over this desk. *Probably hundreds.*

Can I be one of those hundreds? Ugh, Kinsley!

It's hard not to fantasize about Dekker and what lies beneath that solid exterior. Probably an oasis of heavenly rugged plains waiting to be discovered, *by me.*

Kinsley, for the love of God, snap out of it.

I can picture him dominating a woman in every aspect. Commanding her down on her knees, or bent over his desk while he pulverizes her pussy. He'll be ruthless, taking what he wants. There's no softness on his part, but the woman will cum like a freight train, hard and with endless tremors, because it will be the best sex she's ever had. She'll be ruined for all other men. I imagine no one will even come close to Dekker.

In my next life, I'll wish to be blonde with big boobs so I can experience that just once.

The door closes with a soft click, snapping me out of my lustful haze. I need to focus and pray I'll be able to change his mind. I have no doubt, he's merely entertaining this to clear his conscience, if he has one. Why he is giving me the time of day, is beyond me. I was a millimeter away from never seeing him again, and he probably wouldn't have given me a second thought. So why not just let me go?

He sits in his chair and lays out a vanilla colored folder. He doesn't acknowledge me, he's reading over my resume. I sit there quietly as I absorb his facial features and exquisite scent some more.

Beautiful.

Flawless.

Enchanting.

With a side of darkness that's ominous, sinful and a hazard to your health. That's what Dekker is to me.

A minute of silence passes as he flips through the various diplomas I've acquired, before he eases back in his chair, placing his hands in his lap, and studies me for a moment. My hands clam up instantly as I suddenly get very hot under the collar. I clutch my hands together, resisting the urge to fan my face.

Christ, why is he looking at me like that?

I don't know what to make of his silence or expression, or lack of one. He's always stone-faced, and I'm convinced the man doesn't even know how to smile.

"That's an impressive resume you have," he finally divulges in a deep baritone voice that flows through me like a gentle wave.

"Thank you, Sir."

His eyes darken, narrowing for a split second as his jaw twitches. If I didn't know any better, I'd think he likes being called Sir. I'm not stupid or naïve, and I've watched enough porn videos to know men that practice bondage, like being called Sir or Master. If I had to venture, I'd say Dekker is one of them. The ladies do call him the Kink Master. Maybe he prefers Master? It doesn't matter, I'm accustomed to saying Sir from my previous job. Call me old fashion, but I personally think it's more professional.

"I see you have your MBA and that you attended Berkeley. Are you from California originally?"

"I am."

"What brings you to New York?"

"After university, I was offered a job at Calver Stone in New York, three years ago. I researched the company and knew they had great core values honesty and integrity with a family oriented team. They had been around for over two decades and were expanding. They were distinguished and profitable, so I didn't hesitate to take the job. But, unfortunately, they were bought out, and I was handed a severance package three months ago."

I'm pretty sure Dekker is the reason why I'm out of a job. He's the one that bought Calver Stone and then gave everyone the boot. All I got was a measly three-month severance package.

"I see."

He doesn't comment further or show recognition, but that doesn't surprise me. He doesn't need to. It's not his life that was affected. Only more than two hundred people are out of a job because of him.

"It says you also studied law briefly. What made you decide against becoming a lawyer?"

"I found there was too much focus on politics for me. Too shady, too much red tape, and eighty percent of the time, it seems the bad guys are set free on a technicality."

"I would have to agree with you, Ms. Everett. Our legal system is full of dishonest people. You can't grow a conscience in that field, or you may find yourself self-destructing. You need to be cut throat, show no remorse. A business can be very much the same, but with less politics."

Meaning yourself and your company.

I give him a nod, and once again, silence falls as we stare at one another. It's like he doesn't know what to make of me, and well, I have no idea what's going on in his head.

"What do you do for fun, Ms. Everett?"

I frown for a second as his question catches me off guard for a moment. *Fun? What's that?*

"Umm, nothing really, Sir. I live a boring life."

This makes his eyebrow shoot up.

"Don't get together with your lady friends? Have a night out on the town?"

I snort-laugh and then cover my mouth and nose, horrified. The corner of his mouth curls up a fraction, but it's gone in a blink of an eye.

"I'm sorry, Sir, I didn't mean to laugh. No, I don't go out. I'm a bit of a loner."

He nods and then looks down at my paperwork again.

"It says you can type seventy words a minute. Do you have time for a demonstration?"

"Of course."

He motions behind me, and I turn my head, seeing a computer has been set up. I stand and make my way over. I wonder how many other women have actually had to do this. *Blowjob or typing test? Blowjob, hands down.* It won't surprise me if I'm the first to ever use this computer.

As I lower myself into the seat, I wonder if that means he's actually considering me? A thrill of excitement runs through me. It has to mean something, right? *He's humoring you, Kinsley, don't bother getting your hopes up.*

I wiggle the mouse around, and a password is prompted. I turn my head to ask for the password, but I yelp instead, realizing Dekker is standing right behind me. Jeez, he's lethal and light on his toes. I'm surprised his cologne didn't give him away, but I was too busy daydreaming.

"Sorry, I didn't hear you come up behind me."

"Dekker1992."

Another frown creases my brow.

"Oh, password. Thank you."

He nods, and I type in the password. I can only assume that was the year he was born. Makes sense as I'm pretty sure I saw it was his birthday about a month ago. That would make him thirty. I can't even imagine what it would be like being a billionaire at his age. God has been more than good to him in all aspects.

I open the Word document, and he places a single sheet of paper beside me. Five hundred words. That's easy to tell. I look to Dekker for the go ahead. Our eyes connect, and I see that intensity again as his eyes drill into mine. I shiver. I can't help it. It shoots down my spine and into my toes. *Christ, why do his eyes have to be so darkly menacing, but yet alluring at the same time?* It's like he wants to slaughter or devour me. *Both are a frightening thought.*

"Umm, shall I start?"

His nod is subtle as he doesn't take his eyes off mine. I have to force myself to turn around in my seat, feeling anxiety roll through me, but not only that, a wave of desire. It's hard not to get caught up in his seductive eyes.

I clear my throat, wishing I had a bottle of water. My mouth is suddenly parched, while the rest of me is slightly sticky. *Especially between my legs.*

I blink my eyes a few times, clearing away the hold he has over me, and then start reading the words on the paper. My hands dance over the keyboard, typing. I'm a fast reader, and my hands tap away at lightning speed. Within minutes, I'm done. I timed myself, six minutes and forty-eight seconds. Not bad. I'm about to look for Mr. Dekker when my eyes catch a bottle of water sitting on the corner of the desk. *Oh, water!* I immediately uncap it, draining half the bottle, when I get the feeling I'm being watched again. I turn in my seat to see he's sitting behind his desk, watching me. I lower the bottle, putting the cap back on.

"Umm, thank you." He nods. "Is there anything else you would like to discuss or have me demonstrate?" I question since his silence is a little creepy while his damn eyes flay my skin.

"No. That will be all."

His lack of enthusiasm is disheartening. I'm not even sure why I bothered to get my hopes up. He has no intention of hiring me. I let out a sigh, standing and walking over to retrieve my purse. He stands as well.

"Mr. Dekker, it was a pleasure and honor to meet you. Ms. Stellar is a lucky lady, and I'm sure she will be a great asset to your company." I lower my head with a curtsy bow. *He is, after all, a God.*

I head to the door, and just as I crack it open, Dekker's voice booms out, "Ms. Everett, stop right there."

I jump, with my head snapping back and my eyes shooting wide. *Oh man, he looks pissed.*

"Close the door."

My hand is still on the door handle and is now slightly trembling. *Scratch that. My whole body is trembling.* Dekker comes closer when I don't move, and I watch his large hand come up and close the door. His powerful body crowds me, and I instinctively step back, flattening myself against the door. I know my eyes are still wide, I can feel them. He leans in closer, going beyond personal boundaries, and I find myself holding my breath. If I lean forward, our lips would almost be touching.

"What gave you the impression I was hiring another?"

His deep voice reverberates against my face like silky feathers, I have to physically stifle a groan. My pussy skips into overdrive, pulsating with desperate need. Either I'm going to pee my pants or cum on the spot. I'm not sure what I would prefer, bladder relief or orgasm? Probably both.

"I... umm... I just thought," I fumble my words like a moron, so I snap my mouth close.

"Your assumption is wrong, Ms. Everett. I would like to offer you the job."

My mouth falls wide open with disbelief.

"What? Are you serious?" I question.

"Yes. That's if you're still interested?"

Before I can stop myself, I throw my arms around him, crushing him in a hug. "Yes!" I shout.

His body goes ramrod stiff, and I feel my eyes bulge out. *Oh. My. God! What did I just do?* I quickly untangle myself from his steely hard body as my cheeks burn red hot with heat. I drop my head, utterly humiliated and avoid his eyes.

"I'm very sorry, Sir. I wasn't thinking. Please accept my apologies. I promise that will never happen again," I babble out in a rush.

"No need to apologize, Kinsley. You're excited, and rightfully so." Even Dekker seems out of sorts as his voice takes on a different octave, but I also noticed that he called me by my first name.

"Well… umm, I think on that note, I'll leave before I make a fool of myself further and have you regret your decision."

"Kinsley, look at me."

I haven't dared to look at him at this point, still mortified. I slowly lift my eyes to his to find they have softened, along with his facial features.

"I have a feeling I'm going to regret my decision, but not in the way you're thinking."

I narrow my eyes with a frown, not knowing what to make of his comment.

"Well, I'll make sure you don't regret your decision, Mr. Dekker. I'll be at your beck and call whenever you need me. I promise I won't let you down."

And just like that, his damn eyes glaze over with vivid intensity as I watch his jaw clench. It's like I've said something wrong, or perhaps right? Maybe I didn't choose my wording very well. Now that I think about it, it's like I just offered myself, meaning body, to him to use whenever he'd like. *God, I'm such an idiot!* He would probably rather poke his eyes out than be with me.

On that depressing note, I stick out my hand, now that he's put some space between us.

"Mr. Dekker, thank you for giving me this opportunity. I can't express what this means to me."

He takes my hand and squeezes with slight firmness, holding a little longer than normal standards, while his smoky grey eyes penetrate my face. Instantly, I feel all warm and fuzzy as my insides turn to putty. *Christ, I need to get out of here. And, no more touching the boss, Kinsley!* I smile and release my grip.

"I'll see you out."

"Oh, that's not necessary. I've taken up enough of your time," I counter back.

"I'll see you out," he says more firmly, and I snap my yap close.

Instead, I nod, and he leads me out, opening the door. Ivy peeks up from her desk with an expectant look.

"Ivy, please draw up an offer letter for Ms. Everett. Are you able to start on Monday?" he now asks.

"Yes, that will be perfect."

He nods, and Ivy beams at us.

"Yes, Mr. Dekker. I'll email it to you shortly, Kinsley, and congratulations," she says with a wink.

"Thank you, Ivy."

We proceed to the elevator, and I go to push the button, but our hands collide with a zip. I snatch mine back with my eyes shooting up to his. His jaw ticks with dark eyes scorching.

Talk about electric shock.

I thought you only get electric shocks in the wintertime? Maybe it's the air being this high up? I shake off the bizarre feeling as the elevator dings and the doors slide open. I step inside, facing Mr. Dekker, and he puts his hand out, preventing the door from closing.

"Kinsley."

"Yes, Mr. Dekker."

"Maybe you should consider celebrating. Let your hair down and let loose. You deserve it."

I laugh as I touch my bun at the back of my head, that's usually a permanent fixture. It's very rare that I wear it down. It's always in a bun, braid, or at best, a ponytail.

"Now, that would be a revelation for me. Not sure if I'm ready to take that leap yet."

"Change is good and sometimes inevitable."

"Yes, I suppose you're right. I'll give you a maybe. How's that?"

"I'll take a maybe."

I beam at him, and again, I see a ghost of a smile.

"Well, Mr. Dekker, you have a good weekend, and I'll see you on Monday."

"You as well, Kinsley."

He finally removes his hand from the door, letting it close shut. I breathe out a rush of air and slouch over. Good Lord, that man is intense, and now I have to work with him day in and day out. Not sure how I'm going to survive that. It's going to take a miracle for me not to space out and fantasize all day long. I already got one miracle today, so I'm sure I've used up all my wishes for the remainder of my life. Will power, that's all I need. And knowing that he is so far out of my league a chimpanzee probably has a better chance than me. *Now that's a depressing thought.*

Oh well. At least I have a job and no longer have to worry about living on the streets. Yes, I can always move back home, and my parents would take me in with open arms, but that would be admitting failure, and I hate failing. Or maybe it's my pride that would take a blow. Anyhow, I don't have to worry about that now. I just need to keep my spending at a bare minimum until I've built up a buffer. Unfortunately, I have been racking up my credit card these last couple of weeks. That will need paying first, along with my rent.

Before I reach the main floor, I undo the top two buttons of my blouse. I puff it out several times, trying to cool my heated skin. *Hot, too hot.* I remove my suit jacket. There, that's a little bit better. Once the elevator doors slide open, I decide to look around the clothing shops here in the building. I desperately need new clothing.

Maybe that's how I'll treat myself, buy a new outfit for Monday morning.

CHAPTER THREE

Kinsley

A fter returning my visitor badge to Ms. snooty pants, I enter the first clothing store I see. The sales lady hanging up a silk blouse gives me the once over. Of course, she's a blonde knockout, wearing a black, pencil skirt with a white formfitting top, accentuating her endless curves.

"May I help you?" she asks in a demeaning tone. She might as well be telling me I don't belong here.

"No, but thank you. I was just going to take a look around."

She walks away without another word or glance. I roll my eyes and move to the first rack of dresses I see. I'm not going to let some prissy sales lady put a damper on my day. I pull out a dark green dress. It's simple with cap shoulders, a v-neckline and looks to be a slim fit. I hold it up to myself and turn to look in the full-length mirror. I notice right away it brings out the green in my eyes.

My eyes are kind of peculiar. They are a greenie blue, and depending on what I'm wearing or the lighting, one color can be more prominent. Right now, they're shimmering green.

The dress comes to my knees, which means it will most likely sit just above. That's fine. It's pretty, classy, and, more importantly, business appropriate.

I see a white tag dangling from the armpit, and I pull it into view. My mouth drops open. One thousand, one hundred and ninety-nine dollars. Jeez, talk about crushing your spirits. Someone might as well have poured a bucket of cold water over my head. I blow out a sigh, sulking as I put the dress back. I spend a few more minutes checking other items, but everything is way over my budget. *Okay, all the clothing in here costs way more than I can afford.* Depressed now, I put back a black silk blouse that's four hundred and ninety-nine dollars.

The sales lady smirks at me when I turn around. I curl my nose up with a sneer and give her the middle finger. Her eyes pop wide as she gasps, and I hightail it out of there, only to run smack dab into Dekker's hard chest. I grunt on impact as my feet falter, and I feel myself falling backwards. His arms come out in a flash, circling around my waist, and pulling me flush with his body.

Too close! Too close!

The alarm bells blare in my head as our bodies collide. I shiver, closing my eyes, and feeling every solid indentation this man has to offer, even the steely hard vessel plastered against my pelvis. I let out a pitiful sound, something between a groan and whine. *Christ, he's huge!*

I don't want to move or look at him. My body is flaming hot, and all I can feel is his lengthy size digging in, and I swear it's moving, but he doesn't seem too eager to let me go.

"See something you like, Ms. Everett?"

Yes, very much so. I mean no!

I decide to brave it and lean back to look into his smoky eyes. They're hard and demanding as they bore into mine.

"Sorry?"

"In the store. See something you like?"

"Oh, yeah. No. I was just browsing," I say, releasing the grip I have on his chiseled back. His arms drop, and we both take a step back. I avoid looking at his crotch, so I divert my eyes to his left.

"And do you always give the sales lady the finger?"

Oh, bloody hell! He saw that? Of course, he did. This day went from great, too bad, to worse! Okay, it's not all that bad. I got to feel what it would be like to have Dekker's hard body against mine and his prize possession.

I let out a nervous laugh.

"Guilty as charged. Not one of my finer moments. Anywho, I should be going. Have a cat to feed," I blurt out in a rush and step forward to move past him.

He grabs my elbow gently, stilling my movements, and I jump.

"She deserved it. I'll make sure she's spoken too."

My eyes widen for a moment as we stare at one another.

"What? Why?"

"Do you even need to ask? She was disrespectful to you."

"Ah, well. I was rude back, so now we're even. No need to say anything."

He narrows his eyes at me, and I cringe slightly.

"Really, it's fine. Please don't say anything." The last thing I need is to start a new job and have gossip flying around that I'm a tattletale. Being the new girl will be bad enough, and I can't imagine what people will say about me. Especially since I'm not Dekker's usual MO, meaning, blonde with big boobs.

He nods, "I'll walk you out. I have a dinner meeting to attend."

I'd rather he not, considering there are already dozens of people watching us, including many females and the receptionist lady at the front desk. *Oh man, if looks could kill, I would be six feet under.* I swear they are all shooting daggers at me. They probably want to gouge my eyes out and stab me in the back for good measure.

Christ, I think I might need a bodyguard to work here.

I keep my mouth shut and head for the door. Dekker falls in step beside me, keeping a bit of distance between us. Once through the revolving doors, my eyes narrow to slits, having to squint with the blaring sun shining down. Dekker pulls out a pair of sunglasses, sliding them on his face.

Mirrored, of course.

"Okay, I guess this is it. See you Monday."

"Have a good weekend, Kinsley."

I nod and head for the bus stop. Luckily there is one only a few feet away. It will take twice as long to get home, but it beats paying fifty-two dollars. Definitely can't afford to pay that again. I'll have to get up an hour earlier every day, and will have at least an hour and a half commute time, one-way, every day, but beggars can't be choosers. I have a job.

I notice there's a black Range Rover, with tinted windows as dark as can be, sitting out front with a man all decked out in a uniform wearing a pair of aviator sunglasses waiting by the passenger door. Of course, Dekker has a personal driver, and it wouldn't surprise me if the SUV is bulletproof.

You know, precious cargo and all.

I take a seat on the bench and pull out my cell phone. It's quarter to five. To kill some time, I scroll Facebook to see what gossip is spreading around now. A moment later, a large shadow comes into view, and I glance up to see Dekker staring at me.

"Do you want a ride?"

"Oh, no. The bus is fine. I have no place to be," I say right away.

He stands there for what feels like an eternity in silence. From this angle, he looks dangerously powerful as he towers over me. I can't see his eyes, but I feel them boring into my skin.

"I'll call a ride for you," he finally speaks and then does a loud whistle call. A black sedan appears out of nowhere.

"Dekker, it's fine. I can wait for the bus," I quickly retort. I see his brows shoot up, and I realize my mistake. *Shit!* "I mean, Mr. Dekker. It's fine."

He stands for a moment longer, and damn, I wish he would take off his sunglasses. I don't know if I've pissed him off by calling him Dekker. He then proceeds to the vehicle, and I blow out a breath. The driver lowers the window, and words are exchanged. He then opens the back door.

"Ms. Everett, Winston will see you home."

I let out a sigh, somehow knowing there's no point in arguing. I can see him picking me up and putting me in the car. Now that's a crazy thought, but I wouldn't put it past him. I can tell him I can't afford the fare, but that will be too embarrassing. I can't imagine how much this ride will cost me. It's not New York's usual taxi or Uber transportation. Hell, I'm not even sure who this guy is or what company he works for. There's no logo.

"That wasn't necessary, but thank you," I say once I'm standing beside him. He nods, and we stare at each other for a moment before I slip inside.

"Enjoy your evening, Ms. Everett. I'll see you Monday at nine."

"Thank you. And you as well, Mr. Dekker."

He gives me a final nod and closes the door. The driver pulls out a moment later, and I resist the urge to glance back. That lasts for a whopping two seconds, before

I'm cranking my neck backwards. Dekker is standing on the sidewalk watching. The windows are tinted, not as black as his SUV, but somehow I suspect he can see me. I spin around as my cheeks heat. I smile to myself, feeling warm and tingly. Dekker is incredibly intense and unequivocally gorgeous, but I get the feeling there is another side to him he doesn't let anyone see. *Compassion.*

The media says he's a ruthless man with a cold heart. He could quite very well be that, but when you're president of a multi-billion dollar company, you don't get to the top, being kind and compassionate. It's a juggle, and some people may disagree with me, but I know this firsthand. Calver Stone was a great company with morals and ethics, but they were snatched up and abolished in a blink of an eye. I don't know if they were in financial difficulties, but Dekker obviously had his reasons for buying the company. It sucks that so many people are out of a job, but such is life. Nothing is permanent, and all good things must end at some point, right?

I don't expect to work for Dekker long, considering none of his assistants last very long, but I'll deal with that when the time comes. It also won't hurt to keep looking. But now, having spent some time with him, I sense there are multiple layers to him, and yes, I do believe he has a heart.

After we are a few blocks away and out of sight, I tell Winston to pull over.

"I'll take the bus the rest of the way."

"Mr. Dekker has specifically instructed me to take you home, Ms. Everett."

"That's not necessary, Winston. I can take the bus."

He repeats his last sentence, and I roll my eyes.

"I heard you the first time, and I appreciate this, but honestly, I don't have the money to pay you. So if you'll just pull over now, I'll be on my way."

"There is no charge, Ms. Everett. I work for Mr. Dekker."

My mouth drops open.

"What?"

"I'll pick you up on Monday at eight o'clock."

"What?"

"I'm your personal driver, Ms. Everett, for the duration of your employment at Dekker Enterprises."

I almost shout "*what*" again, but I'm sure I'll hear the same mantra again. I'm learning Winston is a one-monotone voice. Almost like a robot. Instead, I sit there stunned and speechless. I have my own personal driver?

"Does all Mr. Dekker's personal assistants get their own personal driver?" I counter back.

He shrugs his shoulders.

What the hell?

I suppose it can be a different driver every time, so maybe he truly doesn't know, and since Dekker is filthy rich, maybe it's one of the job perks. That doesn't sound unreasonable. *Hmm, pretty cool, I guess, and it beats an hour and a half stinky bus ride.* Maybe I'll ask about it on Monday just to be on the safe side. Feeling satisfied, I lean back in my seat with a smile on my face.

CHAPTER FOUR

Kinsley

An hour later, Winston is pulling up to my apartment building. It's an old building, but the owners have done a decent job keeping up with the property.

"Thank you, Winston. Can you pick me up at seven-thirty on Monday? I would like to arrive a little early."

He nods. I climb out and walk up the five steps to the front door. I punch in my passcode, and the door unlocks with a beep. I then trudge up another three flights of stairs. No elevator in this place. I unlock my door and call for my fur baby.

"Mittens, I'm home."

My cat peeks his head out from the cat tower and I giggle. I call him Mittens because his legs are white with black paws looking like he has mitts on.

"Guess what? Mama got the job," I tell him as I toss my keys on the kitchen counter and remove my heels. When I look up, he's gone.

"Yeah, I guess it's not very exciting news for you as it is for me."

I walk up to the cat tree, where he's hiding. It's six feet tall and has an enclosed room at about the five-foot mark. I added a fluffy blanket, and he sleeps in there most of the time, especially when I'm not home. The rest of the time he sleeps on top of me. I lean down and peer inside. He lifts his head and yawns.

"Come here you little bum. Mama wants to snuggle."

I reach inside and scoop him up. He starts purring like a dump truck as he nuzzles my face. I hold him upright, gently squeezing and giving him kisses. It's nice to feel loved, even if it's from a cat. I put him down and grab the treat bag. He meows several times, rubbing up against my leg. I chuckle and put a couple down for him. He gobbles them up in a flash as I plop down on the couch.

"What a day, Mittens." He jumps up on the couch beside me and curls up in a ball for another sleep.

I glance around my place. It's a complete disaster zone thanks to this morning's wardrobe fiasco, and I was just hired by the one and only Mr. Dekker. New York's most eligible and desirable bachelor, and I still have nothing respectable to wear.

I saw how all the other women were dressed. They were sophisticated, elegant and classy, all dressed in their designer clothing. I don't own one name-brand item. Not only is Mr. Dekker so far out of my league, but so are the rest of the people in that building. I really don't understand why he gave me the time of day. He'll probably regret his decision come Monday when he sees I'm dressed in old lady clothing, and I wear big clunky glasses. This outfit I have on now, is my Sunday best. *Ugh!* I'm so going to embarrass him. He's not going to want to be caught dead near me. *Shit!* I think I better start looking for a new job and ASAP.

I first remove my contacts before they give me a headache and then grab my laptop, powering it on. The computer dings, signaling I have an incoming email, and I see it's from Ivy Davis. I click it open and read the email. She first congratulates me and tells me she's so excited I got the job. Enclosed is my offer letter and someone will be by on Sunday to deliver my swipe card, a new cell phone, and a new laptop. My mouth drops open after reading the last sentence.

Oh. My. God! Is this for real?!

After re-reading the sentence again, I give my head a shake. Jeez, I guess Mr. Dekker really goes all out.

Ivy then tells me to review the offer letter and if I have questions, to let her know. If not, I'm to bring in the signed offer letter on Monday, and she'll meet me on the ninetieth floor, same location, at nine AM.

I open the offer letter and immediately look for the salary. I scream, leaping up with my laptop tumbling to the floor. Mittens jumps ten feet in the air and then flies up his cat tower, hiding in his bed.

"Sorry, Mittens!"

I grab my laptop and plop back down, staring at the salary again. This has to be a typo. I quickly close out and hit reply to Ivy's email.

Dear Ivy,

Thank you for your email and this amazing opportunity. I will work very hard to please Mr. Dekker and hope this is the beginning of a long relationship.

I did find one discrepancy with the salary indicated in the offer letter. When I applied for the job, the ad in the newspaper said fifty thousand to start. This letter states eighty thousand.

Could you please send me a revised letter?

Thank you kindly.

Kinsley Everett

I reopen the offer letter and stare at the eighty thousand. At my old job, I made forty-five thousand, which wasn't bad. God, what I would give to make that kind of money. Maybe in your next life, Kinsley.

Everything else is standard, so I wait for Ivy to return my message. In the meantime, I clean up my mess, rehanging all my clothes. An hour passes by, and then another. Of course, she's gone home for the weekend. I guess I'll point it out on Monday. I print off the letter, and my stomach decides to growl. It's almost eight, and I haven't eaten since noon.

Opening the fridge, I see there's nothing remotely edible. I need to go grocery shopping. Maybe I'll just order in. I grab my cell phone to see exactly how much money I have left in my bank account. After signing in, I cringe. I have just under three hundred dollars to last me two weeks. I do recall the job letter indicating I would be paid bi-weekly. I sign out and look in the cupboard. I grab the box of Cheerios. *Cereal it is.*

After eating and feeding Mittens, I decide to call it a day. I move the coffee table off to the side that sits in front of my couch. After removing the cushions from the couch, I pull on the handle easing out the bed. My couch also serves as my bed.

My apartment is actually considered a studio, at five hundred square feet. Virtually one big room with a separate bathroom. It works for me since it's just Mittens and me. I had splurged when I applied for this unit three years ago because it has three oversized windows in a curved design. I pay eighteen-fifty a month in rent, but it's worth it. I'm on the top floor, which also has a nice high vaulted ceiling. It doesn't give you the feeling of being closed in. The floors are real hardwood, and all the appliances were new when I moved in.

I did take a twelve-foot section beside the couch and install a white closet organizer with a drop-down desk bought from Ikea. They really do have great stuff and ideas for tiny apartments at great prices. The closet also has sliding doors so my clothes and shoes aren't on display if I have company. My place is light and airy with white walls, except for the wall with the windows. It's painted a sapphire blue, and it's the first thing you see when you walk into my apartment, and you're also standing right in my kitchen.

After using the washroom and sliding on my pajamas, I climb into bed, turning on the TV. But I can't concentrate on the show as my mind replays my encounter with Dekker. His scent still lingers in my nostrils, and his eyes... good Lord, that man has some intense eyes. I swear they could liquefy you with just one look, or melt the panties right off you.

Being in Dekker's presence made me realize I haven't been with a man in what feels like an eternity. Not that my first time is anything to talk about, but he invokes those certain body parts that lie dormant, arousing you and making you remember you're a woman with needs. Needs that will never be fulfilled in my case.

I could touch myself. Make myself climax, visualizing Dekker's skillful tongue between my thighs, licking me in a heated passion and consuming me until I'm drunk with pleasure. I'll feel the piercing gaze of his dark eyes. He won't look away from me for one second while down there. He likes to watch. He also likes to tease, or perhaps torture is a better word. He'll lick slowly, diving his tongue deep inside, tasting, and taking his sweet time. Building me up, and when I'm about to reach my peak, he'll stop, deflating my orgasm. I'll cry out in frustration, making him chuckle, because he's evil like that. I'll growl at him, and he'll nip my clit, letting me know he's in charge. He'll always be in control. But when he lets me cum, it will be the most epic orgasm ever. I'll see exploding golden stars.

Before I can stop myself, my hand slides underneath the band of my underwear. I'm already soaked. I finger my clit, picturing his tongue, and I cum within a minute. I let out a sigh, sagging back against the mattress. *That was not epic at all.* That was actually pathetic. My sex life is pathetic. *Ugh!* Maybe I need to put myself out there and start dating. There has to be someone that will find me pretty enough. Even if it's just for sex. I really don't care.

I'm going to need some kind of relief if I'll be working with Dekker five days a week or I'll go mentally insane. Or perhaps I should say, sexually frustrated. If I can find a man to satisfy me, maybe I won't be so inclined to drool all over myself every time I see Dekker. Okay, that will probably be impossible.

The man is definitely drool-worthy.

Lick-worthy.

Suck-worthy.

Damn, I'm horny again!

I grumble and roll over onto my side, pulling the blankets up to my ears. I just need to go to sleep and stop daydreaming over the delectable Dekker.

CHAPTER FIVE

Kinsley

I wake up drenched in sweat and slightly sticky between my thighs. I forgot to turn on my fan last night, and my place isn't air conditioned, but I also recall having a few sex dreams of Dekker and being very vivid. I let out a sigh. Is this what my life has turned into? Sleep fantasy sex? I rub my eyes, shaking my head. I'm so screwed.

All three windows are open, but it's mid-June. The temperature didn't dip down much last night. It also doesn't help that I have a cat sleeping on my chest. I open my eyes to see Mittens. He peeks his eyes open, and then yawns, stretching his front legs out. They're long and now they are touching my chin.

"Good morning, sweetie."

He slithers up until his wet nose is almost touching my face. He wants his morning scratches. I oblige, rubbing the side of his face and under his chin with my nails. He purrs like a diesel truck.

My day is non-eventful, consisting of grocery shopping, house cleaning, and in the afternoon, I spend some time making some homemade cards. I have to keep myself busy somehow, or I'll go crazy. I sell them for six dollars on Facebook marketplace. It helps bring in a little bit of money, but I'm running out of crafting supplies. I have a lady coming at four today to pick up two Happy Birthday cards.

Right now, I'm making a *Thank You* card for Dekker. Yeah, it's corny, and I'll probably chicken out and not give it to him, but we'll see. The color scheme I've chosen is cherry cobbler red, black, and a crisp white. I use red cardstock paper for the primary color. On the bottom half is a gorgeous black damask flock paper that feels like velvet, and the top panel, I use white paper with raised white dots. I had applied a mist beforehand, a champagne shimmer for some extra sparkle on the white dotted paper. After adding a red ribbon across the center, I spend the next twenty minutes making the red rose. It's the most time-consuming and very intricate.

Once I'm done, I lightly spray the rose with a rose fragrance and glue it down to the card, adding tiny black scallops with decorative swirl designs. Lastly, I fasten a red cut-out tag on the bottom with a white overlay and handwrite "Thank You" in calligraphy.

I pick up the card and examine it. It looks good, and the rose turned out perfect. It looks realistic, and I love the smell of roses myself. Not that I've gotten any before. I'm not sure if the card is manly, but it looks very elegant. The inside is simple, plain white cardstock paper, a red ribbon, and more of the black damask flock paper.

I put my chin in my hand, pondering what to say on the inside. I write a few sentences on a sheet of paper before deciding.

Dear Mr. Dekker,

Thank you for giving me this fantastic job opportunity.

I can't express how truly grateful I am.

I look forward to a long career working by your side.

Yours truly,

Kinsley Everett

I reread the note and pray I'm not coming across as needy or mushy.

It's not long before the intercom rings. I meet the lady downstairs, and she's happy with her cards. I pocket the twelve dollars as I gaze around the neighbourhood. There are kids playing on the sidewalk, hopscotch, or something like that. I notice a black Audi parked on the other side of the street, a few feet down, and I frown, knowing for a fact, that no one around here drives an Audi. If they did, they wouldn't be living here. The windows are blacked out and the way the sun is angling down, you can't see through the front windshield either. Too much of a glare. I suppose it could be a friend or family member visiting. The apartments across the street are actual apartments and not studios, so they are for the "I'm a little richer than you," people. I shrug my shoulders and head back inside.

After eating a TV dinner of meatloaf, mashed potatoes and green beans, I climb into bed. I never did make my bed this morning. A bad habit that's becoming the norm. I flip on the TV and browse through the channels. There's nothing remotely interesting. It's going to be a long night. I've never wished for Monday to come so fast in my life. This not working sucks.

I think about Dekker. He probably has had a woman in his bed since he left work on Friday. A weekend filled with unadulterated sex.

Hard sex.

Rough sex.

Kinky sex.

Yup, that's what Dekker is probably doing now, while I sit here in my shorts and t-shirt, wishing it was me, yet again. *Christ, I need to get out of here.* There's a small night pub not too far from here. Maybe I'll go hang out there for a while and see if I can pick up a man. I've never been, but have walked by several times. They play decent music, but I won't be able to afford drinks. Maybe I'll get lucky and find someone to buy me a couple of drinks and take me home for the night.

Sounds like a double win to me.

It's four-thirty, so I wait until eight, before getting ready. First, I shower, shaving my body parts again for good measure. I then spend twenty minutes raiding my closet. I don't have anything remotely sexy. After humming and hawing, I decide to go with a pair of black skinny jeans and my red spaghetti strap shirt. I look down at my chest wondering if I can get away without wearing a bra. I guess that's one good thing about being small-chested. No bra, it is. I put on my five-inch high heel sandals and give myself the once over in the mirror. Not bad. My booty looks great in these jeans, if I say so myself. Too bad I'll be sitting down on my butt the whole time.

It's not a nightclub, so no dancing for me. Just good music, pool tables, and a dozen TVs playing various sports. I guess I could play pool if someone asks me. I look at my hair. Up or down? I swipe it off my neck, holding it up. I don't ever wear my hair loose, unless it's first thing in the morning, I'm going to bed, or after I've gotten out of the shower. I'm not sure why. I do have nice thick hair, but I think it's the fire engine red that bothers me. It's just so out there, and I am so not. I decide on a simple braid.

After saying goodbye to Mittens, I lock up my place and walk to the pub. It's a thirty-minute walk, but I'll take the bus home. I don't like walking alone after the sun goes down. When I get there, I take a few deep breaths before heading inside. It's not too busy, considering it's only nine-thirty, but there are a few couples sipping on beverages, having some appetizers, and chatting. Other than that, there are four guys sitting at the bar. There are pool tables in the back, but from this angle, I can't tell if anyone is back there. It's semi-private, with the ability to draw a curtain closed for full on privacy. I glance back at the guys at the bar, and as if on cue, they all turn to look at me. I feel my cheeks heat with embarrassment. I give them a brief smile, and since there's no hostess, I look for an open booth. There is one against the window, and I immediately snatch it, taking a seat.

"Hey there, darling. What can I get you tonight?" a perky waitress asks.

"Umm, how much for a Diet Coke?"

"Five and a quarter."

"Okay, I'll have one, please."

"You got it."

I steal a glance at the gentlemen at the bar. They're talking amongst themselves. They lost interest in me pretty quick. I let out a sigh. *It's still early, Kinsley.* After the waitress brings back my drink, I take a baby sip. I need it to last for at least a couple of hours. Not knowing what to do with myself, I grab my cell, opening TikTok. I watch video, after video, after video. People come and go, the place filling up, but not one guy takes an interest in me.

It's ten minutes to eleven, and I was going to give it to eleven before calling it quits. I glance at my Diet Coke. It's mostly water since the ice has nearly melted. I let out another long sigh. This was such a waste of time. I might as well pack it in now.

I finish off my watered-down drink when I see the waitress approaching.

"Oh, good timing. I'm ready to leave."

"This is from the gentleman at the bar," she says, placing down a colorful pink drink in front of me.

My mouth drops open.

"Really?"

She smiles with a nod.

"Who?" I question.

She gestures over her shoulder to the right. I lean back in my seat, and my eyes immediately connect with the gentleman that I can only assume bought me the drink. His brief nod kind of gives it away. He's standing at the end of the bar, and I take him in. He is tall. Tall as Dekker with a similar build but maybe not as beefy. Dark hair, chiseled jaw, his nose is a little longer and pointy than normal, but overall, not bad. *Yay!* I give him a wave as my heart rate picks up, and he's quick to close the distance.

"Good luck," the waitress says and disappears.

"Hi, I'm James. Do you mind if I join you?"

"Oh, no, not at all. I'm Kinsley, and thank you for the drink. What is it?" I ask once he has taken a seat across from me.

"Cosmopolitan. I hear it's popular with the ladies, but if you don't like it, I'll order whatever you'd like."

"I've never had one," I tell him and then take a sip. "Mmm, it's pretty good. It's sweet with a zip of tardiness. Good combination."

He smiles as he stares at my face.

"I must say, you have some killer eyes. I bet they attract a lot of attention."

I snort-laugh, then slap my hand over my nose and mouth. Unfortunately, I have a tendency to snort when I laugh. It's kind of embarrassing, but James chuckles.

"Cute laugh," he remarks with a wink, and I find myself grinning.

"Sorry, bad habit, and to answer your other question, no, not at all."

He frowns, narrowing his brows together.

"That can't be true. You must have dozens of men throwing themselves at you."

I wish.

"No, but let's not talk about my nonexistent love life. Instead, tell me about yourself, James. What do you do for a living?"

And that's how the rest of my night goes with James. I learn he's into real estate, has his own place in upper Manhattan, drives a BMW, has never been married, and he's thirty. Same age as Dekker. I can't help that my mind keeps detouring to him. As I listen to James, I find I'm comparing the two. James's cologne is different, it's not as potent. It doesn't seize your lungs or invade your senses. Dekker's scent is like a drug that imprisons you, holding you hostage and making you slick with desire.

Before I know it, two hours have passed, and I've drank four Cosmopolitan. I'm on my fifth one, feeling giddy with a light buzz.

"Do you want to play a game of pool?"

"Oh yeah, that sounds great, but I'm not sure how well I'll perform. Feeling a little tipsy," I admit with a snicker.

He chuckles, climbing out of the booth, and helps me to my feet.

"Christ, I didn't realize how tall you are," he states, clearly shocked.

I laugh, standing in front of him, nose to nose.

"Yeah, I get that a lot. All legs."

"And, I hope I get to see them up close in person, very soon," he husks out, flirting, and making my body heat rise or maybe it's just the alcohol.

He gives me another wink, linking our fingers together and guiding me to the back where the pool tables are. As I walk, I'm finding my eyes are going a little cross as the ground shifts. I grab James's forearm to steady myself.

"Easy now," he says, pulling me close to his side and wrapping his arm around my waist. "Do you need to sit down?"

"Umm," I blink my eyes a few times. I'm wearing my contacts which aren't probably helping. "No, I think I'm good now." I blink again, and everything comes into focus.

He nods, and as we draw closer, I see they're two other gentlemen playing a game and another one sitting on a bar stool in the corner watching. They all stare at me when James and I pass through the curtains.

"Gentlemen," James says in greeting.

I give them a brief smile, suddenly feeling uneasy. I'm not sure why. Maybe it's the way they are staring at me. It's giving me goosebumps, but not in a good way. They look like trouble. They're good looking guys, but for whatever reason, red flags are going off in my head. I glance over my shoulder as James closes the curtain.

"Umm, maybe I should head home. It's getting late," I say to James.

He looks at his watch.

"It's only one, darling. How about one game, and then I'll give you a ride home, if you want? Maybe I'll get to see those gorgeous legs in person, if you allow," he whispers that last part in my ear.

I shiver and glance at the other guys. They've gone back to playing their game, and the guy sitting in the corner is also preoccupied, watching them.

Okay, Kinsley, I think you're overreacting, and I thought you wanted to get laid? I do!

I smile at James, giving him a nod and he smiles back, giving my waist a squeeze. He hands me a pool cue, and I use it to steady myself. I watch as he rounds up the balls, setting them in place.

"Ladies first."

"Oh no, you go ahead. I'm not very good at breaking."

He calls solids and takes his shot. *Crack.* The balls fly in every direction, and he ends up sinking one solid. I watch as he skillfully sinks three more before it's my turn.

"All right, Miss Long legs, you're up," he tells me.

I snicker and glance around, trying to decide which stripe ball will be an easy mark. I polish my cue and then take my position at the left end, off to the side. I call my shot and sink the ball effortlessly. James winks at me. I sink another ball, but when I get to the third ball, my vision distorts momentarily as a wave of dizziness crashes through me, and I send the ball flying in the opposite direction. I close my eyes briefly as I stand, clutching the pool table and waiting for the dizziness to pass. I feel James is at my side a second later.

"Kinsley, are you all right?"

"Just feeling a little lightheaded, but I think I'm okay now," I tell him.

"Here, have a seat," he says, pulling out a bar stool.

I thank him, taking a seat, and I notice the other guys are watching me again. I look away, trying to ignore them and sucking on an ice cube from my drink. I watch James drop in two more balls. He has one solid left, plus the black ball. He misses his shot and gestures that it's my time. I get up, slowly making my way to the table.

I find my next shot, but as soon as I lean over the table, my vision blurs, vertigo striking once more. James moves in behind me, blanketing his body against mine. My eyes close on their own accord, as I feel his hand land on my ass with a firm squeeze.

"Need some help there, darling?" he whispers in my ear.

"James, I don't think I can move. I need to go home," I tell him.

His hands travel up my sides until he's pushing my shirt up, and are cupping my breasts. I flinch, with my eyes flying open. They lock with the other three guys that are prowling in. The one sitting in the corner already has his zipper undone and is stroking his cock with his hand. I feel like a bucket of ice is poured over my head as horror sets in.

"That's all right, love. My boys and I will do all the work. You just need to lay there and not make a sound."

His hand clamps over my mouth before I get the chance to scream, and with even faster fingers, they work down the zipper of my jeans. I'm completely paralyzed with his weight bearing down on me, and I'm too drunk to fight back. I close my eyes as tears silently fall. I wanted to get laid, but not like this.

A loud commotion erupts behind me, and then all hell breaks loose with a booming roar. James is torn off me, but I still can't move, and my eyes don't want to cooperate. They stay closed as the shouting continues, and I'm pretty sure fists are flying, hearing several grunts and groans, a lot of cursing, and a piercing howl.

My body begins to shut down as everything fades out. I don't even have the energy to pull my shirt back down as my legs give away, slumping against the pool table. At least my jeans are still in tack, I think. Moments later, another hard body covers mine, and I let out a sob. I know this scent.

"I've got you, Kinsley," Dekker whispers by my ear as he carefully pulls down my top.

I'm eased over onto my side and then hoisted up into his big strong arms. He holds me tightly as I bury my face in his neck, inhaling his scent. A scent that I will now forever associate as my savior. I don't open my eyes for one second or ask where he's taking me as he carries me effortlessly in his arms. Instead, I let myself go, relaxing into his tight embrace, feeling safe.

CHAPTER SIX

Dekker

Kinsley is asleep in my arms before I even reach the SUV. Her head tips back with the bouncing in my arms and I glance at her mouth. She has such beautiful dark pink lips that I would very much like to see wrapped around my cock. My dick twitches in my pants, growing in size and visualizing Kinsley on her knees, sucking me with those juicy pink lips of hers. She'll gag and choke, unable to handle my size and girth, as I force her to take my entire length, but that's okay. They all do.

Chase, my personal driver, already has the back door open of my Mercedes, waiting.

"Home," I confirm, climbing inside and easing Kinsley on my lap.

I'm livid. And part of me wants to wake her up so I can strangle her neck and whip her derriere until it's blistering red. I would then shake her for good measure, asking what the hell she was thinking. I just might do that tomorrow morning when she wakes up.

My blood boils, still reeling from seeing those four guys ready to take turns raping her. I was almost too late.

I'd been watching her when an incoming call I'd been waiting for distracted me. Ever since I laid eyes on her yesterday, I couldn't stop thinking about her. No redhead has ever attracted my interest. I've never given them the time of day. I have particular tastes, and I rarely deviate.

Yes, she looked like a fucking Sunday school teacher with her hair pulled back in a tight bun, and she tries to hide her slender figure in those ridiculous old lady clothes. But her eyes... Christ, does she ever have some iniquitous eyes. I noticed on a few occasions they would alter in color. It has to be the lighting or angle, but one minute they'll be an ocean blue, the next, they'll be teal green. They are striking, and I almost wish she would open her eyes so I can see what color they are now.

But then there is her damn height. It's not hard to tell this feminine beauty is all legs, but seeing her in her tight-ass skinny jeans, I grew painfully hard. Her ass and legs are to die for. I can't help but smirk. The media that believes they know me, thinks I'm a breast man, and while I prefer women with larger boobs, it's their ass I'll gravitate to first. Kinsley's ass is a perfect little round apple that I would like to sink my teeth and my cock in. *Anal.* I can't get enough of anal sex. It's the perfect amount of tightness that my cock needs to climax. God knows I have a hard time reaching my peak with regular intercourse.

I glance down at Kinsley. There's no doubt in my mind this redhead has probably never had anal sex. I can definitely see her forbidding that area. She has an innocent aura that surrounds her, and I highly doubt she's even experienced a good hard fucking. I would destroy her. I want to destroy her in every way possible. That's what I do. Women are nothing but a vessel for me to do as I please, and once I get bored, I discard them. I never get attached, and I don't do relationships.

I gaze down at Kinsley as I feel something unfamiliar stirring deep in my chest. I want to peel back her layers of clothing and learn every inch of her body. I want to go slow. I don't want to miss a thing. I already know her skin is a pearl white, and she has these adorable little freckles across her cheekbones. She has eight on the left side and nine on the right. Yes, I already counted them yesterday and want to discover all her freckles and indents. I need to. And her fingers, they're long and slender, like the rest of her body. Her tits are small, but with this spaghetti strap shirt on, I can tell they are perky little round balls. My hand itches to cup one now. To know what it feels like. I know she's braless, and I want to know how they'll fit in my hand. But something else is brewing, especially with what almost happened at the pub. I feel a sense of possessiveness towards her. She's *mine,* and I will crush anyone's skull that dares to touch her.

I did, starting with that scumbag, James, and damn, it felt good. The guy with his dick out is lucky he still has one, but I made sure he'll never be able to have kids after crushing his balls with my bare hand. Chase handled the other two.

I had been watching her place this afternoon and followed her to the bar. She was completely oblivious that I was there. I was hiding in the corner at the back. I had a perfect view of her, but the pub was poorly lit, I highly doubt she would have seen me. I watched her baby her drink. A Diet Coke.

I know her finances aren't good. She has less than three hundred dollars in her bank account to last her two weeks. Her credit card is fifteen hundred in the hole. I also know she told Winston to pull over. She couldn't afford the fare, and her place is a studio apartment, micro-small. That will change. I'm the reason she's out of a job, and I also know she questioned the salary. Of course, she would. Most women, correction, no woman would ever question that amount, but Kinsley did. She's smart and humble. Two attributes that women severely lack around here.

Chase pulls into the underground parking lot of my building. I have my own private entrance that no one knows about. He opens the door and gives me a nod. I lift Kinsley in my arms and head to the elevator. Bill, one of my security guards, already has the door open for me. With another nod, I enter inside and ride up to the ninety-first floor. Kinsley hasn't moved a muscle. She's out cold.

The elevator door opens, and I take her straight to my bedroom. I place her down on her back, and she lets out a soft groan, wanting to roll over.

"Not yet, sweetheart," I tell her.

I remove her high heels sandals, then her ultra-tight jeans. As I reveal every inch of her legs, my mouth starts to water. *Christ, these legs go on and on.* When I finally tug them off, I devour her porcelain skin with hungry eyes. She's wearing light pink cotton underwear that covers her pussy, and her skin is flawless. Her shirt has risen up slightly, exposing her tiny belly button, and I lean down, spotting a dark freckle on her left hipbone. I trail my fingertip over top. It's not a freckle but a mole, somewhat raised. I let my fingertips glide along her belly. Just as I thought, silky smooth. My hands burn with itch, wanting to remove her top as my cock hardens expectantly. I picture her nipples a dark pink, just like her lips.

Kinsley groans again, trying to roll over. It makes me wonder if she's a belly sleeper.

"All right, Ms. Scarlett," I pull back the blankets and pick her up.

She groans again as her head flops back, mouth wide open. I place her carefully in the middle and roll her over onto her side. She immediately rolls the rest of the way onto her belly with another muffled groan.

I step out of the room, heading down the hallway and into one of my spare bedrooms. I grab a thin pillow. All my pillows are thicker as I sleep on my side most of the time. I come back, and Kinsley is still face down. She's going to smother herself. I place the thin pillow under her head and turn her neck to the side. I tuck her arms in and then step back off the bed.

My eyes immediately drift down to her ass. She's wearing cheeky underwear. A perfect little apple as I suspected. She should be wearing a thong or better yet, nothing. My cock thoroughly agrees, going ramrod hard like granite in my pants. I groan, latching my hand through the fabric of my slacks and around my cock, squeezing harshly. The need to jerk off is strong. *Christ, I haven't jerked off since I was a school boy.* I never needed to. My dick is always getting a workout. Seven days a week if I so desire. All I have to do is make a phone call. I have dozens of ladies waiting.

But not this weekend. For whatever reason, I couldn't get a certain redhead out of my mind as soon as I laid eyes on her. It's driving me mad, quite frankly. She isn't my type. But God dammit, my fucking dick says otherwise. I'm sure her pussy will be like the rest of them—too loose. Not enough friction or restraint. I'll need her tight ass to cum. Kinsley will probably be horrified and think I'm some kind of freak. I am a freak because that's not the only thing I want to do to her. My eyes roam over her delicate skin. It would mark so beautifully. *Christ, I'm a sick bastard.* But that's who I am. I love layering their buttocks with angry welts. Hearing their screams, it's like music to my ears and, when the beast inside of me is satisfied, will I indulge them by claiming their ass.

I pull the blankets up on Kinsley before I do something I'll regret. All the women I'm with give me their verbal consent. I'm upfront, honest, and I make it abundantly clear it will be painful. But, they also know at any time, it can be stopped. *Red.* I glance at Kinsley's hair in a braid. *Redhead. Red.* Where's the irony in that?

Some women will ask if I'll fuck their pussy. I have no problem with that request, providing they take their stripes like a good girl. I'll fuck them until they are comatose. I can go all night.

But Kinsley's different. I'm not sure if I want to cross that line. I can see her being the vanilla type. But on the other hand, I feel a protectiveness around her, like I don't want to hurt her. *Scar her.* I still want to redden her ass after tonight's incident. *How dare she put herself in that situation!* I want to wring her neck and ask her what the hell she was doing. And if anyone dares to touch or hurt her again, I'll lose my Goddamn head. It's an emotion I've never felt before and I'm not sure what it means, nor do I want to find out. My life is perfect the way it is. I don't need this confusion or any of this emotional crap that's spinning around in my head and screwing with my mind.

Jesus, I need a drink!

I leave Kinsley and go search for my bottle of whiskey. I pour a hefty glass, downing half of it. It burns my throat and chest, but it's a good burn, heating my blood and veins. Just what I need. I crack my neck, feeling the alcohol alleviate some of the stiffness in my muscles. Removing my suit jacket and tie, I dial Chase's number. He picks up on the first ring.

"Shut that place down. Burn it to the ground for all I care. I want everyone involved out of my city," I state with no formal pleasantries. Not only is Chase my personal driver, but he's also my own personal bodyguard.

"Got it."

I disconnect the call and look towards my bedroom. The call that distracted me from Kinsley earlier was from one of my informants. I'd been expecting Trey's call and had stepped into the hallway so I could hear better. That's when I found out the pub has had two other incidents in the last month, not reported, and there have been a dozen other attacks on women nearby in the last couple of years. The owner has been turning a blind eye. I should have crushed his skull when I had a chance.

I was almost too late and Jesus, my heart had never thumped so loud and hard in my chest before. I almost lost my mind when I noticed she was gone. I hadn't realized they had a back room with pool tables. The curtains were black and drawn closed, blending in, and the lighting was shit. After Chase had confirmed she hadn't left, I raided the women's washroom. It wasn't until I was practically standing in front of the curtain did I see the dull light shining through the bottom. I peeked inside and saw her with James laying over top of her. I called for backup. This was going to get messy. Chase was at my side ten seconds later. *Ten more seconds, and her bottom half would have been exposed. Ten more seconds and one of them would have violated her.* I squeeze the glass in my hand, rage boiling through me, and the sides give out, shattering to the floor. *Those men are lucky to be alive.*

After taking a few calming breaths, I clean up my mess and wash my hands. Having Kinsley in my bed is a novelty for me. A woman has never slept in my bed before. Not here. Elsewhere yes, but never here. I have half a dozen other places in New York and across the state, but at the end of the day, this is where I retire. Alone. Not too many people know this place exists, and I intend to keep it that way. I like my privacy.

I rub my face with my hands, feeling drained. It's two-thirty in the morning. Unless my dick is drilling into a tight puckered hole with adrenaline coursing through me, I think right now, I need sleep. I strip out of the rest of my clothing and head to my spare bedroom. I can't sleep beside her. She's too tempting, and I won't be held accountable for what I do in my sleep.

I peek in on her one more time. She hasn't moved an inch. I take a moment to scrutinize her face. Her beauty is unique. One that should be appreciated, but I get the feeling she goes unnoticed. I'm one of those guys. If our paths crossed on a sidewalk, I wouldn't have even glanced at her. She's one of those women that fly under the radar until it hits you square in the face, making you look, and I mean truly look until you realize she's a diamond in the rough. *One that should be worshipped and cherished.* She has my attention all right, but I should leave her alone. Somehow, I don't think that will be happening.

I shut off the lights, heading out and closing the door behind me. I will deal with Ms. Scarlett tomorrow.

CHAPTER SEVEN

Kinsley

I let out a lengthy groan, trying to roll over, but my limbs don't want to cooperate. I think someone put lead in them.

"Mitten's, can you help mama out? I don't think I can move," I mumble face down into my pillow.

"Here, take my arm."

My eyes pop open.

"You're not Mittens," I state, already knowing who it is.

Oh my God!

"No, I am not."

"Oh, God."

"I've been called that a few times," he says with a hint of arrogance.

"Dekker."

"No woman has ever called me that."

Shit!

"I mean, Mr. Dekker."

"Yes, Kinsley."

"Do I still have a job?"

"That depends."

"On what?"

"You explaining to me what you were doing last night."

"And if I can't?"

Silence.

I turn my head off to the side, peeking my eyes open, only to inhale abruptly. *Yikes! Dekker is shirtless!* I can't help but stare with my eyes flickering in every direction, unsure what to take in first, as my mouth salivates. His skin is impeccably tanned, with sculpted arms, broad shoulders, down to bulging pectoral muscles, and chiseled washboard abs. The man is a superior God. Powerfully built to heavenly perfection.

My chest constricts, desperate for air I didn't realize I was holding, as my fingers ache to touch him. To run my hands up and down his gorgeous chest and feel his taut skin against my palms. I've seen thousands of pictures of men's carved chests on TV or in movies but seeing one that's real and this close is a different story. It's indescribable. *Dekker is indescribable.* A man of seduction that can make you wet your panties in a blink of an eye, and make you so very hot and needy. *Christ, I need to get laid.* I tried that last night, but it backfired in my face. If it wasn't for Dekker... I shiver, remembering everything. It almost turned out to be my worst nightmare.

My eyes finally connect with his. Oh man, he doesn't look happy. *He's never happy, Kinsley*, I remind myself. True, but his current expression is more harsh and strict. I think I'm in trouble.

"How about you take these, have a hot shower, and we'll talk after," he says, handing me a glass of water and two tablets. "Advil," he adds.

I nod and push myself up into a sitting position. I look down to see I'm still wearing last nights' shirt, but I'm only wearing my underwear below the waist. I can only assume Dekker is the one that removed my jeans. *My new boss!* Heat rises up in my face with utter embarrassment. As much as I fantasize about Dekker, he's the last person I would ever want to see my naked skin. I know he saw my toothpick legs, but that doesn't ease the redness in my face.

I lower my gaze as I reach out for the water and pills. Our fingers lightly brush against each other, and I feel electricity skate through my arms, and down into my belly. My instinct is to jerk my hand back, but I hold strong. *Jeez, why does he have to shock me every time we touch?* I take the pills with a gulp of water, thanking him and handing him the glass back, but avoid finger contact this time.

"The washroom is straight ahead," he says, gesturing to his left.

I nod, and silence fills the room. I expect him to leave, but he doesn't move. I risk raising my head and looking at him. He's staring at me with those dark, demanding eyes. I cringe, turning away, and glancing towards the washroom, then back to him. His expression is deadpan as he doesn't move a muscle.

"Umm, are you going to leave?" I finally brave asking, and I watch his jaw clench.

"I'll be back," he clips out and finally gets up, heading to the door and giving me a splendid view of his sculptured back. My eyes drop further to his silk pajama pants that mold perfectly to his ass. I suck in my bottom lip, biting down as I watch his back and ass flex through his long, confident strides. He glances back for a moment when he reaches the door. He knows I was ogling as a faint smirk appears, but gone a moment later. I put my head down, staring at my lap until I hear the door click close.

I breathe out a puff of air, feeling very hot. *What the hell was that all about?* I get the feeling he didn't want to leave, which is completely absurd. But not only that, I'm in big trouble. I feel it brewing in the pit of my stomach. What is he going to do? Spank me?

Now that's a scary thought, and maybe a wee-bit exciting.

I wait a few more seconds before climbing out of his bed. It's massive. It has to be a California King with black bedsheets that feel like silk. His bedroom is three times the size of my studio, which doesn't surprise me and the color palette is mostly dark. Grey and black with accenting white pieces. The curtains are still drawn closed with a bedside lamp on.

I make my way to his bathroom and my eyes grow wider as I peer inside. On the contrary to his dark bedroom, his bathroom is a sea of elegant marble, mainly in stark white and again, vast in size. There are floor-to-ceiling windows straight ahead that have been tinted. My feet automatically move to the windows, curious to see if I recognize the area where Dekker lives.

As I glance around, I'm quick to identify the buildings surrounding me. I frown, dropping my eyes to look down. I see the yacht-shaped entrance. We're in Dekker's work building. *He lives here?* We have to be on the top floor, but I only recall seeing ninety floors in the elevator on Friday. The building is immensely huge, so I guess we could be on the other side from where I met Ivy and Dekker.

After snooping around too long, I turn on the water faucet in the walk-in shower. Multiple showerheads come to life in every direction. There are so many, I swear it's like going to Vegas and watching the Bellagio fountains without the music. I guess when you are insanely wealthy, you can afford to overindulge.

I peel off my underwear and shirt, then let out my braid before stepping inside. I wish I had my glasses. My contact lenses feel like they're ready to pop, and my eyes are scratchy and dried out. But, if I take them out, I won't be able to see a thing. I guess I'll have to suffer a little bit longer.

I let out a loud, "ahh," feeling the jets gently massage my body. *Now this is the life.* I could definitely use one of these in my next life. It's like being in a Jacuzzi or hot tub, the only difference is you're standing. Although, there is an L-shape bench for seating.

I can't help but wonder how many women he's fucked inside here. *Probably hundreds.* I was snoopy, and looked around for any female products, but didn't find any. Perhaps, he's one of those guys that screw your brains out, and then kicks you out the door. I can't see Dekker being the cuddling type. Nope. That's not him at all. It's no secret he doesn't do relationships. *Doesn't he ever get lonely?*

When you work with hundreds of people day in and day out, and can have a woman in your bed every night, he probably enjoys his alone time. But I wonder if the thought has ever crossed his mind to settle down and start a family. *Probably not.* Why settle down when you're basically a Hugh Hefner. All Dekker needs to do is build his own Playboy mansion and fill it with blonde women with enormous breasts.

I look down at mine. Absolutely pitiful. Small little bumps that catch no man's attention. As much as I wish to have one night with Dekker, I would totally chicken out. There's no way I would want him to see me naked. I would probably scar him for life or maybe he would laugh. *No, Dekker doesn't laugh, so scarring it is.* I have seen a couple of times a hint of a smile, but I'm pretty sure he doesn't know how to. Maybe in the throes of bliss, does he smile? *Still a no, and besides, who smiles during sex?* Not that he looks miserable all the time. I just think he's a hard man to please.

After wasting too much water, I reluctantly shut off the tap and open the door, looking for a towel. There are two white towels neatly folded on a stool about a foot from the shower door. I frown. I don't recall seeing those before I got in. Actually, I don't recall seeing the stool either.

Oh. My. God! Dekker must have come in.

I don't know whether I want to cry or crawl into a hole. Maybe both. Humiliation doesn't even come close to what I'm feeling right now. *How could he come in knowing*

I'm naked? It's not like the shower is closed in. Nope, there's eight feet of temper glass in plain view as soon as you walk through the door. I would have given him an eye full, that's for sure. I glance back at the glass door. They are somewhat steamed up. Maybe I was lucky and he saw nothing.

Okay, Kinsley, you know that's wishful thinking.

I dry myself off, wrapping the towel around my body, and then towel dry my hair the best I can. After running a brush through it, I see a toothbrush sitting on the counter with toothpaste beside it. It looks new. Not wanting to have morning breath any longer, I use it. If it's his, and he complains, I'll buy him a new one.

Making sure my towel is extra secure, I peek my head out of the bathroom. Two of the curtains have been drawn open, casting light in. I see something on the bed that resembles a dress, so I move in to take a closer look. There is a man's belt on the bed by the pillow and at the other end is a black dress with a pair of underwear. I pick up the undergarment. It's a black thong made with intricate lace and silk, but I don't see a bra. I put it down and pick up the dress. *Wow, this feels incredible also.* It must be silk or satin. I can't imagine what it would feel to wear something this soft. I hold it against myself, noticing the pretty ruffle trim in the front with a side slit. I grin, swinging around and looking for a mirror, when a dark shadow catches my eye. I shriek, feeling my heart thump loudly in my chest, realizing Dekker is sitting in the corner, watching me.

"Jesus H Christ, Dekker! What the hell are you trying to do? Give me a freaking heart attack?"

He doesn't move or speak, and I can barely make out his facial features, but I can see his eyes. They're predator-like. I gulp nervously. That uneasy feeling I had last night comes creeping back.

"What are you doing?" I whisper.

A good thirty seconds passes before he stands, taking a couple steps towards me. I take a step back when his face comes into view. His jaw is set like stone, and his eyes look dangerously chilly. *I'm definitely in big trouble.*

"You need to start talking. Beginning with what were you doing at that pub last night?" He cuts me an icy glare that sends shivers down my spine.

"I… I went there for a drink."

"What were you doing at the pub, Kinsley?"

"I told you already. To have a drink."

"Why else, Kinsley?" He takes another step towards me.

"There's nothing else."

"Rule number one, don't ever lie to me. I'll ask you one more time. Why were you at the pub?"

"Why does it matter?" I retort, not wanting to tell him the real reason, but I suspect he already knows. He just wants to hear me say it. Humiliate me some more.

"Rule number two, don't ever talk back. You've got ten seconds to answer the question."

I grit my teeth, as my nostrils flare. Dekker starts counting. *Who the hell does he think he is? No one has ever talked to me like that, and I don't care if you're considered a God!*

"Go to hell, Dekker. You don't own me," I snap and make a charge for the bedroom door.

Dekker is on me a split second later with an arm latching around my waist and a hand wrapping around my throat. He squeezes, as my eyes flare wide and I clutch his forearm and wrist.

"Wrong answer, Ms. Scarlett."

Ms. Scarlett?

The front of his body is pressed against my backside with an unruly hard erection digging into my ass.

"Dekker," I manage to squeak out as my heart races. His grip around my throat isn't hurting me, but there is definite pressure.

He dips his head, diving his face into my hair and inhaling deeply. I freeze, not knowing what to think or what to do. *What the hell is he doing?*

"You know, no woman has ever called me Dekker but you." I feel his warm lips skim across my neck, sending a ripple of tremors through me. "No woman has ever slept in my bed but you." He nips my earlobe, and I gasp, feeling my nipples harden, but that's not the only body part coming to life. I try to look down to see if my towel is in place. I think it is, but I can't say for sure as Dekker has my neck tipped back, paralyzing any movement.

My brain begins to scramble when I feel his tongue slide down, giving me a long lick to my shoulder until I feel his teeth. He bites down, and I shriek, shooting up on my tippy toes, but he doesn't loosen his grip for a second. Instead, he licks the tender spot as a moan rises up from my throat. I try to stop it, but damn, his tongue feels incredible as my body turns to jelly.

"What's the real reason you were at the pub, Kinsley?" His voice drops down to a low rumble, but I can't focus. His hot breath is invasive as his lips and tongue continue to stroke my heated flesh. At this point, I would give anything for him to bend me over his bed and fill this needy void inside of me.

Another sink of his teeth digs into my flesh, and I screech again.

"Answer me!" he booms out.

"Sex! Christ, Dekker, I was looking for sex. There, are you happy now?!"

"Not even close." With his hand still wrapped around my throat, he turns us and walks over to the bed.

Oh God, I'm not sure if I'm ready for this.

"You need to be taught a lesson, Ms. Scarlett. Drop the towel and bend over the bed." He releases his grip from my throat, but his firm body remains glued to my backside, letting me know there's no escaping.

I stand there unmoving, not sure if I heard correctly. I thought he would have bent me over and put me out of my misery, but I think I'm sadly mistaken as I glance over at the leather belt.

"What are you going to do?" I barely whisper out, clutching my towel.

He leans down, putting his warm breath at ear level.

"I'm going to redden that ass of yours. I won't lie, it will be painful. But you need to be taught a lesson after last night's stunt."

"But I didn't do anything wrong," I argue.

"You deliberately put yourself in danger!" he booms out, making me jump. "If I hadn't got there when I did—" He cuts himself off as goosebumps flail my skin.

I would have been raped. Maybe even beaten or worse, killed.

"Do you know I almost killed a man, because of you?"

"I'm sorry," I whisper, tears streaking down my face.

"Shhh," he says soothingly, nuzzling my neck. "This is something I need, Kinsley. Do you think you can handle it?"

"I don't know," I say truthfully. Not sure why he needs this, but all that runs through my head are what women have said about him. *He is the Kink Master.* There's no doubt in my mind he's domineering.

"Red. Shout red, and I'll stop, or tell me no right now."

Apprehension shoots up my spine along with flutters of excitement. We stand there in silence, not moving as I battle my will. Part of me wants to do this. To know what it feels like, even if it's just one strike. I can shout red, and he'll stop. The other part is scared shitless. He already said it will be painful. I'm not sure what my pain tolerance is. I've never been seriously injured. No broken bones or concussions. Yes, I've had my share of bumps and bruises. Scraped knees from falling off my bike when I was younger, but I don't recall them being too painful. There is also another small part where I want to do this for him. I went to that pub looking for sex. I opened myself up and invited trouble. I deserve to be punished.

Before I can talk myself out of this, I quickly bend over the bed, tucking my arms in tightly, but I don't drop the towel. I can't.

I wait, and finally Dekker steps aside, picking up the belt, and then silence fills the room as my stomach turns inside out. I'm not worrying about how the belt will feel at this moment. No. My nerves are taking flight because I know he's staring at my naked rearend. It's in plain view as the towel is bunched around my waist. His silence is deafening as the blood rushes to my eardrums with a pounding roar.

Humiliation cloaks me, knowing after this, I'll never be able to face him again. Whether I survive the belting or not is beside the point. I close my eyes and kiss my job goodbye.

It feels like an eternity passes when he finally touches my butt with his fingertips. I flinch instinctively. I resist the urge to squirm as I lie there perfectly still, waiting. His fingers trail across light as feathers, and I almost expect him to rip the towel off me.

"Your skin is so milky white and soft."

Those are the last words I hear when the belt comes down in a whoosh sound, landing across my butt cheeks with a loud crack. I scream bloody murder, shooting upright, but a large hand is quick to push me back down, holding me firmly.

"This is for putting yourself in danger!" he roars.

The second blow comes a moment later, and I scream again as fire erupts, spreading outward and scorching my skin. I try to wriggle away, but Dekker isn't having none of that.

"Please. I'm sorry," I beg, tears falling down my cheeks at lightning speed.

"You were reckless and irresponsible!"

Another strike comes even harder and I turn into a blubbery mess.

"I'm sorry," I chant repeatedly, but that doesn't stop him.

Blow after blow, he pelts my skin until hiccups develop, and my mouth dries like the Sahara desert, and I struggle to breathe. I clutch the bedsheets, shaking uncontrollably, and try to focus on my breathing. It takes me several seconds as I lay there suspended in shock from the pain my poor bottom is taking, but there's something else brewing. I don't know what to make of it. My brain is a muddled mess of chaos, but I can feel it in my toes. A tingling sensation that's spreading through my legs, and higher into the pit of my stomach.

I close my eyes, focusing on absorbing this new sensation with the timing of his strikes. My body begins to relax as a gush of wetness coats my thighs. My nipples are painfully hard as pleasure engulfs me. I feel no pain, only exquisite sublime. I don't know it's possible, but it's like my butt is welcoming the hard, fast blows as my pussy quivers with excitement. I lay there immobilized, having lost count of how many times the belt has come down, but now, I find myself melting into each delicious stroke and feeling powerful endorphins whisk me away.

CHAPTER EIGHT

Dekker

My breathing is hoarse and laborious as I layer Kinsley's ass with angry red welts. I can't stop as images of the four guys are getting ready to violate my woman. *She's mine!* I'm the only man that will lay a finger on her.

Mine to discipline.

Mine to fuck.

Mine to worship.

I will fucking worship her because she's a goddamn Aphrodite. *Mine.* I've lost count on how many stripes I've given her. My heart is pounding fanatically in my chest, and my cock feels like a steel bat, ready to combust. I drop the belt to the floor, discarding my pants, ready to claim her.

I grip her hips, bending my knees, so my dick lines up, when I glance up at Kinsley. I freeze. She isn't moving or making a sound. My feet falter, taking a step back as my eyes widen.

Her skin is so ghostly pale with red welts that look overly cruel. My chest constricts. I was too hard on her.

What the hell was I thinking?! I wasn't thinking. All the images from last night came crashing down on me. I took my aggression out on her. And, what's even more unsettling, she got eerily quiet near the end. Thank God, I didn't pounce on her ass. God knows I wanted to, but at least I was somewhat coherent and knew she wouldn't be ready for that, yet. I stare down at her motionless body. The sight lacerates my heart with my dick deflating instantly. *Christ, I'm a fucking bastard.*

"Kinsley?" I whisper.

I move around to her right side, leaning down, and peel back the hair sticking to her face. I frown. *Is she smiling?* Her eyes are close, and I swear to God there's a hint of a smile. I scoop her up in my arms to place her in the middle of the bed and slide in beside her.

"Mmm," she mumbles, nuzzling her warm lips against my neck. The contact immediately sends tingling vibrations down my spine, and my dick goes ramrod hard in a nanosecond.

"Kinsley?" She hasn't opened her eyes, and somehow her towel is still safely intact. That will be corrected soon. I know she's reluctant to let go, and why. But I'll show her soon enough. "Sweetheart, open your eyes," I coax her, slipping my hand through her silky strands. She really does have beautiful, vibrant hair, just like her eyes.

"Hmm, I'm sleepy," she murmurs again, leaning into my touch.

"Other than being sleepy, how do you feel?" I question as I keep stroking her hair.

"Umm… like I'm floating on a cloud."

My brows pinch together for a second, and then it dawns on me. My eyes shoot wide, staring at this beautiful creature lying beside me that's captured my full attention. Goosebumps skitter across my entire body as my head tries to comprehend, thinking it's impossible.

Did she go to subspace?

I've never had a woman sink into subspace before. Of course, I've heard about it, but it's really unheard of.

"Open your eyes, Kinsley."

Her eyes finally flutter open as a brilliant smile appears on her face.

"Hi," she whispers with innocent shyness.

I'm completely dumbfounded, as I continue to stare at her. Her eyes are a dark green, but so full of vivid color. Her ethereal beauty almost seems to be intangible and something I want to protect. I certainly don't deserve her, but Christ, I don't know if I can let her go. *I don't want to let her go.*

"Did I do something wrong?" she whispers, pulling away and retreating.

She must be coming down from her high. I don't let her go far, pulling her closer and wrapping my arm around her waist. I take a moment to inhale her delicious scent. She smells like roses with a hint of vanilla. *My Scarlett red rose.*

"You did absolutely everything right, Kinsley." She peers into my eyes with a questioning look. "How was subspace?"

Her brows crease together in a deep frown. "I didn't go to subway."

A rumble shoots straight up from my chest and I burst out howling.

"You do know how to smile and laugh!" she states in disbelief, sitting up on her one elbow, and watching me bust a gut. Her last comment has my stomach aching. I've never laughed this hard in my life, and soon she snickers, finding me humorous. I shake my head, taking a few deep breaths to calm my heart.

I roll over, only to climb on top of her. Her eyes widen, realizing I'm naked with my cock pulsating against her pelvis. This causes her to squirm, and she doesn't know what to do with her hands, so she folds them over her chest. I can tell her nerves are kicking into high gear.

"Who are you?"

She shrugs her shoulders, probably thinking it's a trick question.

"I'll tell you who you are. You are a beautiful, intriguing redhead that's turned my world upside down, but in the best possible way. I'm under your spell, Kinsley, and the feeling is inconceivable."

"Dekker," she says my name with tears brimming her eyes.

I take her wrists, gathering them together in one hand, and pull them up above her head. She resists for a moment as her chest starts to heave.

"I want to try something different. I want to make love to your pussy, Kinsley." This will be another revelation for me. I've never made love to a woman, but I'm willing to give it a try. With my other hand, I move to her towel, slowly loosening the top.

"Dekker, please."

It's a plead not to uncover her breasts. I'm the cause of this. Her insecurity. Yes, she has small breasts, but I know they are perky, waiting to be discovered and paid homage to. I ignore her, unfastening the top, and she closes her eyes. I allow them to remain closed for now.

I peel back the final layer, revealing her taut breasts. The blood rushes to my groin as my dick goes from hard to unyielding hard. I'm pretty sure it could break glass. Her tits are fucking perfect. Dusky pink nipples that stiffen immediately to pointy little peaks. *Christ, I've been depriving myself!*

Tears trickle down the side of her face catching my attention, and I let go of her wrists, cupping her face. I claim her mouth, silently conveying how much I desire her. She gasps at first, eyes flying open as they connect with mine, but I don't stop kissing her. My tongue dives into her hot mouth, tasting her sweet essence. It's my first real kiss in God knows how long. My mouth doesn't usually deliver pleasure like this. It's too personal. I might do hard and fast, and will only last a few seconds, but with Kinsley, I want to go slow. I want to commit everything about her to memory.

I feel her body relax as I watch her eyes drift close. She joins me, lick for lick, tasting, as our tongues mingle in a slow sensual dance. Her hands come up, tentatively feeling my biceps, inching up higher, until her long slender fingers are slipping into my hair. She digs her nails in as she runs them up my skull, and damn, I feel the sensations right down to my toes. I release a low growl, and she freezes, quickly dropping her arms as her eyes pop open. I halt the kiss and peer down into dark green eyes.

"You're so damn perfect, Kinsley. Every single inch of you."

Her hand comes up to cover her breasts, and I catch her wrist in a firm grip, causing her eyes to flare wide.

"Don't ever cover yourself up or hide from me, Kinsley. This is your only warning," I say with a bit of a snarl in my voice so she knows I'm serious. I lift up, straddling the top of her legs and wrapping her hand around my steely cock protruding straight out. She gasps, trying to draw her hand back, and I swear her eyes will pop out now. My hand grips over top of hers, squeezing.

"This is you, Kinsley, and God knows I can't fake this shit. You make me so goddamn hard, and your tits, they're perfect jewels. Mine to suck. Mine to lick, and mine to bite. Your body belongs to me."

With her hand in mine, I make her stroke my cock. Her eyes haven't stopped bulging as she stares at him. She probably didn't even hear me, and I doubt she's ever seen anyone as big as me. *Yeah, I'm a little arrogant in that department.* I'm close to ten inches in length, and goddamn proud of it.

"What's on your mind, Ms. Scarlett?"

Her eyes whip up to mine, and I give her a wink. I slowly release my grip around her hand, letting go, and to my surprise, she keeps stroking. This allows me to cup her breasts, and we both groan in unison. I have to admit, I love the feeling of her soft, supple mounds in my hands. Their perky, beautifully proportioned, and a few more adorable freckles catch my eyes. I drink in her exquisiteness, slowly scanning downward to the satiny toned midsection, to her slender hips and an auburn triangle that leads to another oasis, waiting to be discovered.

I dip my head down, taking her pink nipple into my mouth. It hardens further against my tongue, and I give it a firm flick. Kinsley sucks in a sharp breath with a jerk of her body as she watches me closely. I nip her nipple, sucking it in once more, and pinch the other, hard enough that she lets out a squeak in surprise. I want to test all her boundaries and push her limits. Although after the belting, I believe Kinsley can handle almost anything. She is a natural submissive that's able to slip into subspace. *Subspace!* The thought is still mind-boggling. She is truly one of a kind, breathtaking worldly, and mine.

I focus on her breasts, getting well acquainted with them, sucking, nibbling, and tweaking her nipple and then its twin until my attention is demanded elsewhere. Kinsley's arousal scent is wafting through the air, heavy and thick and smothering all other senses. It's intoxicating, and making me delirious. No pussy has ever smelled this good.

She had let go of my cock a couple of minutes ago as she loses focus, her breathing becoming short and panted. I've been watching her this whole time, and I can tell she's lost in the pleasure, it wouldn't surprise me if she has forgotten where she is, or who she's with.

There's no question, she didn't want to reveal herself to me, probably feeling not good enough. I'll admit, if I hadn't actually stopped and looked her over, I wouldn't have given her the time of day. Yeah, I'm an asshole, and I'll add egotistical to that list. But it was her illuminating eyes that caught my attention first, and then her inner grace. The way she bowed to me like I was a God. I felt a buzz of excitement run through me, and I wondered then if she was a submissive. But the formal way she addressed me, Sir, was another clue. She had my interest piqued.

The more I observed, the more I became obsessed. I've never obsessed over a woman. I knew right there this woman is going to be trouble, but that isn't going to stop me. I need just one little taste. Ms. Scarlett has been promoted to the top of my "must acquire" list. I don't know if this is a temporary infatuation, but right now, I don't care as I have a beautiful woman squirming beneath me and growing hotter by the second.

I slide my hand down between her legs to find she's soaking. I groan, shuffling down her body and pushing her legs wide open as I'm beckoned to play. I don't usually eat pussy, but my mouth is salivating as I hover above, inhaling her glorious scent deeply. Again, I don't think Kinsley is even aware I'm down here. Her eyes have been closed ever since I ravished her tits, making me wonder if she's somewhere between subspace and a state of consciousness. She's been pretty quiet with soft moans and panting breaths.

I open her pussy lips, exposing her pink nub, and blow on her clit. This induces a shutter from her, along with a contented sigh. So far, she's been receptive to everything I've done, and I want to memorize her reaction to all the places I touch. I already know the sight of her reddening ass by my belt had her screaming, and crying until she slipped into subspace. That vision has been permanently embedded into my skull. I will remember this day until my heart stops beating.

I dip two fingers inside her and let out a groan. *Bloody hell, she's tight.* I know I'm not imagining this. The deeper I push inside her narrow channel, the tighter the restriction becomes. If my fingers feel this constrained, I can't imagine what it will feel like with my cock buried deep inside. *Christ, I think I'm going for the biggest revelations revealed in one day.* She is the ultimate enigma that no one has cracked until now. *Jesus, I'm the luckiest son of a bitch alive.*

I strum her clit with my thumb as I finger fuck her at a leisurely pace. I watch Kinsley draw her legs up so they're bent at the knees, feet planted on the mattress, and then she drops her knees wide open. She arches her back, clutching her breasts, and squeezing them. When she starts dancing her ass to the rhythm of my fingers, I feel precum bead as my mouth begins to salivate again. Her heavenly scent is filling my nostrils, and my cock is eager to dance with her. *Fuck me, she's a beautiful sight to watch, and so is that tight little puckered hole.* I'm not sure what my cock is begging for more.

She's already soaking wet, so I withdraw my fingers quickly, sitting up and inserting the head of my cock into her pussy. Normally, I wouldn't give it a second thought, but I don't want to traumatize her any more than I already have.

"Yesss," she hisses, pinching her nipples with a tug, and now, there is no doubt in my mind she is in some kind of suspended unconscious state. Maybe she thinks she's having sexsomnia. She did mention earlier she was sleepy.

"Hey, Ms. Scarlett, you still with me?" I drive my cock home, deep inside her pussy, wanting to wake up sleeping beauty.

Kinsley's eyes fly open in a blink as she lets out a strangled cry, and I grunt heavily, muttering a dozen curses. I swear my cock is caught in the ultimate vice grip, clenching with added conviction. *Jesus Christ, how is her pussy this tight? I've fucked asses that haven't even been this tight!* Her breathing becomes erratic as shock blankets her face.

"Shit, Kinsley, talk to me," I lean down, clutching her face, and it takes a few seconds for her eyes to focus on mine. I repeat myself once until I have her attention.

"Pain," she manages to stutter.

"Where?"

"My pelvis. It feels like I've been ripped open."

"How's the pain now? Is it getting worse?"

She's silent for a moment, and it isn't long before I start to feel her relax beneath me.

"It's getting better. It's like a dull ache."

I blow out a breath, placing my forehead against hers momentarily. It's not uncommon for me to hear a woman say, "You're going to rip me in half." For once, I actually thought I did with Kinsley.

"I thought I was dreaming," she finally whispers.

"I know. I think you were still partially in subspace."

She doesn't comment back or ask what subspace is, as awkward silence settles in, and then she turns her head off to the side, looking away from me.

"You know my first time having sex was... umm, let's just call it a disaster. I think it was his first time too, or at least I wondered, because he was so excited he climaxed even before he was inside of me. I felt most of it on my butt cheeks and on the bed. But he continued on and maybe lasted another ten seconds before pulling out and rolling away from me. I guess he had a little bit left over and it was enough to break through my barrier. I remember lying there feeling... I don't know... ripped off, I guess. It's not how I pictured my first time going. I left his place feeling miserable and robbed, knowing it was something I could never get back. I never did see or hear from him again, and it's been almost three years since then."

An icy chill sweeps through my body, listening to Kinsley as my heart starts to beat faster. My head is spinning, unable to believe what my ears are hearing.

"Then I met you. Of course, I've known about you for a while now. Fantasized over you. Seen you in pictures and have heard what the ladies say about you. You're a God in most women's eyes, gifted with extraordinary... beauty. I know that word may not be fitting for a guy, but you are beautiful, Eric, and a man that is untouchable, experienced, and so far out of my league."

I go to stop her right there, but her eyes briefly meet mine with a shake of her head. I grit my teeth, holding my tongue for now. "Your track record indicates you date blonde women with big breasts. Although, occasionally, you'll change it up and throw in a stunning brunette." She pauses for a moment before continuing. "The point of all this, I'm asking you not to play games with me. Let's not pretend you care. We both know I'm not your type, and I'll only embarrass you come Monday. I'll do us both a favor and quit before I damage your reputation. I'll just gather my stuff and see myself out."

"You're not going anywhere," I snarl, seeing red. If her ass wasn't already layered red with angry welts, I would take my belt to her again and whip her senseless.

This gets her attention as she turns her head meeting my hard glare.

"Let's get one thing straight. This isn't a game I'm playing, Kinsley. If I wasn't interested in you, I wouldn't have been watching you or followed you to that pub." Her eyes grow wide, not knowing that piece of information. "Yes, I've been watching your place since Friday night. I can't get you out of my damn mind ever since I laid eyes on you. You're gorgeous and have the most extraordinary eyes I've ever seen. And, these." We're lying chest to chest, so I lift up, looking down at her perky breasts. "Your tits are fucking amazing, and right now, I want to fuck the shit out of your pussy, until it's raw and swollen. Fuck you how you should have been fucked the first time. And, you're going to cum all over my cock, because I'm going to venture and take a guess and say no man has ever given you an orgasm." She goes to look away, but I capture her chin, holding steady. "It's nothing to be ashamed of, Ms. Scarlett. It just means every guy has been too stupid and blind to see what's been standing in front of them all this time. But I see you, Kinsley. God, do I ever see you. You are sensual, alluring, and sexy as hell."

Her eyes brim with tears, but I'm done talking. I crush my mouth to hers, surging my tongue forward, giving her no choice but to open for me. She does, and I plunge inside, rolling my tongue and entangling it with hers. She tastes divine, and I'm almost tempted to taste her red hot pussy. I haven't eaten pussy or had pussy sex in God knows how long, but for the brief moment my cock had, he recognizes this one is different. He rejoiced and is begging for more. It does make me wonder how long it will take me to climax.

While I have Kinsley distracted, I lift my hips, angling my cock to her slick entrance. It isn't until I start to push inside do I feel her body stiffen as the movement of her mouth stills. I open my eyes to see she's staring at me with a slight alarm in her eyes. I release the kiss.

"We'll go slowly. Tell me to stop if it hurts too much."

I almost half expect her to tell me to stop considering what she told me earlier, but to my surprise, she nods. I inch forward, keeping my eyes trained on her. This will be another novelty for me. I don't do slow, but for her, I will. In many ways she has a virgin pussy, and I want to make this memorable for her. My cock will stretch her, but hopefully not too much because she feels incredible. My body starts to tingle when I'm halfway as Kinsley's breathing starts to pick up.

"Breathe, baby. That's it. Eyes on me. Nice easy breaths," I soothe her, sitting up and drawing her legs up so her pussy opens up for me more.

She keeps her eyes on me, while concentrating on her breathing. Once she relaxes again, I move forward another few inches until I'm fully submerged. I let out a lengthy groan, holding my position.

"How is this? Is it still painful?" I ask.

"It's getting better."

"I can't even describe how it feels for me, Kinsley. It's the most exquisite feeling ever, and I'm telling you the God's honest truth because I'll share a little secret with you. I don't fuck pussy."

She knits her brows for a second until realization dawns on her.

"Never?" she questions.

"Let's just say, it's rare and only at the woman's request."

"Why?"

"I have a hard time climaxing. Not tight enough."

"But I am?" We both know the answer to that question, but I tell her yes.

"I think my dick has found a new favorite spot. I'm pretty sure he doesn't want to come out." This makes her smile, and I give her a wink. "This feels incredible for me. How about we make this feel incredible for you?"

She nods quickly, and I lower my body to hers, cupping her face with my hands and claiming her mouth. She relaxes into me, so I raise my hips, pulling out and pushing back in. I spend the next few minutes gliding in and out of her at a leisurely pace and letting her get used to my size.

Her pussy walls clench around me as she becomes more aroused, and we both let out a series of moans. At this point, I'm not sure how much longer I will last. She's so warm, wet, and crazy beautiful. I think I'm going for a world record here. She's shattering everything I knew and stood for. It's an alarming thought, and I don't know if I can give her what she'll want. *What they always want.* A ring on their finger. I don't do relationships, and the thought has never crossed my mind about getting married or having children. It's something that's way down at the bottom of my list of priorities.

I push that final thought out of my head. I don't want to think about that right now. Kinsley's juices are flowing freely, and saturating my cock. I break the kiss, sitting up.

"Mmm. I can't believe that it feels this good," she murmurs.

"You're about to feel even better." I withdraw my cock, and a frown creases her brow until I'm rolling her over. "Up on all fours, Ms. Scarlett," I instruct her, helping her roll over. Her ass is still glowing red, and my mouth waters. "You have a gorgeous ass. Red looks stunning on you." I run my hand over some of the raised welts causing Kinsley to hiss. "Beautiful," I remark, sliding my cock inside her and making sure to go slow.

Kinsley whimpers when I have two inches left. I stop, leaning over and wrapping my arm around until my finger is thrumming her clit.

"Ohh," she squeaks out, surprised.

"You like that baby? You like it when I play with this beautiful pink nub while my cock strokes you're heavenly pussy?"

She bites down on her bottom lip, nodding yes.

"You going to cum all over my cock, aren't you?"

She whimpers, nodding again. I keep teasing her clit with my thumb as my cock receives the best massage ever. She's clenching around me greedily and soon I feel her body stiffening with short pants.

"Oh, God. Dekker,"

"That's it, sweetheart. Let it go," I tell her, flicking the swollen nub faster.

That does it for Kinsley as she detonates seconds later, letting out a beautiful cry. I increase the speed of my cock, stretching her to the fullest and pounding into her.

I grit my teeth as waves of pleasure milk my cock, squeezing without mercy as her body quivers and shakes. *Too fucking tight!* I feel the sensations shoot down my spine and into my balls. *Fuck, I'm going to cum!* I can't stop it even if I try. I come fast and hard, letting out a roar, exploding, and seeing white spots dance before my eyes. *Jesus, I didn't realize God had a cloud for me to float on.* But, holy shit, that's what I'm feeling right now. I'm floating along in a state of bliss, savoring her pussy for as long as possible.

When I finally open my eyes, I see her front arms have given out as her face lays smushed against the mattress. Her eyes are closed too. I pull out my softening but elated cock.

"Come on, baby," I say, helping her roll over onto her side.

"Hmm, I'm sleepy now," she murmurs.

This makes me smile. She's beautiful when she's dopey or sleeping. I crawl in beside her, pulling her close and covering us up with the blankets.

"Okay, Ms. Scarlett, you have a little sleep. We'll go for round two, soon," I whisper to her.

CHAPTER NINE

Kinsley

I'm having one of those fabulous dreams where you don't want it to end. *Dekker.* He's everywhere. The heat of his body is warming my skin while his decadent scent fills my nostrils. His touch is surprisingly tender as he glides his hand down the side of my body and over the curve of my hip. I feel his eyes on me, taking everything in, but... oh God, this isn't a dream. *I'm in Dekker's bed, and he's lying beside me.*

I'm hesitant to open my eyes. My brain is trying to tell me this isn't real. Dekker does not have sex with small chested women, or redheads. But he did, with me. My bum and pussy are a physical reminder. I think about what he did earlier. My poor bottom taking abuse from his leather belt. God, the pain was horrendous at first, but then, something else took root, spreading its wings. It's like my body had hit a plateau as the inferno manifested into something greater. I felt myself drift into this trance-like state, like having an out of body experience while my endorphins kicked into high gear with all these new heavenly sensations.

I don't even know how it's possible. Logically, it doesn't make sense, but God, it was the most extraordinary feeling, and I would most definitely love to experience that again, *providing I'm able to push past the burning pits of hell.* And, speaking of burning, I reach behind me, brushing against Dekker's hand to touch my butt.

Oh, that's tender!

"I'll get some cream," Dekker says, climbing out of bed.

I still haven't opened my eyes, and my bottom isn't the only thing burning. My eyes are itchy, and severely dried out. My contact lenses have overstayed their welcome. I instinctively rub them with the back of my knuckles, trying to produce moisture. Unfortunately, this causes my lenses to shift, and they both pop out when I blink, trying to put them back in place.

"Shit!" I curse, sitting up, and then curse again with my tush burning. I grit my teeth, fumbling my fingers down my chest to find them, but I can't see a damn thing.

"I can do that if you like," I hear Dekker say in a playful tone.

"I can't find them."

"Find what?" he asks, climbing back onto the bed.

"My contacts. They popped out, and I can't see without my glasses or contacts."

"Do you have another pair in your purse?"

"No."

Luckily, I'm blind as a bat. It's bad enough, sitting here while my naked chest is on display, but at least I can't see his facial expression. Once he finds them, I quickly pull up the blankets.

"Can you see anything?" he questions.

"Not much. Everything is blurry."

"Here, I'll help you to the washroom so you can put them back in."

"They won't go back in. My eyes are too dried out and scratchy. They have overstated their use. I need my glasses."

"I'll send Chase to grab them for you."

I let out a sigh. "I should probably go home before this gets weird and awkward."

"The only one getting uncomfortable is you, Kinsley, and you probably still think you don't belong here or something along those lines. But I meant what I said earlier, and I don't want you to leave."

"It's just—" He silences me with a kiss.

"I want more, Kinsley. A whole lot more, and as for this Monday, you'll come to work and be at my beck and call. Isn't that what you offered?" he whispers low by my ear as I feel him move in, crowding me with his divine scent. My body reacts instantly, craving more from this man.

"Drop the blankets, Ms. Scarlett, and sit back against the headboard."

I find his request a little odd, wondering what he's up to, but I do as I'm told. I let out a groan with my bum protesting, wiggling it to get into a comfy position. At least Dekker's sheets are ultra-soft, and soon the burning sensation settles down.

Dekker clears his throat. It takes me a moment to realize I still have the blanket tucked under my armpits. I'm reluctant to let go. I heard what he said, but it still hasn't sunken in. There are a lot of things my brain is having a hard time processing, but I'll need to work through them once I'm alone. With Dekker this close, he's too distracting. He muddles my thoughts, only eliciting heavy desire.

I drop the blanket with my nipples hardening and wish I could see his face. The eyes reveal the truth. I saw it earlier, and I do believe him, but I need reassurance. *Blonde. Big boobs.* These pictures are constantly running through my head.

"You have beautiful tits, Kinsley, but the next time I ask you to do something, I expect it to be done without delay, or there will be consequences."

I swallow the thick lump at the back of my throat. I don't think my bum is up to another spanking session quite yet. Hopefully, by Monday, I'll be good to go.

His hand brushes along my cheek before he's cupping my chin.

"I see your self-doubt, Kinsley, and I will correct that. If I have to spank the insecurity out of you, I will. You're perfect the way you are." He removes the rest of the blanket, exposing my lower half. "Now, bring your legs up, and wrap your arms around each one." I do without delay, planting my feet on the mattress and then wrapping my arm as he instructed. "Open your legs. I want to see everything."

Jesus, he can't be for real!

I shut my eyes, splaying my legs wide open, keeping my arms locked around each leg. A burst of heat rushes to my face with embarrassment when I feel my pussy lips peel apart.

"Mmm, now that's a pleasant view, Ms. Scarlett," he drawls out with a hum, and I feel my cheeks inflame hotter. "Now, normally I would tell you to keep your eyes open, but I recognize you can't see much, so I'll let that slide. Open your mouth there sweet thing," he says, and I obey once again. He inserts two of his fingers into my mouth. "Suck," he orders.

Embarrassment keeps burning through me, but I close my lips around his fingers and suck. Dekker lets out a low groan as I coat his fingers with my saliva, licking and rolling my tongue.

"Jesus, I can't wait to test out this hot mouth of yours," he husks. I'd be lying if that remark didn't worry me a wee-bit. *Okay, maybe a lot!* I've never given a man a blowjob, and Dekker is undeniably huge. If my pussy had difficulty taking all of him in, I can't imagine how my mouth will fair. "Enough," he commands, and I stop, opening my mouth so he can withdraw. The next thing I feel is his two wet fingers at my entrance.

"This is so pretty," he murmurs, running his fingers against my wet slits, and giving a tug. My breathing catches in my throat as my body jolts. He slowly submerges his fingers in until they can't go any further. I release a whimper, feeling my pussy spasm and tightening as I clench around him. Even his fingers feel impossibly big. Dekker lets out another deep groan.

"An Enigma," he rasps, making me wonder where that comment came from. *Is he referring to me?* But I don't have time to ask or dwell on it as he starts to pump his fingers. Instead, my insides turn to jelly as thick desire sweeps through me.

"Oh." Dekker draws out several moans of pleasure from me as all my muscles tense, and I suddenly wish I could close my legs as I become embarrassingly wet, with a lot of squishy noises. I've been sex deprived for so long it doesn't take much, and well, Dekker's fingers feel like magic, working me over, and pushing up on a tender g-spot that feels incredible. Soon I'm a panting mess.

"Oh God, I think I'm going to cum," I groan as my head swims, my body already drifting into bliss.

As soon as the final word leaves my lips, Dekker withdraws his fingers, leaving my pending orgasm hanging.

"NO!" I shout, my eyes flying open, even though I can't see jack shit.

"I think I'll keep you like that for a while."

"What? You can't do that!"

He chuckles. *The smug bastard chuckles!* Although I'm blind, I see his dark shadow move away from me as the bed dips with his weight, and he's no longer on the bed.

"I'll be back. And, don't think about moving or closing your legs unless you want more layers added to your ass and no touching yourself."

"No, Dekker, please, you can't leave!" I shout as I see his figure retreating further away.

"Patience there, sweetheart, and no more talking. I'll be back."

"Dekker—"

"Quiet!" he booms.

I jolt, clamping my mouth shut, and he's gone a second later, with the click of the door being closed.

Did he just yell at me?

Dekker's dominant side is a bit scary, I have to admit. Of course, I've never experienced this before, and it's a little unnerving. There are too many ups and downs. I don't know what to expect or what he expects of me. What if I end up being a huge disappointment to him? Come Monday, he'll be ashamed to even associate with me, and cast me away like all the others. Is this a one-time deal or will he want more? Do I want more? Too many questions storm through my head, making me even more insecure. Of course, I want more. Who wouldn't? But Dekker doesn't do relationships. That fact is well known. Even if there is a chance that he entertains this for a month or two. Then what? *I'll be sent away.* It's not exactly known where his past assistants have gone, but rumors say they're sent to a different country with a generous severance package.

I don't want to leave New York. I love it here. Yeah, I miss my parents, wishing I could see them more often, and yes, I also live in a micro-small place, but New York is my home. Can I give up everything for a fleeting and insanely intense affair with Dekker? I'd like to say no, but I can't. I don't believe there is one woman out there that would be able to resist him, but not only that, I love how he makes me feel. *Alive, desirable, and wanted.* Yes, the belt was scary as hell and painful, but it ended up being the most remarkable feeling ever. I want to feel that again and again. *After my rearend heals.*

I let out a huff as my pending orgasm deflates. What's that saying, "absence makes the heart grow fonder?" I snort-laugh. I don't know about the heart growing fonder, but the absence sucks. I consider myself a patient woman, but being open and exposed like this is enough to crack my composure. I don't like it. The position isn't uncomfortable, but how do I know he doesn't have cameras recording me? *He probably does, Kinsley.* He probably records all his women. *Now, that's a depressing thought.*

My mind continues to kick into overdrive, wondering how many women he's had in this exact position, needy and waiting. I hate that I keep thinking about all the other women he's been with and comparing myself to them, but I can't help it. Dekker doesn't do redheads with no boobs. What if he leaves me here for hours and the joke is on me?

Tears come out of nowhere, spilling down my cheeks as my thoughts drastically take a turn for the worse. I close my legs, locking my arms around them tightly and rock on my heels, wishing I could turn back the clock.

CHAPTER TEN

Dekker

After making a quick phone call to Chase, I wait ten painfully long minutes as my dick grows impatient and too bloody hard. I'm stark naked, itching to get back to Kinsley. She has a seductive pull I've never felt before, and Christ, I want more. I already have a serious obsession with this redheaded beauty, and I've barely touched the surface with her. I can't get enough, and at this rate, I just might tie her to my bed until I have my fill of her.

I glance at the clock seeing it's shortly after noon. If it was late afternoon, I would pour myself a drink to take the edge off. My cock throbs, so I grab it, squeezing harshly and trying to alleviate some of the pressure. Her mouth is going to get a workout and soon.

I'm going to assume she's never given head, but that doesn't bother me. I have no problem teaching her how to suck cock. A thrill of excitement courses through me. Although Kinsley wasn't technically a virgin, she is in all other aspects. She's a blank canvas that I can teach and mold into the perfect submissive. So far, she's blowing all other women I've been with out of the water, starting with the ability to reach subspace.

I realize she has some insecurity issues because of my track record. But, I met the confident woman with grace and dignity at yesterday's interview. I just need to help her overcome that insecure feeling in the bedroom. Show her she is a desirable woman that I'm very much attracted to. Christ, dress her in a runway gown, and she could be a supermodel. She has the height and build. And, there's no doubt, she would be a goddamn siren draped in a deep, crimson red gown with painted red lips.

I groan, crushing my cock. I've never been this hard daydreaming about a woman. Enough of this waiting shit. Time to see Ms. Scarlett and see if she's been a good girl, and followed my instructions.

I silently move to the bedroom door, opening it, and my stomach drops, seeing Kinsley's tears as she rocks back and forth. I'm on the bed in a flash.

"Hey, what's wrong?" I cup her face with my hands, but she pulls away.

"I want to go home, Dekker. Please call me a cab."

I sit there stunned for a moment. *Is she pissed that I didn't let her cum?*

"Talk to me, Kinsley. What's going on? Are you pissed that I didn't let you cum?"

"No. Well, kind of, but that's not the real issue."

"What is it then? Tell me what's going on in that head of yours."

"It's everything, Dekker. I have so much crap floating around in my head, I can't deal with it. I don't *want* to deal with it."

"Because of the women I've dated. You can't get past that?"

"Yes! We both know I don't belong here, but it's not only that. All I can think about is how many other women you have had in this exact position waiting, or the countless blondes you've fucked in this bed. That this is not real, and it's some kind of cruel joke. But, if there is a one percent that this isn't all BS, I don't want to be sent away when you're done with me. New York is my home. But also, come Monday, I'm going to embarrass you publically because I dress like a nun, or even worse, I'm going to make an ass out of myself in the bedroom. I know nothing of this world."

Wow, that is a lot!

"Okay. Calm down," I say gently because she's huffing and puffing after giving me an ear full.

I know I'm to blame for much of this, but I think I know what will help put her mind at ease, or at least I hope.

"Come here, sweetheart." I move in beside her, taking her hand. I feel her reluctance. "Lie with me, Kinsley," I say more firmly, stretching out and urging her to follow suit.

She uncurls her long legs and scoots down on the bed. I pull the blanket up, and she's quick to grab it, pulling it up to her chin. I shuffle closer eliminating the space between us. She tenses next.

"You're naked still," she remarks with shock.

"I am, because I wasn't finished with you."

"What were you going to do?" she hesitantly asks.

"Don't worry about that right now. Right now, I want to hold you."

She turns her head, looking at me. "I hate that I can't see your face."

"I know."

We stare at each other for a long moment before she finally flips over, facing the opposite direction. That's fine. I press my entire body against her backside, and Kinsley whimpers. I'm sure it's because my hard length is pressing on her tender butt, causing her discomfort.

I run my fingers through her fiery red locks. It's dry now, and I see she has natural, full waves. I don't know what kind of shampoo or conditioner she uses, but I swear she smells like roses with a hint of vanilla. I lean in, inhaling deeply. *Exquisite, just like her.*

"You have gorgeous hair," I whisper after a minute of silence. Kinsley remains dead quiet, but I can tell her body is relaxing. I wait a few more minutes, letting her get comfortable.

"You know, you're the first woman I've ever had in this bed or at my place for that matter. No one knows this place exists except for a handful of people that work for me directly." I let this sink in for a moment. "Do you know where you are?"

"In your office building," she says quietly.

"Yes, we are on the ninety-first floor."

"But the elevator out front only goes up to ninety," she questions.

"There's a private elevator at the back of the building that leads to this level. It's not visible to the public and is guarded with several security cameras." She's silent again, so I continue on. "I won't ever lie to you, Kinsley. I know this is all hard for you to believe, but everything I tell you is the truth. You're breaking down everything I've stood for and teaching me there's more to life than what I've known. I can't tell you where this is going or how long, but I don't want this to end. And, as for embarrassing me, never, Kinsley. You're a beautiful woman even if you dress like a Sunday school teacher, but I think that Sunday school teacher is hot, and I very much look forward to disciplining her with a ruler."

Kinsley shivers with that comment.

"What do you say? Are you willing to take a chance?"

"When this ends, promise me I can stay in New York, and I'll promise you, you won't ever see me again."

That final comment from Kinsley leaves me chilled to the bone. *When this ends.* Part of me can't imagine letting her go, but a long term commitment is just as chilling. It's not that I have anything against marriage or kids, I'm just not ready to settle down. I like being a bachelor and having whomever I want. It's the thrill of excitement when I have a new pretty doll. Someone at my beck and call, and I can do whatever I want to them. And when I'm bored, and *I always get bored,* or they try to push me for more, I move on to the next one. It's simple. No strings, just sex.

"If that's what you want, I give you my word."

She turns her head and looks at me. "It is what I want, but I also have one more request."

"Anything."

"I want two months. Nothing more, nothing less."

Two months is usually the norm for me, but when I hear Kinsley say it, it sounds like the end of the fucking world.

"I can commit to two months."

"I don't want any special treatment either. Treat me like you would treat the others."

I treat them like they are nothing because in reality, they are nothing to me. I don't know if I can do the same with Kinsley. She's different. I already know that much. She invokes a side of me that I didn't know existed. I feel the need to protect her, and there's a strong pull of possessiveness. S*he's mine.* Two things I've never felt before with another woman.

"That's fine, but if we're making deals here, then I have a request to add." She nods for me to continue. "No more insecurities. When we're behind closed doors, I want the confident woman I met yesterday afternoon. I want all of you and no shyness. I want to explore all your desires and test your boundaries. You'll follow my rules. Can you handle that, Kinsley?"

She's silent for a good minute as I wait with bated breath.

"Yes. My answer is yes."

Goosebumps plague my skin. I have two full months with this redhead, and I'll be damned if I waste another moment. I roll her over with swift hands, claiming her mouth in a fervent kiss as I blanket her body. She opens for me, not holding back as she wraps her arms around my neck and legs lock around my waist. We devour each other as hunger and passion intensify at lightning speed. I'm quickly learning there is more to this beauty as she matches my thirst. She has fire racing through her veins as we lick, nip, and bite, the flames continuing to blaze, burning so hot, it's scorching. She's moaning and shuddering beneath me, and I swear my dick is going to combust. Her sounds are like an aphrodisiac, deliciously seductive, and I can't wait to hear them again and again.

I break the kiss with my breathing ragged and see Kinsley's breathing is just as labored. *Christ, I could kiss this woman for the rest of my life.* The thought comes out of nowhere, shocking my system momentarily. *Jesus, I need my head examined!* I swear being around this woman has seriously fried my brain cells. But at this point, I no longer care. She's mine for two months. I'll screw her out of my system and move on like I always do.

"I want you in the same position as before," I say once my breathing has adjusted.

I roll off her and expect her to hesitate or protest, but she moves into position with eagerness. I let out an audible groan when she spreads her legs, and I see her pussy lips pull apart, inviting me to play and glistening with arousal. Her cheek turns a shade of pink, but other than that, she remains quiet, holding her position.

"Are you comfortable?" I ask, running my hand over her kneecap and down her leg. I love the feeling of her skin. So soft and milky white.

"I'm comfortable. Just wish I could see you."

"I have an idea," I say, climbing off the bed and heading to my dresser.

I pull out two items that I bought recently. I'm constantly buying new play toys. Replacing. Upgrading. Adding. I like a variety. I'm glad I left this stuff here, not having made time to get it over to my other place. After taking the one item out of the wrapper, I head to the washroom to clean it. Like all new things, it should be washed before using.

I come back to the bed and move in front of Kinsley.

"Are you allergic to Silicone?" I always try to make a point of asking because once, I learned the hard way, having to take a woman I was with to the hospital for having a severe allergic reaction.

"Not that I'm aware of."

"I have a vibrator I'm going to insert inside of you. Tell me right away if you feel a burning or itching sensation."

Kinsley nods, and I can almost guess she's putting two and two together why I'm asking. *Yup, learned from experience.* I hold the next object a couple of inches from her eyes.

"Can you see this?"

"Umm, is it some sort of cloth?"

"Kind of. It's a blindfold. Thought you would feel more comfortable with it on than having to strain your eyes."

She nods again, and I slip the black silk blindfold over her eyes, tucking her hair back. I lean down so my lips hover above hers. She inhales deeply and then bites her bottom lip. I dart my tongue out, gliding across her seam until she releases that plump bottom lip, and then I suck it in. She whimpers as I give it a little nip, pulling out and grazing my teeth along.

"Ready for step two?" I ask, and she nods.

I pick up the We-Vibe vibrator. It's purple, but I make a mental note to look specifically for red play toys. It's her color, no doubt about that. I slide it along her pussy lips, lubing it up. She's still wet, and after probing in and out of her pussy a few times, it glides in effortlessly. With two fingers, I push up, making sure it's in the correct position. Kinsley releases a low moan, and then I wrap the front piece around, so it's flat against her clitoris.

Show time.

I turn it on low, selecting the pulse mode.

"Oh!" she cries out softly as her body jerks to the stimulation.

I find myself smiling, watching her reaction. She's beautiful as a light pink blush creeps up on her face.

For the final step, I stand up on my feet and move between Kinsley's wide open legs, so my cock is directly in front of her mouth. It starts to strain, bobbing with anticipation. I plant my hands on the wall, coming in closer so the head of my cock touches her lips. Kinsley gasps, mouth dropping open, and I almost thrust instinctively. I would have, under normal circumstances, not caring if she chokes or gags, but I don't do vomit. I make a conscious effort to learn their limits and pull out when needed. But I do like throwing in a couple deep thrusts. Pushing past their boundary for a fleeting moment.

"Will this be another first?" I question.

"Yes," her answer comes out in a bit of a squeak as she wiggles a little. I smile, figuring as much and also wondering how long she'll last before reaching her peak.

"We'll take this slow and make sure you don't let go of your legs," I tell her, even though it will likely kill me. But I'll do it, for her. "Open and stick your tongue out." She does, and with one hand, I direct my eager cock to her tongue.

I move the head of my cock around her tongue, and soon, Kinsley takes over, swirling her tongue around the large crown. I inch forward, dying to know how much this beauty will be able to take. I have no problem climaxing when my dick is shoved down a hot little mouth. I'm not sure where the logic is in that, seeing how I can't when I'm in their pussy. *Exception to that rule, Kinsley.* Maybe it's because they can create a vacuum suction effect.

"That's it, sweetheart, you're doing great," I encourage her.

She lets out a moan, and then flattens her tongue, sucking and massaging the underneath of my shaft. It feels great as my cock pulsates, and I continue to inch along. She's almost three quarters of the way when I reach her tonsils. Kinsley groans again, and I feel the sensation drift down my shaft, causing me to groan in return. *Jesus, maybe the vibrator wasn't such a good idea.* I pause for a moment to regroup myself and Kinsley squirms again.

"Breathe through your nose and try to relax your gag reflexes."

I slowly push past her tonsils, sliding in another half an inch or so when she chokes. I pull back immediately, letting her catch her breath. She inhales sharply, gulping down air.

"That's perfect, Kinsley," I say, cupping her chin and rubbing my thumb against her soft skin. She was able to swallow more than most women, but I should have known that. This goddess is full of surprises.

We start again, and she's eager to try out new techniques with her tongue and getting well acquainted with my length. I pump in and out of her mouth at a steady pace, making sure not to breach her boundary. I love watching my cock disappear into her hot mouth as she continues to learn and work me over. She's stunning and I can't take my eyes off her.

It's not long before Kinsley's breathing turns choppy with the vibrator wreaking havoc on her clit. She'll stop sucking, losing focus, and then start again. Soon her moans and whines take on a different octave, elevating and more persistent as she really starts to squirm. She's going to cum any second.

"Let it go," I grit out, reaching down to tweak her nipple.

She flies apart with muffled screams reverberating down my shaft, causing a spine tingling effect to rocket through me. I take over, gripping her head and riding out her climax as I pump feverishly down her throat.

"Fucking hell!" I bellow, feeling my muscles coil and spasm with the first spurt of cum rushing to the head of my cock.

I withdraw from Kinsley's mouth, fisting myself harshly and cumming all over her tits. My movements are jerky as I grunt and groan, decorating her chest with my semen. By the time my wheezing has calmed down, I hear Kinsley whining and mewing. I drop to my knees, removing the vibrator. She releases her legs, slumping forward with a huff.

"Beautiful," I whisper against her lips as my fingers massage her tender pussy. She whimpers and shudders again as a post-orgasm ripples through her. "Let's get you cleaned up," I say, removing her blindfold.

She squints, blinking her eyes a few times, and then rubs her jaw.

"You're too big. My jaw hurts a little."

I try not to laugh, I really do, but there's no stopping this one. This woman literally knocks me sideways. She flew in like a graceful swan, demanding my attention and stirring up so many emotions. *Laughter is one of them, and it feels good.*

Living in the social media eye for a good chunk of my life and running a multi-billion dollar company has a tendency to toughen up your exterior and your heart pretty damn fast. I didn't get to the top playing Mr. Nice Guy, and that includes social affairs. Any dates or charity events I have gone on, I found the conversations to be mundane and predictable. My competitors fishing for information or the normal work related chatter.

Ms. Scarlett is full of surprises.

"I'm guessing I'm the first woman to say that to you, or at least, admit it out loud?" she remarks after I've stopped laughing.

"You are, but I'll take it as a compliment."

"I don't think you need any more of an ego boost," she says with a hint of humor in her tone.

I chuckle, shaking my head.

"All right, Ms. Scarlett, let's get you cleaned up."

I help her to her feet, and she grips my arm. I feel bad that she can't see, but I had no idea she wore contacts. If I had known earlier, I would have sent Chase to collect, but he'll be here soon enough. I guide Kinsley into the bathroom and start the shower.

"I don't want to get my hair wet again."

"Do you happen to have a hair elastic in your purse?"

"I think I left the one I was wearing this morning on the counter."

I turn and see the black elastic, so I pick it up, handing it to her. She gathers her hair, pulling it back, and twisting it into a bun on the top of her head, and then fastens it into place. I smile, watching her. She's stunningly naked, and although I prefer her hair down, I can appreciate her long, elegant neck. My eyes skim over every inch of her. With the natural sunlight shining in, her skin seems to have a soft glow. My eyes catch a few more freckles, but I haven't taken the time to explore her backside. I'll be sure to do that now. Her entire body is slender, with narrow hips and deliciously long legs.

Jesus, I'm hard again!

"Umm, I'm ready," she says, fidgeting with her hands.

I can tell she's starting to feel uneasy with the silence lingering because I'm too busy gawking, but it probably also doesn't help that she can't see me. So far, she's been doing very well, and I can only assume she's taking our deal seriously.

I take her hand, guiding her into the shower, and I spend the next several minutes washing her body. She's quiet the entire time, and I wonder what's going on in her head.

Is she having second thoughts? Did I hurt her?

"Is everything okay? You've been pretty quiet," I venture asking.

"Why didn't you... cum in my mouth?" she finally says after a few seconds of hesitation.

I turn her around so she's facing me.

"Is that what's bothering you?"

She shrugs her shoulders.

"Anything else?"

She looks down at her feet.

"Was it okay?" she barely whispers, I have to strain my ears over the sound of the water pelting down.

I lift her chin back up with my fingers and I see her cheeks are pink again.

"It was more than okay, Kinsley. It was incredible, just like you are," I say before pressing my lips against hers for a kiss. "And, as for the other part, I forgot to ask you beforehand whether you wanted to swallow or not. Is that something you want to try next time?"

She nods timidly, and I can't help but smile. I have no doubt this beauty will try about anything.

CHAPTER ELEVEN

Kinsley

I feel my cheeks still flushing with heat. It was embarrassing to ask, but I had to know. I guess everyone needs an ego boost once and a while, providing you get good feedback.

Dekker turns off the water and then takes both of my hands, leading me out of the shower. I hate that I can't see his beautiful face, or that I have to rely on him. It makes me feel helpless. If I was in my own home, it's not a big deal. It's tiny, with only a few steps here and there. I should really go home.

After drying off, Dekker applies this cooling cream to my bottom. Instead of feeling embarrassed as he works the cream in at eye level, I'm finding it soothing. It feels magnificent as it works its magic, alleviating the burning sensation. He then carefully guides me back to the bedroom, and holds up the dress I saw earlier.

"Here, let's get this on you, and then we'll go out for lunch."

"That's not a good idea," I immediately say.

"Because you don't have your glasses? Wait right here," he says, leaving me before I have a chance to interject.

I decide to slip on the dress while he's gone. *Holy cow, talk about buttery soft!* The dress feels heavenly against my skin and my bottom, which is even better. I untie my hair, deciding whether I'm going to braid it or tie it back.

Dekker comes back a minute later as I'm tying up the side of the dress. The next thing I feel is a pair of glasses sliding on my face. I blink a few times. *Hey, these are mine!*

"Where did you get these?" I ask, shifting them higher up my nose.

"I sent Chase to get them."

"Who's Chase?"

"My personal driver and security guard."

"How did he get into my place?"

"We have our ways," he says with a wink, but I frown. "Chase told your landlord he was a friend, and you were in dire need of your glasses. She retrieved them and locked up afterward."

"Well that's a relief," I remark.

"Don't you look stunning," he says with a sly grin, glancing me up and down.

I eye him up in return. It's the first time seeing his entire naked body, and good Lord, it's a sight to behold. My body reacts instantly, buzzing with heat from my toes and into my cheeks. I suddenly feel a little light headed as I take in his lengthy package. I watch it grow hard and extend before my eyes, and Dekker releases a low growl.

"I suggest you stop staring at him, Ms. Scarlett, or you'll be bent over this bed in two seconds flat, and I'm not sure what hole I'll go for first."

My eyes snap up to his face, shooting wide at his bold statement. *Anal sex.* It's something I've never thought of, but hearing Dekker's confession earlier, I know it's only a matter of time before he wants to claim that body part. It's a scary thought, but I'll try just about anything for him. I have just two months and I'm going to make the most of every second we are together. Experience all of it because God knows I'll never have this again after him. Maybe I'm overreacting, but it won't surprise me if I compare any potential guy to Dekker and find myself ruined. No one will ever come close to the extreme ecstasy Dekker has made me feel, and it's only been one day. Two months and I'll probably be ready to live my life as a real nun.

"The dress is pretty and velvety soft. Thank you," I say, changing the subject. The other topic can wait a few days, maybe a week or two. Dekker softens, giving me a splendid smile and it warms my heart. He really should smile more often. He has a killer smile, but that doesn't surprise me. *Killer smile. Killer body.*

I watch Dekker get dressed and continue to gawk when he isn't paying attention. He slides on a pair of tailored pants, medium grey in color, and then a black fitted dress shirt that molds to his body, accentuating his biceps. He's definitely drool worthy clothed and unclothed.

"All right, darling, let's go for lunch."

"No," I immediately say, causing Dekker to narrow his brows together.

"Excuse me?"

"I'm sorry, but I don't think it's a good idea to be seen together."

Shock registers across his face momentarily, and I am a little surprised by his reaction. I would have thought he'd be on board, keeping our affair a secret, considering I'm not his usual type, and I certainly assumed he wouldn't want to be caught dead seen with me.

"Why are you surprised?" I question.

"It's just... I guess I wasn't expecting that."

"You don't agree?"

"Yeah, it's fine. Whatever you want."

I frown, not liking his vague response. For the life of me, I can't understand why he would object. We are talking about his reputation that he has worked so hard for, socially and business wise. I can only imagine how the media will react. They'll tear him apart, and I certainly don't want to be responsible for that, or put under a microscope myself.

"I just don't want to deal with the backlash from the media or the employees that work for you." He seems to understand this as he gives me a nod. "Well, I guess I should probably go home, so my cat doesn't think I abandoned him."

"I don't want you to leave. I was hoping you would stay another night," he says, catching me off guard. "I'll order in, and can send Chase to pick up your cat."

"Really?" I state in disbelief.

"Yeah, really. Why does that surprise you?"

I shrug my shoulders.

"I just thought—"

"That I've changed my mind or I've had enough for one day? No. Our arrangement starts now and that means I want to spend as much time with you as possible."

I have to admit that thought crossed my mind or that he'd rather spend his Saturday with one of his blonde beauties and then realize what a huge mistake I was.

"Are we exclusive?" I ask, needing to know. He doesn't have to worry about me, but the thought of him screwing other women while we're together doesn't sit well. I'm not catching any diseases. "And, when was the last time you've been tested? We should have discussed this before, and you didn't wear protection," I add.

"I was actually tested on Thursday. I'm clean." Relief washes over me.

"Are you on birth control?"

"I am, but I'll need to pick them up as well. How about I go home, make sure my cat is fed and grab a change of clothes? My cat won't come to Chase anyways."

"I could always stay the night with you," he counters back, but the word "no" is out of my mouth like a speeding bullet. The last thing I want is Dekker to see how miniature my place is. I swear his bathroom might almost be the same size.

"If it's the size of your place you're worried about, then don't. I know not to judge a book by its cover," he replies, already knowing where my thoughts have gone, but that still doesn't change my mind.

"Your place is fine."

"How about we eat first, and then we can head out?"

I nod and while we wait for our food to arrive, Dekker gives me a tour of his place. I'm pretty sure my mouth would have been gaping open the entire time if I hadn't made a conscious effort not to. Instead, I walk behind him, silently taking in the luxury of wealth surrounding me. Dekker has spared no expense to soaring ceilings, with oversized skylights and floor-to-ceiling windows facing the front of the building and to our right.

A state of the art chef's kitchen in dark grey and white that even includes an entertainment bar area and a secret passage to an extensive wine cellar. Contemporary furniture pieces are strategically placed, following the same color pattern as the kitchen, with splashes of color in oversized artwork hanging on the walls. For the most part, his place is open concept, and he even has his own private gym.

The doorbell rings, signaling our food has arrived, and Dekker leads me back to the kitchen.

"I'll show you the upstairs later, and there's also a fire exit stairwell that will lead you to the parking garage in case of an emergency or the elevator malfunctions. The elevator does not stop on any other floor, except for my office, here, and the garage."

I give him a nod as I take a seat on the kitchen island bar stool, waiting. It's not long when two servers come into view, carrying two big platters full of food. Dekker tells them to set them down on the island, and my mouth instantly starts to water, eying everything up. There is an assortment of deli wraps, including egg salad and tuna, and a bowl filled with taco salad. A third platter is set down, and my stomach grumbles when I see the mountain of desserts on one side and an assortment of fruits on the other. I clutch my stomach as my eyes shoot wide. The young gentleman smiles at me and then turns to give Dekker a slight courtesy bow.

"Will that be everything, Sir?"

"Yes, Philip. Thank you."

He sees him out, and I can't stop drooling, eyeing all the food. It feels like I haven't eaten in days.

"A little bit hungry, Ms. Everett?" Dekker remarks as a flicker of amusement passes through his facial expression.

"Maybe just a wee-bit."

"Sorry, but that would be my fault. Our morning was a little tied up."

I feel my cheeks flush recalling every vivid detail. It was definitely worth not eating. Dekker grabs two plates and peels off the plastic wrap, giving me the go ahead to dive in. I select a tuna wrap, and a turkey and cheese wrap, and scoop out some taco salad for now. Dekker chooses what looks to be roast beef and some taco salad. I suddenly feel embarrassed and like an oinker for taking two wraps and a bigger salad serving. I debate putting one back, but that would be obvious and even more humiliating.

He sits beside me, placing a bottle of water by my plate. I can't look at him, and for once, I'm thankful my hair is down. I lower my head with my hair hiding my face.

Jeez, Kinsley, of all times to make a pig out of yourself, you choose now!

"Aren't you going to eat?" Dekker asks when I haven't touched my food.

I pick up the tuna wrap, taking a bite, and my stomach decides to growl again, desperately wanting more.

Oh. My. God!

"When's the last time you've eaten?" he questions and I can feel his eyes boring into me.

"Last night."

"Look at me, Kinsley."

I reluctantly lift my head, turning to look at him. Somehow, I know where this conversation is going.

"What did you have?"

"Food."

"Kinsley," he says with annoyance in his tone.

"It was a TV dinner," I whisper, feeling ashamed.

"TV dinner? That's hardly a meal." I know he's chastising me, but I buy what I can afford. "I'm sorry, Kinsley, that was insensitive of me," he says, taking my hand, giving it a gentle squeeze. "Eat, sweetheart."

I nod, and again, I try to make a conscious effort not to devour my food in seconds. It turns out that after eating the tuna wrap and salad, I feel pleasantly full.

"Sorry, but I can't eat the second one. I guess my eyes are bigger than my stomach."

"Are you sure?" I give him a nod. "No worries. I'll just pack everything up, and we can snack on the desserts later."

After Dekker puts everything in his fridge, we head out. I'm introduced to Chase and notice he barely glances at me, nor does he offer his hand. A swift nod of his chin is my welcome. I'm not sure if I should be offended or if that's the way he is, but I'm kind of glad we didn't shake hands. He's a touch scary looking if you ask me.

Once we're in the SUV, Dekker pulls out a laptop and tells me he has some emails to attend to. I give him his privacy, staring out the window. Forty-five minutes later, I start to get antsy the closer we get to my apartment. I don't want to be caught seen with him, nor do I want him to see my place.

The SUV finally pulls up to the curb, coming to a stop and Dekker closes his laptop at the same time, causing me to cringe.

"Ready?"

"Actually, I'll just run in by myself. I'll only be a couple of minutes."

"Kinsley," he narrows his eyes at me.

"Please, Dekker, there are too many people around, and I would like to avoid rumors if possible."

"Fine, but I want your security code."

"Why?"

"Just in case you forget something, I can send Chase to pick up." It's my turn to narrow my eyes. That's a lame-ass excuse if I've ever heard one. "My rules, Kinsley," he reminds me, and I grit my teeth.

"Fine. 0258520."

He nods, and my passenger door opens on cue. I slip out and beeline up to my apartment. Mittens peeks his head out from the cat tree as soon as I open the door.

"Hi, baby!"

He scurries down and comes running. I bend down, scooping him up in my arms and snuggling him. I actually missed him as he purrs like a diesel truck in my ear.

"I'm sorry, sweetie, but I've got to make this quick. I'm spending the night at Dekker's place, but I promise I'll come home as soon as possible."

"Why don't you pack up all his stuff, and you and your cat stay with me for the next two months?"

My stomach drops hearing Dekker's voice behind me.

"You promised me you'd stay in the car," I barely whisper.

"No, I didn't. You told me you didn't want to be seen together, so I waited until you left and then came up. No one even glanced at me."

I close my eyes. *Son of a bitch! He's got me there!*

"Kinsley," he moves in so the front of his hard body is pressed against my backside, and he wraps his arms around my waist, "you have a nice place, but more importantly, you have a roof over your head. It's nothing to be ashamed of."

He moves my hair off to the side so he can press his warm lips against my neck. A tingling sensation spreads through me, sending a shiver down my back. *How can I be mad when he does this?* He turns my brain to mush as his rich cologne surrounds me, making my body come alive with desire.

Mittens decides he has had enough, jumping down from my arms. I turn around, linking my arms around his neck, and bring his mouth to mine. Dekker reciprocates with a low groan, picking me up swiftly and carrying me to the bed. He lowers me down, and his hands move to untie my dress, exposing my nakedness. A moment later, they're latching onto my breasts, squeezing firmly until I feel a sharp twist of my nipples. I break the kiss sucking in a gasp, and feeling a gush flow between my legs. Dekker takes the opportunity, undoing his belt and lowering his pants and boxer briefs enough to claim me.

His movements are hurried as my legs are wrenched up by his head, and with one hard thrust, he buries himself root to tip, deep inside of me. My mouth falls open as a burst of pain detonates in my lower abdomen, and I see stars explode behind my eyes. Its sensory overload as my body goes into shock. He's too big. I can't even tell you if I screamed or not, but I'm pretty sure I blacked out for a split moment.

"Fuck!" he bellows, setting off a ringing in my eardrum. "Shit, Kinsley! Are you all right?" I lay there paralyzed until I feel fingers digging in, and gripping my face. My eyes come into focus, seeing Dekker's face is inches from mine. "Kinsley, talk to me, baby."

"I'm okay, I think," I finally say, taking stock of my body. The pain and shock are dissipating. *Christ, will I ever get used to his size?* "Just sensory overload. Having a little hard time accommodating your size."

He lets out a sigh, placing his forehead against mine.

"Sorry. The last thing I want is this to be painful for you."

I'm surprised he cares, and I don't mean that in a malicious way, but we are talking about Dekker. From what I've learned so far, he's domineering in the bedroom. He likes to inflict pain, but not scarring emotional pain. Obviously, he does have a compassionate side, I have seen that, but I do wonder if he's like this with other women he's been with or is it just me.

I can feel his cock pulsating inside of me, so I give him a squeeze. Dekker lifts his head up with a growl.

"I'm good now if I haven't killed the mood."

"Don't have to ask me twice," he states, standing back up. "All right, Ms. Scarlett, ready for this pussy to take a beating?"

"As long as I can still walk afterward," I remark.

"Can't make any promises," he says with a chuckle.

I cringe slightly, but Dekker winks at me. To my surprise, he eases himself in and out a few dozen times. It still feels like my lower abdomen is being split open, but the discomfort is fading. He's stretching me, but hopefully not too much. I'll give anal a try, but I don't think it's something I would want to do all the time. He has already admitted regular sex is a novelty for him. I wonder how long it will be before he has trouble climaxing.

Dekker picks up his pace once my body has surrendered and soon my insides are gushing with pleasure. I never knew sex could be this amazing, but that's probably his doing. The tingling sensations that are buzzing through me feel incredible. It's like a drug, feeling medicated and buoyant as my pussy quivers in excitement.

Dekker pulls out so he can roll me over, thrusting my hips up so he can dive back in. I go to grip the bedsheets, but he has other plans, gathering my wrist and locking them behind my back with one hand as he really lets loose. His hips are like pistons, jackhammering into me and driving in deep. At least I was able to remove my glasses before they became embedded into my face.

My face is shoved into the mattress as more exquisite pleasure ricochets through me until I'm lost in a sea of lust and desire. Dekker's breathing becomes hoarse with the sound of slapping skins, and a number of guttural grunts and groans fill my tiny apartment. It won't surprise me if my smoke alarm goes off as we ignite flames.

"Oh, God," I mumble, knowing I'm seconds away from cumming.

"Cum for me, Ms. Scarlett. Cum all over my cock," he growls, and I do, crying out as my orgasm consumes me.

Dekker's movements are sporadic as he curses a couple of times before letting out a booming roar seconds later, finding his own release.

I lay there trembling slightly as my orgasm diminishes and feeling completely sated. *So good!* He frees my wrists and pulls out his softening dick. I feel semen seeping down between my thighs, but I don't want to move just yet. I'm still in a state of euphoria and feeling slightly drowsy. My body isn't used to this kind of physical and demanding activity. I really should start working out, or at least take up jogging.

I feel a warm wet cloth cleaning between my legs, and I hadn't realized Dekker had stepped away.

"Do you need another nap?" he questions with a hint of humor in his voice.

"Maybe. I'll let you know once I wake up." He chuckles behind me. "All right, all right, if you insist, I'll get up," I say, pushing up with my arms.

I grab my glasses first and as I turn around, Dekker smirks. I roll my eyes, picking my dress off the floor and putting it on again. Dekker has already tucked himself back in.

"I really need to get a new set of contact lenses. My glasses almost became a permanent fixture on my face," I say, sliding my glasses up my nose a bit more and I see Dekker cringe.

"Sorry. Not used to a woman wearing glasses, but they do look cute on you. Maybe you can dress like a naughty Sunday School teacher for me sometime." I snort-laugh, causing Dekker to smile. "Don't you have an extra pair?" he now asks.

"No. But even if I did, I really need to have my eyes examined. It's been three years since my last one. That's probably why I can't wear my contacts for more than three or four hours. They give me a headache and these..." I take off my glasses to clear the smudge on the left lens, "these need to go also. They hurt my nose bridge after a while."

"Well, let's go. I'll take you to my optometrist."

"That would be great but it will have to wait a while longer, until I've been paid a few times," I say with a smile, but Dekker frowns.

"It's on me. I don't need my new assistant getting headaches and missing work."

"That's not necessary—" I go to say, but Dekker cuts me off

"It's not up for discussion, Ms. Everett. We are going if I have to drag you there."

I roll my eyes. *Such dramatics.*

"Fine. Let me grab a bag and we can head out."

"Have you given my earlier request any thought?" I frown, not recalling anything particular. "Stay with me for the next two months."

My eyes grow wide. *Yeah, I totally missed that request.*

"What about my place? I can't lose it."

"I'll pay your rent since I'm the one asking. That would only be fair."

"I don't know what to say. I'm in shock. Do women usually stay with you at your other places?" I ask, needing to know.

"That doesn't matter. I'm asking you to stay with me."

I narrow my eyes briefly, not impressed by his lack of reply, but I get the feeling I'm the only one, which really doesn't make sense. *Why me?*

I look around my place. This place is only going to get stuffier when the real heat hits. I don't mind it during the daytime, but it does suck sleeping at night. I also get the feeling I'll end up staying at his place more often than not. And what's even better, I'll be minutes from work.

"And, you don't mind that Mittens comes too?"

"No, not at all."

"All right, but only if you're really sure. I don't want to impose on your life."

"I insist."

I give him a nod and wonder if I've truly lost my mind. I've never lived with a man before, and we aren't just talking about any regular guy. But at least this way, we should be able to be more discreet, considering no one knows that Dekker lives in the same building as he works in.

I glance around my place once again deliberating what I should pack. My clothes are an embarrassment, and I still think there's a good possibility he will be embarrassed by my appearance come Monday. I'm about to change my mind when Dekker speaks first.

"Pack your personal belongings and the cat food. You won't need anything else," he tells me.

I furrow my brows together, and then it dawns on me.

"No way—"

"Do not fight me on this, Kinsley. I have no problem using my belt again," he cuts in, cocking his eyebrow, daring me to try.

I clench my teeth, knowing he probably won't think twice about doing that again. *Domineering arsehole.*

"Fine, but I have one thing to say," Dekker nods for me to continue, "just because you're Mr. Money Bags doesn't mean I asked for any of this. I could care less if all you had was two pennies to rub together. I want the man, not his money. And, as for the clothes, I will take nothing when our deal is up, and I'll pay you back for the eye exam and contact lenses after I save up enough money, and don't you dare argue with me about that or I'll walk."

Yeah, I'm pissed! I certainly don't want to be betrayed as some kind of gold digger in his eyes.

Dekker lunges, hoisting me into his arms and stealing my breath away with a ravenous kiss, it has my heart thundering in my chest. It's fierce and savage as my back gets crushed against the wall, and I forget how to breathe for a moment. My thoughts are muddled as he invades my mouth with firm lips, and a tongue that not only lacerates mine but my heart as well. My pussy clenches with hunger, needing this man to claim me once again.

My legs are securely wrapped around his hips and my arms are locked around his neck. I grind my core against his hard erection, and only then does he tear his lips from mine with a low rumble vibrating through his chest.

"Christ, Kinsley, what are you doing to me?" his words are hoarse and uneven as we both gasp for air.

My lips feel swollen and bruised, but at this point, I don't care. I want more. He drops one hand down, gathering my dress until his hand is squeezing my bare ass. I gasp as my tender bottom ignites with flames.

"Show me your fucking tits," he growls in demand, and my fingers fumble, untying my dress and opening it wide for him. Somehow, he balances me with one arm so he can free his cock. "Don't let go." Is the only warning I get when he drives his hips upwards, impaling himself in one deep thrust, and burying himself to the hilt.

My head drops back as my mouth opens in a silent scream.

"Fuck," Dekker grunts but doesn't stop as he ruthlessly takes me hard against the wall.

His eyes lock onto mine, blazing with liquid fire as I grip him tightly. I can't look away as his dark grey eyes demand all my attention, paralyzing me to my very core. His ripped muscles work overtime, flexing and bunching while I'm at his complete mercy in his powerful embrace as he takes and takes and takes until I'm a quivering mess. I can't stop moaning. The electric current flowing between us continues to kick up, crackling with energy as our entangled bodies become one. Nothing else matters as I feel him penetrate my soul, cracking it wide open. I know it will be beyond repair. Eric Dekker owns me. I didn't want to give it away and I'll be devastated when this ends, but if this is all I get, I would do it a hundred times over.

I'm the first to reach my peak, tipping my head back and letting go as exquisite pleasure rushes through me. Dekker curses a few times, grunting and groaning as he continues to plunge into me until his orgasm crashes through him.

He lays his forehead against mine while he slowly releases my legs. They feel like jello as we try to calm our racing hearts and labored breaths. I swear I feel like I've just run a two hundred metre dash.

"Did I hurt you?" he asks, pushing my hair off my face and neck gently.

Him asking that question almost brings tears to my eyes. Dekker may be a lot of things, but he has a side of compassion that speaks to my heart. I cup his face, kissing his lips softly.

"Never," I whisper.

We hold each other's gaze for the longest moment, and I wonder what he's thinking. Was it as intense for him as it was for me? Probably not, but that's okay. As long as he finds his release, that's all that matters.

Once we're dressed again, I pack up my personal belongings and get Mittens in his cat crate. He's pretty good as he walks in, lying down right away.

"Okay, I'm ready."

He takes my backpack since I don't have much to bring. I then make a pit stop at my landlord's place, telling her she won't be seeing me much for the next couple of months, but ensuring her, I'll be back. Dekker hands over four grand, telling her it's the rent money for the next two months and to keep the change. Selma's mouth drops open when the cash is placed in her hand.

Dekker doesn't waste another moment, guiding me out and into the waiting SUV. We first take Mittens back to his place, and I spend some time showing him around. By the time we get back to the main living area, I see a six foot tall cat tree already put together. It's almost identical to the one he has at home, including a cubby hole for him to sleep in. When I peer inside, there is a fluffy blanket for him. I look back at Dekker, from where he's sitting on the couch, watching us.

"Did you do this?" He nods. "That was sweet of you, thank you." He gives me another brief nod, and I turn back, showing Mittens his new spot.

"Here you go, sweetie. You're new home for a couple months," I say, helping him into the cubby hole.

He turns around in a circle a few dozen times, pawing at the blanket before he decides it's good enough to lay down. I lean back, smiling. Looks like he's happy. Now that Mittens is comfortable, I turn back to Dekker. If I didn't know any better, I would say he looks pissed. His facial expression is impassive and I wonder if he's having second thoughts.

I attentively approach him, and he doesn't take his cavernous eyes off me. Once I'm standing within an arm's length, he reaches for me, wielding me to straddle his lap. I do, and run my hands up the length of his strong arms.

"Are you having second thoughts? Because if you are, I'll understand. It's really no big deal."

His hand comes up, caressing the side of my cheek, until he captures my chin, leaning in to give me a tender kiss. It's surprising how gentle he is, but it doesn't explain why he looks troubled.

"Dekker?" I probe again.

"No, Kinsley. I'm not having second thoughts."

"Then is everything okay?"

"Everything is perfect, including you."

I smile at his compliment.

"All right, did you want to show me the rest of your place? You mentioned you have an upstairs?"

He stares at my face for the longest time, remaining silent, and it reminds me of the first time we met. I still don't know what to make of it. My face is plain Jane as I don't wear a stitch of makeup, and with these big gaudy glasses on my face, I probably look even more unattractive.

"My optometrist said he'll fit you in today, but we need to leave now."

"You know, it's really—" A finger is placed over my lips, silencing me.

"We're going."

I give him a nod and can't help but wonder if the glasses do bother him. I would completely understand if he did, and honestly, the thought of ditching these clunky frames is kind of exciting.

No more achy nose bridge.

CHAPTER TWELVE

Dekker

I need to get Kinsley out of here before I rip her dress off and claim her again. My appetite for sex has always been vigorous, but with Kinsley, it's off the fucking charts. I want her endlessly. I don't know if it's because I haven't felt a pussy like hers in probably close to a decade. It's like having sex for the very first time. You're hooked after the first dose.

The feeling I get when I'm inside her is indescribable, and I'm already counting down the minutes until my next fix. But first, she needs her eyes tested. I don't need her getting headaches because I plan on taking her as often as possible—at work and here.

Once Kinsley is comfortable with Dr. Paul, I pull out my cell phone and respond to a dozen emails, it doesn't matter if it's the weekend or after hours. The emails continue to come in. My job never ends. I'd be lying if there weren't times when I wish I could throw in the towel. I've got more than enough money. It's actually sick how many zeroes I have in my bank account, not just one account either. I have a number of investments in stocks and bonds, and in offshore accounts. I think I need to take a break this winter and skip out of town for a few months. Maybe I'll take up residence in Bora Bora. I haven't been there in eight years, and I'm sure I'll have no problem finding a woman to warm my bed for a couple months.

Kinsley giggles and has my eyes snapping up to see she's trying on glasses. The thought crosses my mind on taking her with me.

"I don't know about these. They almost look like cat eyes frames in leopard print. Dekker, babe, what do you think?"

She turns, striking a pose for me, and I'm stunned momentarily by her beauty. It doesn't matter whether she is wearing big gaudy frames or contact lenses, she has radiance that shines.

"Dekker?"

I put my cell phone away and close the distance in three long strides. I take her face in my hands and kiss her lips.

"You're beautiful," I whisper.

Kinsley turns a shade pink and then looks for Dr. Paul. He's smiling, but I don't care. He's an old man that should retire, but I don't have to worry about him spreading gossip. I think Kinsley realizes that as well as she smiles back.

"Well, do you have something a little less dramatic and light on the nose bridge?" she asks, removing the glasses.

Dr. Paul shows her dozens of pairs, and she finally decides on a semi-rimless frame, dark brown in color with actual nose pads and super lightweight. The lenses will be ready by next Friday, but in the meantime, Dr. Paul is able to fit her with contacts. I order six more sets. That should last Kinsley the entire year. Of course, she goes to protest, but I give her a firm glare. She locks her mouth close, and clenches her jaw. I give her a wink trying to smooth things over, and she screws up her nose with a little huff. I chuckle, loving her annoyance.

"Dr. Paul said I shouldn't have any more headaches. That's the reason why I was getting them because my prescription has changed quite a bit. I'm even blinder than I was three years ago," she says with a snicker as we climb into the SUV.

I don't let her get too far, pulling her on my lap so she's straddling my legs, and when I peer into her enticing eyes, I see they are dancing with lust and desire.

"Take out my cock. I want you to ride me," I tell her as I untie her dress, exposing her naked breasts. I need to buy her a whole wardrobe of this style of dress. Easy access, and what's even better, she doesn't need to wear a bra. A definite plus to being small chested that I never thought of before. My eyes travel down her naked body, soaking up every detail and down to a revealing pussy. My eyes whip back up to hers, and I see she is biting her bottom lip, nervously. I hadn't realized she didn't put her thong back on at her apartment.

Naughty little vixen.

I grab her ass, clutching firmly with a low growl, and Kinsley gasps, lifting up on her knees for a second.

"Have you been bare this whole time?"

She nods, still biting her bottom lip until her face breaks out into a grin.

Holy hell! Someone has a little devil streak flowing through her.

"Well, aren't you full of surprises, Ms. Scarlett. If your ass wasn't already tender, I would take you over my knee and spank some more naughtiness into you." Her face reddens further as she squirms on my lap. I chuckle. "Not today there, sweetheart, but once that gorgeous derriere heals, I'm taking full advantage once again." Her eyes glow a turquoise shade, shining vibrantly, and I'm stunned by the vivid color.

Her beauty may be simple, but the extraordinary color of her eyes is something that makes my heart beat faster. Breathtaking doesn't quite cut it. It's like I'm looking into the depths of her soul. Eyes that hold so much light and power, it steals something from you without asking for permission. It holds you like a prisoner and I'm not sure if I can break the spell, which is unsettling.

Shaking those troubling thoughts away, I tear my eyes from hers. I take her hand, placing it on my swollen erection and reminding her what I asked for. Her gasp is subtle as her fingers remain still, hesitant at first until she's reaching for my belt. Slowly, she gathers enough courage until her fingers are slipping inside the band of my briefs, clasping around my cock in a firm grip. I groan, closing my eyes and savoring the feeling of her touch. I can sense her eyes on me every second as she squeezes, adding just enough pressure, I feel pleasure tingling up my spine. But I don't want her hand, I want her pussy.

Lifting up, I dislodge her hand so I can push my pants down enough to set my cock free. He bobs with eagerness as Kinsley drops her eyes to him, darting her tongue out to lick her bottom lip.

The tingling sensations continue to flutter, finding that simple act sexy and alluring. Grabbing her hips, I lift her up, so her heavenly heat hovers above the head of my cock. I don't thrust her down like I'm itching to do so. No. Instead, I hand over the reins. Something I don't do, or at least, not very often and it's a struggle. I don't like giving up control. I live and breathe for control, power, and dominance in all aspects of my life.

I peer into the eyes of the woman that has bewitched me.

"Take me, Kinsley. I'm all yours."

Her breath hitches before she places her hands on my shoulders. Sucking in her bottom lip, she slowly and most painfully lowers herself until my cock is entirely submerged in her sensual heat and we both let out a throaty groan.

My mind and body still goes into shock every time I'm inside of her. I keep thinking next time will be different. That the first couple of times were a fluke, but so far, there's no change. Her pussy greedily consumes me in her strict confinements, and when she squeezes, I swear I see spots dancing before my eyelids.

This time is no different as Kinsley takes charge, bouncing up and down on my cock, letting pleasure build until we're drowning in ecstasy. I torment her pink nipples with harsh pinches and twists until she cums hard and fast, taking me with her.

By the time our breathing has returned to normal, Kinsley notices the vehicle isn't moving any longer, but I knew we were back in my private underground parking lot. Her cheeks are already flushed, and once I help her get dressed, and Chase opens the back door, her face burns crimson red, knowing he knows what we were doing. I don't give a flying fuck what he hears or thinks. He's paid an obscene amount of money to keep his comments to himself. But I know I don't have to worry about Chase.

He's an ex-military man that's been in the middle of a war and seen gruesome shit no person should ever see, and because of that, the man rarely shows any emotion. He's always stone-faced, and I'm sure he suffers from PTSD. Once, I mentioned to him about getting some help. His response was a rough gruff and I never asked again. But I did hand him a business card for a psychologist I knew quite well. Dr. Sylvia Sinclair has been helping men and women just like Chase for over a decade now. I've known her since high school, and her reputation succeeds her, saying she is a miracle worker. I've never had to use her services, but I do know she is damn good at her job. She's so good, that there is a one year waiting list. I told Chase to drop my name, and they will get him in whenever he's ready. To this day, I have no idea whether he took my advice or not. But I'm guessing not, since it's been three years and he's still just as cold as the day I met him.

The rest of Saturday and Sunday seem to fly way too quickly for my liking. After being dropped off from seeing the optometrist, I showed Kinsley the fire exit and then the second level that leads up to the rooftop, with a sunken in swimming pool that has retractable windows that can be closed during the cold season or when it's raining and my own private dining and lounge area.

Kinsley squealed seeing the pool, and then her face dropped. I asked her what was wrong, and this is when she tells me she doesn't have a bathing suit. I almost burst out howling. *So freaking innocent.* Instead, I give her a wink and tell her that her birthday suit will be just fine. Her face turned another shade of red, and then she snickered, saying, "oops, had a blonde moment for a second."

I then took her back to my bedroom, revealing her own personal walk-in closet filled with brand new clothing, shoes, and accessories while we were gone, along with her own personal dresser filled with lingerie and undergarments. She got eerily quiet as I watched her walk into the closet, standing in the middle and not moving. Needing to touch her, I moved in, wrapping my arms around her waist, and expecting a big grin, but instead, I found silent tears running down her face. I felt her tears twist in my heart. Instead of being ecstatic and racing to see everything she got, she was overwhelmed and humble. I should have known. She lives a modest lifestyle, and not only that, she questioned her salary, thinking it was incorrect.

When I turned her around to face me, she couldn't talk, but instead, she poured her gratitude in a soul stirring kiss. I felt it bone-deep. From there, we tumbled into bed, where we had wild, hot sex until we were both spent.

That night we laid in bed, snuggling close and talking for hours. Something I've never done, nor had the desire to. But yet, I found myself enjoying every second, even when we were talking about mundane stuff like, what's your favorite color, food, middle name, and so on. Kinsley talked a lot about her childhood growing up in San Diego and her parents. Her mother is a PSW and her father works in construction. They've done fairly well for themselves and were able to pay half of Kinsley's tuition without burdening themselves.

In school, Kinsley was the quiet, reserve type with a few constant friends in her life. But when she moved to New York, all connections dwindled away until there was nothing. Now it's just her and Mittens, which she's content with, but as I listen to her story, I can tell she misses her parents the most, only seeing them maybe twice a year.

She asked me about my childhood and parents, and I told her I lived a spoiled life as my dad was the founder of Dekker Enterprises Holdings Inc. but handed over the reins to me. The first question out of her mouth was, "But you're so young."

I was almost twenty-eight when I took over the billion dollar company, but I didn't have a choice. My dad made sure I was primed early for his position, sparing no cost for schooling and sending me to Harvard University. I spent countless hours in a classroom studying economics, accounting, and even engineering, along with achieving my MBA, to satisfy my dad. I then spent another two years shadowing his every move. At the time, I didn't mind. I was money hungry and was more than happy to take over the golden reins and live the high life. But now, sometimes, I regret it. I can't go anywhere without the paparazzi hounding me and thinking they have a right to butt into my personal life. Yeah, I can get laid whenever I want, but because I've been thrust into the limelight, I try to keep myself hidden as much as possible. I have all but one close friend, Jonas Mindfield. We've kept in touch since high school, but it kind of helps that I hired him as my financial controller.

My mom was a stay at home mom and the best mom anyone could ever ask for. While my dad was more of a hard-ass and strict, my mom was a gentle soul with so much love to give. My biggest regret was being a pain in the ass and not spending more time with her. Time that I took for granted and will now always regret.

When Kinsley asked what my parents were doing now. I told her that was enough talking for one night as I rolled her over onto her back, claiming her once again.

When my eyes open Sunday morning, I see it's almost ten. I shake my head. I've never slept past eight on the weekends, and even that's a stretch. I look over to my right, realizing I don't have a certain redhead in my arms. I see her cat is curled up in a ball sleeping on her back and I smile. She's a belly sleeper, as I suspected yesterday. I don't even recall her moving away from me. She was snuggled up against my side when we fell asleep, but now, her face is turned sideways, her arms down at her side, and her legs are spread wide open.

I take that as an invitation, blanketing her body as I slip into her sacred heat. Kinsley wakes up in a flash, arching her back with an 'ooo' of surprise while I let out a raspy groan. Although, I don't think her cat was too pleased with me when I lifted him up, moving him out of the way beforehand.

We then enjoyed a morning swim, and after doing a dozen laps, and knowing Kinsley was butt naked, I grab her, turning our swim into a make out session until a loud gurgling noise freezes my tongue midway down her throat.

Her eyes popped open in a flash, with her cheeks turning a bright pink with embarrassment. I withdrew my tongue with a little chuckle and decided food was definitely more important than sex. It's apparent Kinsley eats like a bird due to her finances. I need to make a conscious effort to make sure her belly is full more often than not. The last thing I need is for her to burn herself out with all the sex we're having or worse, become ill.

After a smorgasbord of hot and cold food for breakfast and lunch combination out on the rooftop balcony, Kinsley's new computer, cell phone, and swipe card arrived shortly after one in the afternoon. It was perfect timing because, unfortunately, duty was calling. I haven't neglected work this much in years, and the emails in my inbox reminded me why.

This is also when Kinsley asks me about the salary. The wariness in her voice said it all. She was praying it was a mistake. I kiss her temple and tell her to get familiar with Outlook and my schedule. She will be required to attend some of those meetings and to browse around my company website. More tears pool in her eyes as she mouths thank you. It was so damn hard to walk away from her when I simply want to take her in my arms and claim her again.

CHAPTER THIRTEEN

Kinsley

I was thrilled when my new laptop, cell phone, and swipe card arrived. That was when it really sunk in, I would be working beside Dekker for the next two months. I know I should keep looking for another job, but I can't bring myself to quite yet. I think part of me hopes that two months will turn into four, six... *permanently.*

A girl can dream, can't I?

The women before me have probably all done the same thing. It's wishful thinking. But... I am different. I'm not his usual type, and he's already told me things I don't believe he's shared with anyone else, including his home.

That has to account for something, right?

The last forty-eight hours of my life have been a whirlwind with so many incredible highs. The sex. I close my eyes, letting my mind drift to all the times I've been with Dekker. It was better than I could have ever imagined. He's gentle one minute and rough the next. I love both sides of him.

The last time we tumbled into bed was insanely hot. He had my legs pinned around my head as he drove himself in so deep I saw stars flash before my eyes. I'll admit it had initially hurt. My body still wants to reject the hostile invasion, but Dekker knows how to open me up. His thumb finds my clit, rubbing circles until my body gives in and surrenders. If I thought he was deep before, this last time had my mouth hanging wide open, and my toes stayed curled the entire time. I still marvel at his ability to pound into me without breaking a sweat and his strength... good Lord, I love watching his hard muscles contract and flex fluently.

Once again, he commanded me to cum and I did. I swear all he has to do is look at me with those dark, brooding eyes or I hear his velvet candescent voice, and I can cum on the spot. I came harder than ever, leaping off the cliff and soaring right along beside him.

The sports bar incident, I've decided to permanently erase from my mind, but I have Dekker to thank for that. It seems like I have a lot to be grateful for because of him, and I search my mind, wondering how I can pay him back. The thank you card I stuffed into my bag without Dekker noticing while we were at my apartment seems insignificant, childish, but without any real funds, I don't have any other options. I highly doubt I will ever be able to afford something meaningful. The gifts he is accustomed to receiving are probably worth thousands of dollars, not a couple hundred. *Besides, what do you buy for a guy that has everything?*

Pushing those thoughts aside, I pull out the *Thank You* card. Dekker is in his office, and he said we'll have dinner together and to make myself at home. After reviewing his schedule for the next two months, I'm starting to wonder if the only time we'll actually have together is on the weekends. The man is insanely busy with meetings after meetings. Whether it's a conference call, office meeting, board of directors gathering, or Dekker meeting his clients off premises, his days are virtually jam packed. We start at nine in the morning and end at five. I also noticed he has a business trip coming up in one month to Las Vegas. He'll be leaving Thursday afternoon and returning late Sunday. I don't figure I'll be going, which is fine, it just means we lose out on three days.

I reread Dekker's card and the part where I indicated '*I look forward to a long career working by your side*,' has me cringing. I wrote before my life drastically changed, but I can't change it now. I didn't bring any of my craft supplies. I place it back in my bag, still undecided whether I'll give it to him or not.

After getting well acquainted with Dekker's schedule and his company, I find myself getting antsy and needing to stretch my legs. I grab my earbuds and cell phone and head upstairs to the rooftop. I gaze out, looking at the colorful city before me. I have never been to the Empire State Building but I can see it standing tall and proud from his rooftop.

The sun is still shining, as a cacophony of sounds fill my eardrums, from sirens blaring, and horns honking, to musicians singing or playing an instrument below on the sidewalks. It's wonderful. I've always admired the people that set up shop on the sidewalks and sing their hearts out, not having a care in the world.

I see Dekker has a Bose Bluetooth speaker outside and I wonder if I can hook up my cell phone to listen. After fumbling around for a good five minutes, I finally manage to connect. I hit play on my music list, and the speaker comes to life. It's almost four-thirty, and I'm guessing I have another hour or so before he is finished.

I tie up my hair in a bun and then remove my dress, slipping into the hot tub naked. I let an '*ahh*' sound once I'm fully submerged, and the jets are gently massaging my backside. I didn't realize how tender my body is, especially between my legs, until the warm water relieves some of the aches.

I close my eyes and think about Dekker. We talked for a few hours last night, and when I asked about his parents, the information he gave was limited. From what I remember, his childhood was good, spoiled, of course, but it sounds like his dad was rather strict with him regarding his schooling, whereas his mom was a softy. But when I asked what they were doing now, since his dad had retired from the business, he didn't want to talk anymore. It makes me wonder if his parents are going through a rough patch, but I'm not about to pry into his personal life. If he wants to tell me, I'll listen with an open mind and heart.

And, speaking of hearts, I really need to lock mine up, or I will pay dearly when this ends. I already feel more than I should for him, and I need to stop it before it consumes me entirely. When we are at work, I need to focus all my energy on the job and when we are alone, let it be about sex, and only sex.

Even as I rationalize this in my head, I know I'll be fighting a constant battle. Sex with Dekker is consuming.

He makes me feel things I never knew existed. Things I never knew about myself, and I only want to discover more, with him.

I always thought of sex as intimate and passionate, and although I feel those things with Dekker, it's so much more. It's like you're caught in this rapturous world where only the two of us exist. I can only breathe because he is my oxygen. He possesses every one of my senses while he dominates my body and keeps me in a perpetual state of euphoria. He's deadly, intoxicating, and my antidote to everything I've ever wanted. That's what I feel when I think about the times I've been with him. *I'm so screwed!*

Letting out a heavy sigh, I try to shut my brain down. It's already starting to hurt because of my growing obsession and my stupid heart.

I don't know how much time has passed when my nostrils suddenly fill with Dekker's delicious scent. I'm about to crack my eyes open, when a strong hand wraps around my throat, tipping my head back as his hot lips land on mine. I gasp, startled, and Dekker takes full advantage, surging his tongue down my throat, kissing me harder than ever. I instantly moan as my skin prickles, and feeling like I'm being sucked into a vortex. A cyclone of passion, spiraling through me, making me feel like I'm weightless but yet, drowning at the same time.

His hand remains on my throat in a firm grasp, letting me know he's in control, while his other hand slips down to my breast, palming it at first until his dexterous fingers tweak my nipple with an urgent tug. My nipples pebble instantly to stone as my core clenches and sparks ignite. I let out a deep moan and he breaks the kiss with a low husky growl.

"Get out, Ms. Everett. I want to fuck that hot pussy of yours." His harsh breath fills my ear before he bites down on my earlobe.

I let out a squeak of surprise as he sucks in my lobe, causing me to shiver next.

"Out now," he whispers, his voice low and full of authority.

You don't have to ask me again, turning around to climb out as quickly as possible but without slipping.

"You're going to get wet," I tell him, realizing he's fully clothed, but he is already reaching for me and plucks me out as if I weigh nothing.

He places me down on my feet and then lays out a towel across the hot tub ledge. I already know what's coming next as adrenaline spikes with anticipation. I love it when he takes me from behind, but I also know it will hurt like an S.O.B until my body gives in.

He turns me around, and with a firm hand, he presses down on my back until I'm bent over the hot tub. His fingers roam my backside, down to the crack of my butt, and I freeze, feeling my butt cheeks spread apart and a thumb grazing over the forbidden area.

Oh God, not yet!

"Soon," he breathes out, his voice thick with desire, and I wonder if Dekker has the ability to read my thoughts. Either way, my body relaxes, saying, "Thank God."

His hands leave my body, and I turn my head, looking over my shoulder. When our eyes connect, I see fiery lust burning in his. Electricity flares through my body, bursting at the seams. I'll never get used to the way he looks at me. Eyes that clearly say he wants to devour me. *Me!* That's a reality I'm still finding hard to grasp, but even as I gaze into his dark and smoldering eyes, there's something more I can't seem to decipher.

He unfastens his belt, zipping down his pants and freeing his swollen erection while his eyes never leave mine for a second. I wish he would completely shed his clothing. He's beautiful with an immaculate body, and I love drinking in his extraordinary physique and feeling his heated skin against mine. But since he's only revealed his prize possession, I know he wants this hard and fast.

I turn back around as his hands grip my hips, and he nudges my legs further apart. I obey, opening my stance wider, and he aligns the head of his cock with my entrance. I brace myself for impact, squeezing my eyes shut.

Shit, this is going to hurt.

I jerk without thinking, expecting him to thrust immediately, but instead, his hands spread out, gliding up my side until they're cupping my breasts, and his cock is safely lodged between my thighs, pulsating against my pussy, and waiting anxiously.

"Relax, Kinsley. I know your pussy is tender, and your body struggles to accept me. I can feel the tension rolling off of you." He leans down further so his warm breath tickles my ear. "But, I promise you, it will get better, but until then, I'll try not to break you." I hear the sincerity in his voice, and my pitiful heart takes another hit. "Lift up and place your hands on the edge," he tells me, and I do so.

He trails his lips down my spine, leaving open mouth kisses, and my body quivers in reaction. His thumb finds my clit, rubbing soothing circles and eliciting my body to relax. I let out a hum of approval, feeling pleasure snowball and arousal seeping out. Dekker slides a couple fingers against my slick folds, already knowing his effect on me. He doesn't stop stroking my sensitive clit as he takes the opportunity to ease himself inside me.

All I feel is the continuous stretching as his huge shaft electrifies every single nerve ending of my pussy walls. We both let out a groan when our bodies have completely joined together, and he can go no further.

"Christ, you feel amazing." His voice is hoarse as he withdraws, only to push back in. "You're going to cum all over my cock, Kinsley. Then I'm going to take full advantage of you and fuck your pussy until it's raw."

My mouth drops open with his blunt statement. The man doesn't hold anything back, but I appreciate his honesty.

True to his word, he has me falling apart within minutes. His thumb dances on my clit while the base of his shaft pumps in rapid pulses, pushing me over the edge. I let out a strangled cry, feeling a tidal wave of pleasure rip through me, and Dekker is quick to take control, unleashing himself and thrusting his hips mercilessly.

I drop my arms, letting him use my body as I lay across the hot tub, still trembling in the after effects. Seconds later, he's hoisting my right leg up, hooking it over the hot tub, pushing even deeper inside of me.

My eyes shoot wide as my mouth drops open for the second time. *Holy shit!* He's deeper than ever, and oh my God, I swear he's splitting my womb wide open. There will be no way I'll ever be able to have children after this. The feeling of fullness doesn't even describe what I'm feeling now. It's too much, too hot, and sweet Jesus, I feel blinding pleasure build once again. He fucks me harder and faster until another orgasm barrels through me, and I scream his name. His hips drive more frantically as his rhythm becomes choppy.

"Fuck! No!" he bellows, fingers digging into my flesh until he explodes a moment later with a deafening roar.

His body jerks several times as he tries to steady his breathing. My eyes are already half-lidded with exhaustion taking over.

"So perfect," he murmurs in a ghost of a whisper, pressing a kiss against my spine before he lifts me up in his arms.

I should object. Tell him I can walk, but at this point, I'm not even sure my legs will work, and well, my eyes have already closed. Instead, I snuggle into him, inhaling his heavenly scent. He chuckles, carrying me with ease and making his way down the stairs and to his bedroom.

"We'll eat when you wake up, darling," he says, placing me down and pulling up the blankets, but I reach for his hand.

"Lie with me."

He doesn't hesitate to shed his clothing. If I wasn't so tired, I would be drooling over his delectable body. Something I'll never tire of seeing. He peels back the blankets, and gathers me close so he's spooning my back and I let out a contented sigh.

I will definitely never tire of feeling his warm body against mine.

CHAPTER FOURTEEN

Kinsley

When Monday morning rolls around, I find my brain is a little scattered when I'm thrusted into Dekker's business world.

The morning starts with Dekker waking up at six AM to work out for over an hour. Since I don't have that kind of energy, and my legs, and pussy are kind of sore after this weekend's vigorous activities, I opt to take a long hot shower. Besides, I'm a guest, and I don't want to intrude on his personal time or regular routine.

As I place down the blow dryer, Dekker saunters in with a towel around his neck and sweat beading down his entire body. I can't help as my mouth drops open as I blatantly gawk at him. He gives me a wink, coming in, and presses his hot lips against my neck.

"Good morning, beautiful. Hope you slept well?" he murmurs, running the tip of his nose along my neck, and inhaling. "You smell extra delicious." His teeth sink into my flesh, causing me to yelp and snap out of my lustful haze. "Next time, wait for me," he tells me, loosening my towel, so it puddles around my waist. His fingers pinch my nipples, and I grow instantly wet, letting out a moan. I lean my head back against his shoulder, closing my eyes. With the towel loose, I open my legs, inviting him to play, but he '*tsk, tsk,*'me. My eyes flash open with confusion.

"Good girls who wait for me in the shower get played with."

My heart drops down to the pit of my stomach, realizing I've made a mistake. I don't like the feeling of disappointing him.

"I'm sorry," I whisper, and a moment later, my breath is stolen as his lips crash down on mine, his tongue seeking entry. I part my lips for him in a moan, and he dives in, tasting and taking as he always does. By the time he's done, I'm panting for air, and my need for him has amplified. He strips off his jogging shorts, and my eyes drop to his steely hard erection. He then turns, walking away from me, and enters the shower without a backward glance.

At first, I'm stunned, thinking he was going to fuck me. His cock wants me, but I guess that doesn't matter. I know enough that he's punishing me, but he's also punishing himself. I swear I'll never have another shower again unless he is there to join me.

With a heavy heart and a throbbing ache between my legs, I look back at the shower where steam is filling the stall. I want to join him. Make things right, but I don't think I can handle another rejection. Hanging my head, I wrap the towel around myself, and head to the walk-in closet that Dekker was so gracious to fill. I suddenly feel overwhelmed as I size up all the brand new clothing again. I don't know a way to thank him that really says, I appreciate everything you've done for me, and I'm sorry for disappointing you in return. I turn around, biting my nails, contemplating. I'm in his bad books now, and the need to fix things weighs heavily on me. There's only one idea I can think of that will hopefully put me back in his good graces. If he continues to reject or ignore me, I might seriously have a mental breakdown.

Hanging my towel over a rack, I pad over to Dekker's closet and get down on the floor. I tuck my legs beneath me and place my hands on my thighs. I'm thankful that there is a thick area rug beneath me. I believe this is the normal stance for a submissive to be in, but I'm not positive. *Oh, wait!* I think I'm supposed to spread my legs, so he has a clear view of my private area. I spread my legs and wait expectantly.

Being in this position is a little unnerving, but when I hear the shower water turn off, my heart starts to beat like a drum in my chest. *Christ, Kinsley, deep breaths.* He's seen you naked a hundred times. This is no different. But there is a difference. I'm trying to suck up for my mistake and I only hope I don't make things worse. The last thing I want is to start my first day with tension between us.

I hear the bathroom door open and his feet smacking on the hardwood floors. I lower my head, staring at the floor, and focus on my breathing, but my heart is pounding so loud that all I hear is *boom, boom, boom,* thumping in my eardrums. It isn't until his feet come into view, my heart decides to jump into my throat.

I resist the urge to look up at him as a moment of silence passes. My hands start to sweat, and when I can't take anymore, I start lifting my head.

"What's on your mind, Ms. Scarlett?"

A shiver runs down my spine, his voice smooth like butter but timbrical deep. I lift my head, slowly taking in his body. He has a fluffy white towel wrapped around his narrow waist, and when I meet his dark rich eyes, goosebumps break out across my skin causing my nipples to harden painfully. They're full of hunger while they penetrate mine.

"I... I have something I want to give you."

He raises his brow in question.

"An apology, if you will."

"Kinsley, you don't need to apologize again," he says, cupping my chin with his hand.

"But, I don't want you to be upset with me or have tension between us."

"Never, sweetheart, and I owe you an apology as well. That was a dickhead move on my part, and I should have known better. You're learning, but more importantly, you're teaching me patience and guidance. Direction that I didn't give you."

My damn heart swells hearing his kind words. Whoever thinks Dekker is an ass doesn't know him at all, but that's probably because he only shows the side he wants seen.

"I appreciate that, but I would still like to please you."

He groans, tipping his head back and closing his eyes for a moment.

"Please," I beg.

"Fuck, Kinsley, you're way too good for me."

"No. We're perfect for each other," I blurt without hesitation and instantly regret my words. Dekker's eyes flash open with his facial expression completely blanking out. I gulp, feeling my hands clam up while my heart accelerates.

"I'm sorry, that didn't come out right at all. What I meant to say, is you're way too good to me."

His face remains unreadable and I curse a dozen times in my head. I recognize it was my foolish heart speaking freely, but deep down, I know this man completes me. But I'm sure every woman that's been with Dekker feels the exact same way. They dream about being his wife, and having him all to themselves. I just hope he doesn't read anything further in my stupid comment.

I reach my hands up to the top of his waist, knowing we both need the distraction. I tentatively loosen the towel, waiting to see if he's going to stop me, but he doesn't. The towel falls to the floor, and I close my eyes for a second as butterflies flutter. He's so incredibly beautiful. Perfect from head to toe, I still don't know what I did to deserve this, but here I am, about to worship this divine man.

I wrap my hand around his cock, daring to raise my eyes as I start stroking his length. Our eyes connect, and the expression on his face has morphed into hunger, with lust burning as we fixate on one another in an intense stare. I lift up on my knees so his cock is directly in front of my mouth, and I open, darting my tongue out, and licking his slit. Dekker's thighs tense, and I lick around his large crown, before opening my mouth as wide as possible to take in his enormous length and size. I wasn't lying after the first time when I told him my jaw hurt. It ached, and every so often, it felt like I had locked-jaw.

As soon as I start to descend, Dekker wraps his fingers in my hair, taking charge and inching further down until he hits the back of my throat.

"Relax, and breathe through your nose," he reminds me.

I nod, inhaling deeply, and he pushes past my gag reflexes another inch. I sputter, almost choking, but he's quick to draw back. He tells me that's perfect, and I trust he's telling the truth. I suck and lick, scraping my teeth along as Dekker controls the pace. Soon he's grunting and groaning as his abs and leg muscles contract, and his thrusts become more urgent, leaving me no choice but to wrap my hands around his backside for leverage, sinking my nails into his granite ass.

"Jesus, your mouth is so fucking good," he rasps with his head tilted back, pumping my face faster, and it feels like my jaw is going to split in half as he stretches it to the max, and I have to force myself to stay focused, and not choke.

"That's it. Suck me harder."

Just when I think I can't take another second of his throat beating, his body turns to stone, and with a sharp jerk of his hips, he slams his entire length down my throat. I choke on impact, and he pulls back enough before blowing his load, and letting out an animalistic grunt. I gulp, working my throat as fast as possible, and making unattractive slurping noises as I swallow and try not to choke.

When the final drop is swallowed, he releases the grip on my hair. I sit back on my heels, trying to calm my labored breathing, and my thumping heart, as the last wave of orgasm shivers through Dekker with a soft groan. He opens his dark eyes, meeting mine with a sated, pleasing look. He's breathing just as hard when he reaches out, cupping my chin gently, and brushes his thumb over my lips.

"Beautiful," he soothes, causing me to smile. "I believe I owe someone an orgasm, but it will have to wait, because if we don't get ready now, we'll both be late for work."

I'm about to tell him it's not necessary as he helps me to my feet, but he silences me with a soft kiss.

"Go get ready, Ms. Scarlett. This will be continued later."

Knowing enough not to argue, I nod instead, heading out, but I don't get far before he's pulling me flush against his naked body and diving his tongue down my throat. A throat that's raw and sore, but I don't care as my body molds to his, and I let him consume me in a maddening kiss.

By the time he breaks the kiss, my sex hormones are in full swing again, and we're huffing for air. He releases me with a light slap on my behind, sending me away with a wink. I want to pout as I leave his closet, and reach mine. I never realized being sex deprived could have this kind of effect on me and quite frankly, it sucks ass. I'm tempted to relieve the throbbing ache between my legs, but doing it myself always leaves me unsatisfied. I'm going to have to suck it up because I know Dekker will make good on his promise, and it will be phenomenal. I always cum hard when he's inside of me, but I wonder if he'll ever use his sharp, skillful tongue on me. I shouldn't complain. *I can't complain.* Sex with Dekker is earth shattering, and he always makes me cum every time we're together, but never with his tongue. I can only assume it's not something he likes to do, but I'd be lying if I didn't wish I could feel it just one time. To know what it feels like to have a tongue induced orgasm.

Pushing those thoughts out of my head, I'm already so thankful for everything he has given me, including this closet full of brand new clothing. I quickly glance over everything, and my eye is quick to latch on to something that looks familiar. I grab the hanger with a dark green dress and recognize it from the clothing shop where the sales lady was snobby towards me. The tag has already been removed but I remember this dress costing over a grand. Looking at the clothing once again, I now realize I'm standing in a closet that's probably worth a million dollars or more. It's kind of unsettling, and I'm certainly not deserving of all this. But to argue with Dekker would be a waste of time. He bought this stuff for a reason. *So I don't embarrass him at work.* I get it. Image is everything, especially when you're in the public eye, but there are tons of clothing shops that have stylish clothing without breaking the bank.

I let out a sigh, slipping the dress off the hanger. Either way, it doesn't matter. I won't be taking any of this stuff when our time is up.

I open a drawer selecting a black embroidered mesh bra with decorative lace and the matching thong. I then wonder if I should be wearing stockings. I've never worn a garter belt or stockings before, because all my dresses or skirts were always floor-length. I eye up the matching mesh decorative suspender belt and stockings, thinking I probably should. My white legs will stand out like a sore thumb.

After putting on the undergarments, I can appreciate the difference between generic brands and high-end. The material quality is like night and day. I slip the dress over top of my head, and before I can turn my neck, wondering how I'm going to zip up the back, I feel Dekker's hands.

"Mmm. I can't wait to strip this off of you later," he says, zipping up the back.

I smile, smoothing down the front of the dress with my hands, and I see it sits just above my knee caps.

"Well, do I look okay for the office?" I ask, turning to face him, and I see he looks like a million bucks in his well tailored black suit.

"You look beautiful, Kinsley. But for what it's worth, you already were."

"Well, we both know that's not true, but I'm fine with that. It's obvious clothing makes a world of difference."

Dekker frowns for a moment, and I go to move past him and head to the washroom, but he grabs the back of my arm, stilling my movements.

"I would have noticed," he says, but I shake my head.

"No, you wouldn't have. Be honest with yourself, Dekker. If you saw me in an elevator or on a sidewalk, you wouldn't have given me the time of day."

His nostrils flare as we stare each other down, and I can tell he's clenching his jaw. I reach up, cupping his cheek with my hand.

"It's okay, Dekker. It's really no big deal," I say, planting a kiss on his lips. "I've gotta hurry. I still have my hair to do and scarf something down my throat. I don't want to be late for my first day," I say with a wink.

Before I can walk away, Dekker hauls me into his arm and crushes his mouth to mine. It's a dominant kiss, powerful and poetic, but yet, I feel his remorse. *An apology.* By the time he releases the kiss, my head is spinning, floating up in the clouds. I could kiss this man for the rest of my life and it still wouldn't be enough.

He gives me a subtle nod, and I return a gentle smile.

"Give me five minutes, and I'll meet you in the kitchen," I whisper before standing up on my tippy toes to give him a quick peck on the lips.

I don't bother waiting for a response as I rush out and into the bathroom. I decide to toss my hair into a ponytail, and with a bit of hairspray, I'm ready. I give myself the once over in the full-length mirror, and I actually see I have an hourglass figure in this dress. Even my breasts look moderate in size. Clothing really does make a huge difference. After sliding my feet into a stylish pair of black high heels, I find Dekker in the kitchen, making a couple bagels with a tray of fruit already set out.

"What would you like on your bagel?" Dekker asks as I slip onto the kitchen barstool.

"Oh, butter is fine." He nods, and while he's doing that I snack on the fruit.

"So, are you ready to be thrusted into my world?" he questions.

"If I can handle you, I think I can handle just about anything," I say with a smirk, and he chuckles.

"You're probably right."

After eating breakfast and brushing our teeth, I tell Dekker I think it will be best if I come and go through the front entrance like everyone else. That way, it won't raise any suspicions. He nods his agreement, and after another toe curling kiss, we part our ways.

CHAPTER FIFTEEN

Kinsley

D ekker had offered Winston or Chase to drive me around to the front of the building, but I politely decline, saying this will be my daily exercise. After entering the vast structure, I immediately notice the place is bustling with people that are all decked out in their designer clothing, ready to start their week. As I make my way to the elevators, I glance at the reception lady to see her staring at me with a dumbfounded look. I beam at her, holding my swipe card up in mockery. *I too can be a bitch.* But if she knew I'm sleeping with the boss, she would probably want to slit my throat.

As I approach the elevator, I see dozens of people waiting, and I quickly become aware I'm attracting a lot of attention. Some are polite, giving me a nod or good morning in greeting, but there are several doing double takes, sideways glances, and some are blatantly gawking. Men and women. I'm not sure if I should be flattered or alarmed, but soon the whispering starts. I try to ignore them, and it's not long before three elevators become available. I slip into the first one, pressing the ninetieth-floor, and immediately tuck myself against the back wall in the corner.

Once it's comfortably full and the doors close, more hushed whispers are shared and backward glances. I plaster a smile on, suddenly feeling hot under the collar. I hope it isn't going to be like this every day, but I suspect it will and will only get worse once everyone finds out who I'm working for. Finally, after stopping for the seventh time, it's me, one other man, and a woman left. I see they are one floor below Dekker.

"Hi, I'm Courtney, and this is my co-worker, Miles. We both work in marketing. Are you Mr. Dekker's new assistant?" Courtney sounds chipper, and they are both smiling, but hopefully she's not one of those women that are nice to your face but talk behind your back when you're not around. She's wearing what almost looks like an elegant black jumpsuit with gold accent buttons and cap sleeves, whereas Miles is dressed a little more casual in dark brown trouser pants and a white dress shirt, no tie.

"Yes. Today is my first day."

"Congratulations. You must be super excited." I nod as the elevator comes to a stop on their floor. "Good luck on your first day. I'm sure we'll see you around," Miles says as the door opens.

"Yeah, and maybe we could have lunch together sometime, and by the way, I love that color on you. It really makes your eyes pop," Courtney adds.

"Thank you, and that would be great. You two have a nice day," I say as they exit and say bye.

Once the doors close again, I breathe out a sigh. They both seem nice and genuine, but I guess time will tell. Seconds later, the door opens, and Ivy is already waiting for me with a wide grin on her face.

"Kinsley! It's so lovely to see you again."

"Hi, Mrs. Davies."

"Oh, Kinsley, please call me Ivy. How was your weekend?"

For a moment, my mind freezes, skipping into overdrive and suddenly wondering if she knows about Dekker and me. That's impossible, Kinsley. She's just making conversation so relax.

"Oh, you know, same old, same old. House cleaning, laundry, grocery shopping. Nothing too interesting."

"Ah yes, story of my life. Weekends are always too short."

I smile as I put down my laptop bag and purse.

"Okay, IT will be in touch this morning to get you access to the network drive and connect your laptop to the printer. But in the meantime, we'll go over Eric's schedule. Mondays are always important because that's when the board of directors meet for their weekly meeting."

"Yes, I did see that. I spent some time getting acquainted with Mr. Dekker's schedule for the next couple of months."

"Oh, good, and I got your email this morning about the salary, and yes, it is correct," she says with a wink. "Now, Eric likes his coffee every morning. Black, one sugar. He should be arriving shortly. The coffee pot is already made. I'll let you bring his coffee to him. I need to check the copier machine. I'm printing off some documents for today's meeting."

I give her a nod, and pour Dekker his coffee as she leaves. I quickly pull out his Thank You card and enter his office. He hasn't arrived yet, and I glance around, now seeing the elevator door. I hadn't even noticed it Friday because it almost blends in with the wall being a dark bronze finish and a matching cabinet on the left side.

I set his coffee down, placing the card beside it, and head out before he catches me. I don't want to be here when he reads it. It's bad enough I'm giving it to the most coveted bachelor in New York that I'm sleeping with, but the words I wrote are null and void now. But I still owe him a thank you for giving me this amazing opportunity, even though it's temporary.

Ivy returns a few minutes later, the same time Dekker mysteriously arrives in his doorway. When our eyes connect, I know instantly he has read my Thank You card.

"Good morning, ladies. Hope you had a good weekend. Ivy, could you please bring me the sales data report from finance? I told them I wanted a hard copy to review later this morning?"

"Oh, certainly. I'll be back in five minutes."

When Ivy leaves, Dekker retreats into his office as he beckons me to join him. I suddenly want to crawl underneath my desk and hide as my heart rate accelerates to warp speed. I shouldn't have given it to him. He's probably taken it all the wrong way, not that I blame him.

I follow, stopping two feet from his desk as he takes a seat. I see my card is lying directly in front of him as he glances at it for a few seconds before lifting his eyes and meeting mine. I swallow thickly, nerves taking flight as I clasp my sweaty hands behind my back.

"Before you say anything, I wrote that card before we made our deal. It means nothing," I manage to say before he can question me.

Dekker's eyes never leave mine for a second as his face remains impassive, and he doesn't say a word. I don't usually suffer from anxiety, but right now, my stomach is coiling into knots, where I feel like I could actually throw up. *The card was a big mistake.* I leap forward, lunging for the card, and just as I have it in my hand, Dekker's arm lashes out, wrapping around the base of my neck and holding me in place.

My eyes shoot wide as a small gasp escapes my lips. *Jesus Christ, he's lightning fast.* I'm virtually bent over his desk with a vice grip locked around the back of my neck. I try to lift up, but I can't move an inch. I glance at him, gritting my teeth, and then I look at the card in my hand. I'm about to crush it, when his other hand snatches it from me in a blink of an eye.

"Give that to me! It was a stupid idea."

"I'll decide what's stupid and what's not," he growls.

I grumble back. *The man can be one stubborn ass.* "It was a stupid idea, Dekker. Just give it back to me, and we can forget I ever gave it to you."

He releases my neck, and I quickly stand back up, checking the door behind me. Of course the last thing I need is Ivy to catch us or anyone else, but I think Dekker is thinking the same thing or I'm sure he wouldn't have let me go that easily.

"The card stays with me, and don't you dare touch it again, or I'll bend you over this desk and redden your ass, and I don't care who sees or hears."

I shiver with that thought, knowing he wouldn't think twice about doing that. I straighten my spine, smoothing down the front of my dress.

"Fine. Keep the stupid card," I say and turn around marching away.

"Thank you, Kinsley."

I halt in my tracks hearing his thank you. That's the last thing I thought I would ever hear from his mouth. Honestly, I expected him to throw it in the trash. It was stupid and corny. I glance over my shoulder and see a hint of a smile on his ever gorgeous face. He truly is a beautiful man.

"You're welcome, Mr. Dekker," I smile with a slight bow of my head and then slip out of his office.

The following eight hours are somewhat of a blur, a galloping whirlwind of information and people. It started with a grand tour of the building and meeting what seemed like hundreds of people in various departments. So many names and faces I'll never remember them all. Although, there were a few gentlemen that took an interest in me right away. The way their eyes would travel the length of my body several times without a care in the world was one hint, but seeing the evident hunger in their eyes was also a dead giveaway. I even had one guy in the sales department boldly ask if I was seeing anyone. His name was Calvin, and I'm sure I won't forget him, because I must admit, he was pretty nice on the eyes. Ivy chastised him, telling him to leave me alone, or she'll sick security on him. He then cozied up to her, slinging his arm loosely around her shoulder, telling her he is still waiting for that hot date of theirs. Ivy rolls her eyes, swatting his arm away, and then giggles. Before we leave, he tells me not to be a stranger, or he'll have no problem seeking me out, he adds with a flirtatious wink and a dazzling smile. It's easy to confirm Calvin is a ladies' man, but I can't imagine what Dekker will think if he does seek me out. We said we are exclusive, and I wouldn't want it any other way, but I know when our secret love affair ends, I will be devastated. Maybe befriending another man or two won't hurt. I'll need someone to lick my wounds and nurse my broken heart.

After returning to our level, Ivy shows me numerous tasks as I get propelled into a never ending job. I only see Dekker a few times briefly, with the board of directors meeting taking up much of his time, but it doesn't stop the occasional daydreaming of him, and before I know it, it's five o'clock.

"Okay, dear. We'll pick it up from here tomorrow. Go home and relax. You're doing great," Ivy tells me as she packs up her stuff.

I give her a nod, and start closing out our projects as Dekker's office door opens. I can't help that my heartbeat quickens at the sight of him. I've missed him and can't wait to be alone with him.

"Ladies, I hope you're calling it a day?" he asks as his dark eyes flicker between us before latching onto mine.

"Yes, I just told Kinsley to shut down. I'm sure she's mentally exhausted from meeting most of your team and learning what you have on the go now." Dekker nods. "All right, you two, I'll see you in the morning. I'm exhausted, and I need to find the nearest couch so my husband can rub my feet and then make me dinner."

I smile at Ivy. I did learn that Ivy is fifty-nine and she and her husband, Patrick, have been married for forty years and have two children, who now have children of their own. She also let me in on a little secret, telling me she's thinking about retiring in the spring of next year.

After saying goodbye, I look over at Dekker.

"And how did your day go? No issues, I hope?"

"Well, I got a lot of raised eyebrows, whispering, you know, the usual, when Ivy introduced me as your new assistant, but overall it was good," I say, standing up and grabbing my purse to leave. "Are you working late, or will I see you shortly?"

"Actually, I would like to see you in my office for a few minutes," he tells me, stepping back into his office. I set my purse down, figuring he wants to discuss work, but as soon as he closes the door behind me, I'm pushed up against the door. I gasp in surprise, and Dekker doesn't waste a second, thrusting his tongue down my throat in a hot and demanding kiss, I all but submit to his dominant side instantly. His nimble fingers zip down the back of my dress, and another two seconds later, it's pooling around my feet. I kick it away as my hands reach for his belt with eagerness.

"Jesus, Kinsley, you make me so fucking hard," he rasps, breaking the kiss, but I barely register his words as I work on his belt and zipping down his pants, desperately needing the same thing he wants.

I swiftly slide his trousers and boxers down enough, freeing his engorged erection, and gripping his steely hard length in my hand, squeezing harshly. Dekker hisses, swatting my hand away and thrusting me in his arms. I lock my arms and legs around him, claiming his mouth in a frenzy kiss, our teeth all but clash together as our tongues battle in a ruthless war. Gripping the back of his hair and pulling callously, I wish I could climb into his body and never leave.

Dekker breaks the kiss with a venomous growl as my butt hits the board room table. He drops my legs, turning me around in a flash and bending me over the hard surface. My thong is ripped off with such force it feels a bit like rug burn, but a second later, a large hand comes down, smacking my ass so hard the burning sensation I felt a moment ago ignites into an inferno.

I cry out, bucking against the table, but Dekker pins me down, raining a series of lethal strikes, and battering my ass once again. The harsh slaps resonate throughout the office, along with my echoing cries, until my voice is hoarse and I see spots dance before my eyes. My whole body feels like it's on fire until I feel a familiar tingle start to spread. I close my eyes, concentrating on my breathing, and soon the blistering sensations take on a new purpose. I'm floating in delirium when I hear Dekker shout.

"Fuck, Kinsley, how the hell do you do that?!"

His booming voice is enough to pull me back to the present just as Dekker buries himself in my slick wetness. My eyes shoot wide as I let out a squeak in shock, and Dekker curses a few more times.

"Your pussy feels like goddamn heaven," he rasps, breathing hard, and I'm quick to follow along. "You with me, Ms. Scarlett?"

"Oh, God, yes."

"That's good because I'm going to make you soar so fucking high, it will be better than subspace," he says, wrapping his hand around my ponytail and pulling back, it feels a bit like whiplash.

He grinds his hips against my ass, inflicting fiery sparks, and I groan, clenching greedily around him. He hisses, pulling back, only to slam into me, setting the rhythm of his relentless pounding and making me dizzy with arousal.

My breathing is labored and my heart is beating so fast, I swear it will either stop functioning or break free from my chest. Dekker grunts and groans, reefing on my ponytail and using it as leverage to drive home every time. I moan hard, feeling the first shudder cresting through me as every nerve cell amplifies to new heights. Our skins are slapping, and I feel sweat beading in all the wrong places, but I'm too far gone to care as euphoria infuses and the first wave of ecstasy is sweeping through me.

"Oh God, Dekker. I'm cumming!"

He growls, letting go of my hair, to grip my hips, pumping faster. I detonate a second later, crying out his name and seeing white stars flash before my eyes. Waves of pleasure shudder through me when Dekker reaches his peak, letting out a savage roar and digging his fingers into my flesh. I know I'll have bruised hips and a sore butt after this bout of vigorous sex, but I don't care. I would let him do that to me again in a heartbeat.

"Come on, beautiful, time to go home," Dekker says, lifting me up in his arms.

I lay my head against his chest, listening to the beat of his heart. My home is right in his arms, but I'll keep that little secret to myself. I'm already in way too deep and have fallen head over heels, but that doesn't surprise me. My heart will be crushed, but it's a small price to pay to feel this kind of passion and be desired by the most extraordinary man ever. A man that will forever hold my heart until it stops beating.

Yeah, I may find love with someone else and he'll make me happy, we will have children and grow old together, but I know deep down I'll never have this intense, magical chemistry again, and a piece of my heart will always belong to Dekker.

"How about I start a bath so you can soak and relax, and then we'll have dinner," Dekker suggests as he places me down on the bed.

I grab his shirt, wrapping my legs around his waist before he can walk away.

"Only if you're joining me," I purr seductively in his ear, causing him to growl.

He gathers my wrists, pinning them above my head, and I'm already lifting my head up so he can kiss me.

"Fuck, Kinsley, I can't get enough of you," he breathes against my lips before diving his tongue inside my mouth.

We don't make it to the tub for another fifteen minutes, and then I pass out on him when he gives me my first neck and shoulder massage. It's glorious, and I never want this day to end.

CHAPTER SIXTEEN

Kinsley

The next three weeks pass by swiftly as we fall into a routine with my day filled with scheduling meetings, screening telephone calls, responding to emails, and managing Dekker's already full calendar. I sit in on several meetings, silently taking notes, and typing up memos. I even prepare PowerPoint presentations and various reports.

I always find it interesting when I sit in on one of his meetings. You can tell we both struggle to concentrate, stealing fleeting glances, and once, I was brave enough, or maybe call it stupid on my part, and stuck my pen in my mouth, doing inappropriate things with my tongue and mouth, and pretending like I was sucking his cock. Dekker was in the middle of a sentence and literally fumbled with his words, turning slightly red in the face.

He excused himself as I sat there paralyzed, and I watched him walk out of his office with a raging hard on that couldn't be missed. I almost half expected him to haul me onto the boardroom table and punish me right in front of his client, but he didn't. He returned five minutes later, minus an erection, and I watched him smooth down his tie, taking a seat, and apologized to his client. He ignored me for the rest of the day while I sat on pins and needles, knowing what was coming.

He waited until after work, taking his belt to my ass and giving me new blistering welts. I screamed bloody murder, until eventually, I slipped into another dimension, feeling nothing but sweet bliss, but unfortunately, that only lasted so long. I felt the welts for the next two days, and my pussy was so raw, I couldn't walk the next day.

Luckily for me, I have the best boss ever and he told me I wasn't going to work. I tried to protest, telling him I'll survive, but he wasn't having any of it. And to ensure I listened to him, the little bugger stayed home with me. He never left my side for more than a few minutes, showering me with affection, making sweet love to me, pampering me with a full body oil massage, and bringing me whatever I wanted to eat in bed.

Hell yeah, I would do that again.

I have now earned a new nickname 'dirty little minx' along with Ms. Scarlett. Apparently, I have a devilish side that he enjoys thoroughly. Although, I have to admit, I kind of like it myself.

When the work day ends, I'm beckoned into his office for what's become our daily ritual. Something I look forward to very much, and sometimes I have trouble concentrating on anything. I'll stare at the clock, counting down the minutes and then seconds as my hormones kick into high gear. He'll open the door, our eyes will connect, and I all but cream myself with anticipation. He has killer eyes that are super intense with a mixture of danger and primal lust.

He'll bend me over his desk or the boardroom table, or sometimes he'll let me take charge, where I'll straddle him on his chair, and we'll both soar so freaking high it's the most exhilarating feeling ever. There have been a few times where he has demanded me on my knees, and he fucks my face until he is cumming down my throat. He's rough, sometimes brutal, but I don't mind. Seeing the extreme pleasure on his face makes it all worthwhile, and I'm getting better at taking his length and choking less often. But when he's done, he's always caring and nurturing. I love every side of him, but I know all I am to him is his personal fuck toy while I dig myself a bigger hole, but if this is all I get, then so be it.

The office whispering never stops, although it's not as bad as the first week, and I actually make a few new friends. Courtney and Miles being two, and this is when I also find out they are dating. I've run into Calvin a few times, and we even ate lunch together once, but it was in a group of eight, but he did make a point to sit beside me. I find him funny, charming, and quite handsome so it makes me a little optimistic that maybe there is life after Dekker.

Last week, I got a shocking but nice surprise from Dekker. It was Friday, shortly after lunch when he opened his door and tells me to clear his schedule for the rest of the day. I was concerned, thinking there was some kind of business crisis, and quickly called all his clients, canceling the afternoon meetings and rescheduling.

Once that was done, he tells me to pack up.

"Is something wrong?" I question logging out of my computer. Of course, his expression remains deadpan and my mind is working in overdrive, thinking the worst.

"No, Ms. Everett, everything is perfect. May I see you in my office?"

I frown, now feeling completely lost, but I follow him.

"What's going on?" I ask, closing the door.

He pulls me into his arms and whispers low by my ear.

"What's going on, is we're going to play hooky for the rest of the day."

My mouth drops open in shock.

"Hooky? As in skip work? But you had important meetings." Dekker chuckles.

"Yes, as in skip work. Did you never cut a few classes in high school?" he questions, and I shake my head no, causing him to smile. "Of course not. You're too innocent and pure for that, but I have no problem corrupting you," he says with a wink. "Besides, the meetings can wait until next week. We're going to enjoy the nice weather and start our weekend early."

My cheeks warm, along with my heart. He takes my hand, leading me into his private elevator and we ride up one floor. I don't even protest or worry about what people will think when they see both of us are gone. I'm too excited to see where he's taking me. When we're upstairs, he tells me to put on a bathing suit but wear something over top and to pack an overnight bag. Nothing fancy, it will be just the two of us. I get all giddy, heading to my dresser and selecting a leopard print string bikini. It's a thong style, and I hope he will approve. I then throw on a pair of cutoff jean shorts and a royal blue t-shirt, so he can't see the leopard print. Finally, I pack an overnight bag and head out to find him.

He's in the living room talking on his cell phone, and I stop dead in my tracks, mouth gaping open once again. His back is towards me, but that's not what has me stunned. He's wearing charcoal grey, cargo-style shorts that mold perfectly to his butt, along with a muscle shirt. By the time he ends the call and turns around to face me, I'm drooling like an idiot. He smirks, giving me another flirtatious wink, and I close my yap, suddenly feeling overheated. *Jesus, he's too damn hot for his own good.*

He comes in close and tries to steal a peek under my shirt.

"I need to see the goods," he states, but I swat his hand away.

"No peeking." Seeing Dekker actually stick out his bottom lip and pout, has me busting a gut. He chuckles in return, giving me a kiss on the nose. There are definitely multiple layers to this hard, demanding man, and I love when he lets out his sense of humor.

After loading the SUV and Chase is merging into the heavy traffic, I ask where we are going, but of course, his comment is, "you'll see." I roll my eyes, and he tells me he has a couple more phone calls to make. I leave him to his business as I watch the pedestrians and traffic flow by. An hour later, I see we are nearing the Hudson River Park. I glance at Dekker, but he only smiles, and soon Chase is pulling into the parking lot.

"We're here," he says as Chase opens the door, and we climb out.

"I've never been to this park. Are we going to take a walk?" I ask.

"Even better, we're going to rent bikes."

"Really! I haven't ridden a bike in like ten years," I practically shout, super excited.

"That makes two of us," Dekker says with a chuckle, and then he tells me to give him a minute. He needs to speak with Chase. I narrow my eyes, wondering what he's up to, but he only gives me that panty melting wink, and then the two of them have a private meeting out of earshot. I see Chase nod a few times, but other than that, his face remains expressionless, not saying a word. I haven't asked Dekker what his deal is because, honestly, he kind of gives me the creeps. He has to be six foot four and one scary-ass beast.

"All right, my dear. Ready to start our adventure?" Dekker asks, sliding on a backpack.

"Absolutely, but why did we need an overnight bag?"

Again, I receive another cryptic response that has my eyes rolling. This earns me a sharp smack on the butt and I yelp.

"Behave, or I'll bend you over my knee and spank that naughtiness out of you."

I raise my brows, tempted, and Dekker growls, taking my hand and virtually dragging me away. If I didn't have my running shoes on, I surely would have tripped, doing a face plant on the concrete. Although, I'm sure Dekker would have caught me.

"Christ woman, you know how to make me hard in two seconds flat," he grumbles, and I glance down at his crotch. *Oops! They are slightly tented out.*

Fifteen minutes later, and Dekker receiving several eye snaps from ladies' unabashedly gawking at him, we reach the bicycle rental. Not one guy glanced my way, but at least Dekker was kind enough to ignore the ladies, only giving me his attention. While he is busy paying for the bicycle rentals, I nonchalantly glance down and see someone has finally calmed down.

"Stop looking at him, Ms. Scarlett."

My eyes snap back up to his.

"Do you have eyes at the back of your head?" I ask.

"For you, yes."

I laugh, and he shakes his head, smiling too.

For the next two hours, we ride along the bike path, taking in the beautiful scenery, and I think I have a permanent grin on my face, loving every second. It makes me feel like a kid again. And seeing Dekker smile as well, I know he's enjoying himself too and that this day excursion wasn't just for me, but for the both of us.

We even stop for ice cream along the way, slightly ruining our supper, but he assures me we are not on any schedule. Hearing that from him sounds weird, considering most of Dekker's life revolves around tight deadlines and schedules. But on the weekends, he does relax, especially when we spend hours naked in bed rolling around. But sometimes duty calls, and he's pulled away from me, and come Monday morning, he's back into his daily grind.

Once the bikes are returned and we're back in the SUV, we start traveling down the road. I see a massive white yacht that you can't miss, currently docked at pier fifty-nine. I practically plaster my face to the window, gawking at it, never seeing one so close.

"That's huge," I remark and then feel the SUV slow down. "What are we doing? Why are we stopping?" I spin to face Dekker.

"Why don't we check it out?"

"We can't do that. I don't think the owner will appreciate people snooping around."

He ignores me, climbing out of the vehicle.

"I'm serious, Dekker. What if we get caught?" I say, not budging from my seat.

"Stop worrying, Ms. Scarlett, and live a little."

"You know you can be an arse sometimes," I retort, and the little bugger laughs at me. *Asshole!*

I reluctantly climb out, and Dekker ushers me to the enormous yacht that seems to tower over us and is rather lengthy. A gentleman is standing by the boat's door, all decked out in a sailor uniform, and he tips his hat in greeting as we draw closer.

"Do you know this man?" I whisper.

He squeezes my hand, not responding, and I grit my teeth. Being left in the dark is starting to tick me off, but I don't get a chance to question him further because the other gentleman speaks first.

"Mr. Dekker, it's nice to see you again. It's been a while."

"Too long, Captain Jamison, and it's good to see you as well." The guys shake hands, and I'm relieved they know each other. "Jeffrey, this is my girlfriend, Kinsley. Kinsley, this is Captain Jeffrey Jamison, a former commanding officer, and the owner of this beautiful vessel."

We shake hands, sharing pleasantries, and then Jeffrey tells us to climb aboard. Dekker smirks.

"Arse!" I whisper, and he laughs.

Jeffrey gives us a tour, and I try to remember my manners and not gawk with my mouth gaping open, but Dekker catches me a couple of times, using his finger to gently close my mouth. The yacht is virtually a floating city on water that has everything from a full-size kitchen, including all major appliances, and a kitchen island that sits two people. There is an area that Jeffrey calls the Salon. It has U-shaped seating in white leather on the starboard side, that's encased in glass and a dinette on the port side, and there is a separate entertainment living area with a wall mounted TV.

You then walk down seven steps to the master cabin with a king size bed, a spacious ensuite bathroom, and a separate closet. It has two large windows on either side that you can open, and down the hall, there are two more bedrooms. One has a queen size bed with another private bathroom, and the third has two twin beds. And, to top it off, hidden behind a closet is a stackable washer and dryer, and the entire yacht is fully air conditioned.

I suddenly feel underdressed as we head back upstairs to the main deck, seeing enough seating for eight people with a raised bar area. This yacht is luxurious with superior class and most likely cost over a million dollars. But since Dekker is at ease in his cargo shorts and muscle shirt, obviously, he is not too concerned.

"Make yourself comfortable. We'll head out shortly," Jeffrey tells us, and I feel my eyes shoot wide with my skin prickling as I turn to Dekker.

"Surprise," he whispers with a sly grin as he nudges me forward, so we can sit on the U-shape couch.

I'm in complete shell shock as I sit there staring at Dekker, but then my sensitive emotions catch up, as tears well in my eyes, realizing Dekker did all of this for us. I don't know if it's something he always does with all his women, but for me, it means the world.

"Hey, what's wrong?" he says, cupping my cheek and running his thumb over a teardrop.

"Thank you," I manage to say, and he smiles, leaning to kiss me.

"You're welcome, beautiful."

I lean into his side, laying my head against his warm chest, and he wraps his arms around me, holding me tight. Ten minutes later, we're pulling away from the pier and heading down the Hudson River.

"Why don't we head to the top level? There is a cushion lounge pad that we can lie back on and watch the views go by."

"Sounds perfect," I say, removing my running shoes and socks and then ditching my shorts and top. "Did you bring any sunscreen?" I ask, bending over to retrieve his backpack on the ground and looking inside.

A few seconds later, there are two strong hands on my butt, squeezing firmly with a rumbling growl. I yelp, jerking out of his grasp and whipping around to see his face is full of primal thirst.

"Christ, Kinsley, you're lucky we aren't in a public area, or I would have to beat the men off of you."

I snort-laugh. "Says the guy that turned all the ladies' heads at the park."

"I only noticed you gawking," he says with a smirk.

"Well, you are definitely eye candy for the ladies," I say, letting my eyes slowly scan down his naked torso and down further. He has removed his clothes, leaving him in his swim shorts, boxer-style briefs in nylon material. It's the first time I've seen him in broad daylight in such little clothing, and although I've seen every inch of his well toned body, he looks even more scrumptious. And how the hell is his body so tanned?

"Do you have a tanning bed at your place?" He's sporting a nice bronzy tan, and I don't know how he maintains it.

"I do. It's upstairs on the rooftop in a separate room. I must have forgotten to show you."

I roll my eyes. *Of course he does.*

We head up to the top level and I squeal in delight seeing a lounge area that virtually has a built-in bed, flush with the flooring, and I love how there is a canopy for some shade and privacy.

"I want to sleep up here tonight!" I exclaim, already lowering myself to the soft bed. I stretch out, letting an *'ahh'* sound, and hear Dekker chuckle behind me, but I don't care. A girl could definitely get used to this. "Come and join me, handsome," I say, patting the spot beside me, and he does, pulling me flush against his body.

"You're crazy beautiful, and I can't wait to be inside of you with only the stars as our witness."

I shiver with that thought. It will be like a wild fantasy with Dekker making love to me out in the open, beneath the midnight sky and the stars and moon shining above.

"I can't wait," I whisper before pressing my lips against his.

Before we get too comfortable, I get Dekker to apply a coat of sunscreen to my backside, and he spends far too much time on my derriere with a few deep groans and growls. By the time he's finished, his swimming shorts are tented like a mountain. I can't help but wonder if tonight will be the night he'll ask for permission. I know he will ask, he's a gentleman like that. I also know it's coming soon.

I finish my front side, and for the next hour or so, we take in the majestic views that New York has to offer, including the Statue of Liberty and Ellis Island, until we're navigating through the vast ocean. It looks and feels surreal as you drift further away from civilization, and all you see is an endless ripple of blue water.

I take a few pictures of my surroundings and then hold my cell phone out.

"All right, gorgeous, smile for the camera." I put my arm around his neck, bringing him closer so our cheeks touch. He indulges me, and I click away.

"See how beautiful your smile is?" I point out, practically sticking my phone in his face. He chuckles, shaking his head. "I'm just saying," I remark, shrugging my shoulders and looking at our picture again. He's beautiful, looking so relaxed, and I must admit, it's a great picture of us together. It almost looks like we belong together.

The yacht decreases in speed, coming to a crawl, and Dekker tells me this is where we'll be anchored for the night. I put my cell down, glancing around. It feels like we're in the middle of nowhere, but at least I can still see the coastline. Vaguely. It isn't until the motor is shut off do I realize a jet ski, and a much smaller scale boat have been ahead of us the entire time. I'm not sure why they are here, but I think I'm about to find out. Jeffrey drops the anchor as we make our way to the back to meet him and the other guest also arriving.

"Mr. Dekker, she's all yours for the night. I'll be back around noon to take you guys home. Of course, you can contact me via CB radio if you run into issues."

"Thank you, Jeffrey," Dekker responds, shaking hands, and I give my head a little shake. Did I hear correctly?

I then watch the gentleman on the jet ski climb off, tethering it to our yacht, and then he climbs aboard the other boat. Jeffrey follows suit, giving us a salute in goodbye. Dekker bows, and then we watch the three of them sail away. I suddenly feel like we're in a movie where you're left alone to survive. Hopefully, the night doesn't take a turn where a violent storm comes out of nowhere. You know, like the movie, *The Perfect Storm.*

CHAPTER SEVENTEEN

Kinsley

"This is ours for the night?" I ask Dekker as soon as they are out of sight.

"It is. Care to go for a ride?" he asks, gesturing to the jet ski.

I let out a squeal, forgetting my train of thought, and the yacht being ours, or asking if the weather is supposed to be good tonight.

"Really? I've never been on one."

Dekker smiles, not saying a word but taking my hand instead. I'm again confused as we head to the lower level and into the master bedroom. As soon as I step inside, I'm tossed onto the bed and pounced on by Dekker. He whips down his shorts in a nanosecond and plunges deep. I cry out in both pleasure and shock, feeling my entire body ignite with vivid sensations.

"Fuck!" Dekker bellows, stilling for a moment before our eyes connect. "I was trying to be a patient man and wait until later, but Christ, you make me so goddamn hard. I've wanted you the moment you revealed that cunning thing you call a bikini."

"You're the one who bought it," I say with a little giggle, and he shakes his head.

"All right, beautiful, this is going to be hard and fast," he says as he withdraws and flips me over, so I'm on all fours.

He grips my hips, positioning the head of his crown at my entrance, and tells me to hang on. I do, bracing my body while my hands grip the comforter, and a split second later, he slams into me with such force, I almost buckle instantly. My mouth drops open as the air leaves my lungs, my back bowing with flames erupting from one end to the other, detonating torpedo style. His body is a powerhouse with hips thrusting, not stopping for one second as he pounds into my delicate body, mercilessly. It's brutal, ravage, but I wouldn't have it any other way. I love it, and he knows precisely how to make my body sizzle with heat and soar.

The sounds coming from Dekker are like a fierce beast. It's heady and only heightens the adrenaline pumping through my veins. I can't stop moaning as the pleasure builds too fast. Our flesh smacks together as the scent of arousal floods the room, and soon he reaches up, clapping one hand on my shoulder for leverage and the other reaching around to flick my clit. It's enough to send me over as I scream incoherently with waves of pleasure all but consuming. My body gives out moments later as I face plant the mattress, and Dekker takes over, holding my hips up until he finds his release soon after. I've never felt so deliciously used and spent, it's fabulous.

Dekker withdraws, telling me to stay, and I grunt into the comforter for a response. He chuckles, disappearing for a minute and coming back with a warm cloth.

"Now, that's a lovely sight, Ms. Scarlett."

He refers to my derriere that's shamelessly still up in the air, giving him an X-rated view.

"Yeah, well, I'm not sure if I can move," I mumble into the blanket, feeling no remorse.

I receive another humorous chuckle, and I roll my eyes, even though they are closed.

He's gentle as he cleans between my legs and then helps me roll over.

"Hi," I say, peering into his gorgeous eyes and still feeling like I'm on cloud nine.

"Hi there, yourself," he whispers, gathering me closer, and I close my eyes, laying my head against his chest, listening to the steady beat of his heart.

I could lay here forever. No, correction. I could lay in his arms forever. I feel completely at ease with him, safe and warm, even though we have no covers on. He runs his fingers up and down my back as we lay there in silence for several minutes. I love how he allows me this time, knowing I get a little sleepy after our intense bout of sex. I always am, and I should really start working out to boost my energy level, so it's more equivalent to his. The man is like the energizer bunny. *He keeps going and going and going.*

"Feeling up to going for a ride?" he finally asks after my twenty-minute power nap.

I lift my head. "Absolutely." Then stretch up, pressing my lips to his. "Thank you."

He gives my bum a squeeze, already knowing why I'm thanking him. After redressing and meeting back upstairs, he hands me a life jacket to wear. When I ask why he isn't wearing one, he tells me he doesn't need one. I give him an eye roll. If anyone is precious cargo, it's him, not me.

For the next hour or so, we cruise around on the jet ski. It's fun, exhilarating, and soon I'm feeling a little mischievous. My arms are already wrapped around his waist, and I easily slide my hand underneath the band of his shorts, gripping his cock. It doubles in size instantly as he jerks, letting out a hiss, or maybe it was a growl, but I heard something.

"You're asking for trouble," he shouts over the noise.

"I am trouble," I whisper back at the shell of his ear before sucking in his earlobe and nipping it as I keep stroking him.

He slows the jet ski, coming to a stop, and then plucks my hand from his shorts. Two seconds later, he's twisting around and hoisting me in front as he slips into the back seat.

"You're going to be the death of me," he growls, lifting up to expose his rigid cock. "Suck," he commands, his voice stern and full of authority, and he is already pushing my head down on him.

I open wide, and he pushes past my boundaries without hesitation, making me swallow him whole. Root to tip, he's lodged in my throat. This is my punishment for tantalizing him. He likes to be in control and rarely hands over the reins. I'm a millisecond away from choking as he lets out a guttural groan. I try to hold it, but a second later, I'm gagging, and only then, does he withdraw my head, allowing me oxygen.

"One more time." Is the only warning I get as he pushes my head back down his entire length.

I dig my nails into his thighs as I gag, making an embarrassing retching noise and slobbering all over him with my eyes watering. But he doesn't seem to care as he pulls back, allowing temporary oxygen, and then sets a grueling pace, giving me no choice but to keep up, but at least he's not breaching my boundary.

"Fuck yeah. Suck it real good, my dirty little minx." He grinds through clenched teeth, pumping my head faster.

I suck and lick as fast as possible until he's shooting his load. I almost choke again, but I quickly work my throat muscles, swallowing. He finally releases my head, with his shoulders slumping forward slightly, and I take the opportunity to fill my lungs with much needed air. When I look at him, I can tell he's still in la-la-land with a hint of a grin on his face. It warms my heart knowing I pleased him.

"You're so sexy when you look like that," I admire, and only then does the lustful haze lift from his eyes. "Do I get to drive now?" I ask with hopefulness but half expecting him to say no.

"I think after that outstanding performance, I'll let you drive whatever you want."

I snicker and go to turn around, but he captures the back of my neck, pulling my lips to his.

"You continue to surprise me, Ms. Scarlett. Don't stop. I like it," he admits with a devilish wink. "Now, turn around before I change my mind."

You don't have to tell me twice as I quickly shift around and then get a quick lesson on how to operate the machine. It seems pretty basic, and soon I'm cruising around with the wind whipping through my hair.

"Of all days, you don't wear your damn hair up!" Dekker shouts, and I glance back for a second to see him trying to pick my hair off his face. I snicker, and finally, he gets my hair under control, gathering it in one hand, and giving it a little tug.

After another thirty minutes on the jet ski, Dekker tells me to head back. The sun is just starting to descend, so I'm figuring it has to be around seven or later.

"I was really hoping to see dolphins," I say absently, gazing across the vast water as Dekker secures the jet ski to the boat.

"I know of a place a few hours from here. I'll take you some time," he states and then turns around to face me.

When our eyes connect, I see the unsaid words we both think of immediately. *There won't be a next time.* It's disheartening, but I refuse to think about that right now. I need to focus on the present and I'll worry about the future later.

"Yeah, that would be nice," I say with a smile, shoving my emotions in a box.

That evening, Dekker insisted on hand feeding me. At first, I wasn't too keen on the idea. The last time I checked, I wasn't a dog. But of course, I gave in, and after the first few bites and licking his fingers clean, it quickly became a sensual game. Seeing the hunger in his eyes as he fed me chunks of filet dipped in garlic and butter was almost enough to cream myself. Liquid desire emanates from him as the electricity kicks up a few notches, crackling between us. Needless to say, we abandon our dinner, succumbing to our heated attraction.

That night, below the moonlight and twinkling stars, he let me take control. I was surprised, so sure tonight would be the night for anal sex, but he didn't ask. I wasn't about to question, so instead, I climbed on top of him, straddling his hips, and rode him until ecstasy claimed both of us. That was the first of three more times, all under the midnight sky with only the moon and stars as our witnesses. I think it was the most romantic thing ever, and I know it will be something I'll never forget. If I could wish upon a star, I would freeze time and stay like this forever.

But something this good never lasts.

CHAPTER EIGHTEEN

Kinsley

It's Friday afternoon the following week, almost home time, when I glance at the clock for the fourth time. The minutes tick by, and soon five o'clock comes and goes, but Dekker's door remains closed. I check his calendar again. He had a telephone call scheduled at four-thirty, but it should have only lasted fifteen to twenty minutes.

I'm about to send him a text message when I hear the elevator ping and the doors open. A *hot* blond guy steps out and heads in my direction. He's as tall as Dekker and built the same, but he's casually dressed in blue jeans and a fitted t-shirt. I know Fridays are dress down days, so I don't know if this guy works for Dekker or if he is a visitor.

I stand up as he approaches my desk.

"May I help you?"

"That depends," he says, sizing me up as he comes around my desk and has no quarries about invading my personal space.

"On what?"

"What your plans are for tonight?"

"Excuse me?"

"The name is Jonas, and I guess the rumors are correct."

"Rumors? What rumors?" I frown, not liking where this conversation is going.

"Don't worry, love. They are all good," he says, eyes roaming for the third time.

I'm about to give this *hot* guy a piece of my mind when Dekker's door opens.

"Jonas, stop hitting on my personal assistant, or I'll fire your ass."

Jonas barks out a laugh, stepping away from me, and I watch the two of them share a quick hug with a slap on the back. I stand there in shock. I've never seen Dekker hug anyone, except me and I wonder if Jonas is his brother. The two of them could definitely pass it off. The only difference is Dekker has wavy dark brown hair and Jonas is more a dirty blonde.

"How was your trip?" Dekker asks.

"Ah, you know, never long enough. I need my boss to give me a few extra weeks of holidays," he says with a wink, and Dekker shakes his head.

"Kinsley, this is Jonas. My financial controller, but we've been good friends since high school."

"Oh, it's very nice to meet you, Jonas," I say, sticking out my hand.

Jonas takes it, but instead of shaking, he brings it up to his lips, kissing the top of my knuckles.

"The pleasure is all mine, love."

I see Dekker clench his teeth beside him with an exaggerated eye roll.

"Well, umm... I'm just going to be heading out. Have a good weekend, Mr. Dekker."

"Yes, I have a few things to wrap up here. Have a good weekend yourself, Ms. Everett."

I give him a nod, understanding his hidden message, but it actually pains me to leave. I was looking forward to being bent over his desk or getting rug burn on my knees. Five PM is turning out to be my favorite pastime, but not only that, it's the start of the weekend, and call me greedy, but I want to spend every waking minute with him. Unfortunately, come this Thursday, Dekker will be leaving for his Las Vegas trip, so there goes that weekend, and then we're down to one month.

It's a depressing thought as I make my way to the elevator and slip inside. When I turn around, I see both of them standing there, watching me, but I only see Dekker. As good looking as Jonas is, I'll only ever see Dekker.

After making my way around the building, and giving the security guard that sits in his booth all day long a quick wave, I'm back upstairs calling out for Mittens. Slowly but surely, he comes sauntering my way, yawning once, and when he's close enough, I scoop him up in my arms, giving him snuggles and kisses. I've noticed these last few weeks he has adjusted very well, and I frequently find him sprawled out on the bench that Dekker has in front of the floor-to-ceiling window, sunbathing. Or at least, that's what I assume when I come up to rub his belly and ask if he's working on his tan.

My cell phone dings so I put Mittens down and pull my phone out of my purse. I see it's a text message from Dekker.

Dekker – *Going out with Jonas for a few drinks. I'll try not to be too late. Sorry babe, I'll make it up to you.*

I let out a sigh, plopping down on the couch and rereading his message. I don't want to sound like a bitchy, possessive woman, but really, that sucks ass. This is our time, but it's also not fair to Dekker, and I can't expect him to stay home with me twenty-four seven. He has his own life and is allowed to hang out with his guy friends. I really need to make a few myself. I only hope he'll stay true to his word and not hook up with another woman. I think that's where my insecurity truly lies. Even if Dekker and I were an actual item, I would be terrified to let him out of my sight, knowing thousands of women are waiting to sink their claws in him. *Thousands of full figured, blonde women at his disposal,* and I'm sure he knows it.

I let out another sigh, texting him back.

Kinsley – *No need to apologize or rush home. Have fun, and I'll see you in the morning. XX*

He doesn't text back, and I sit on the couch, looking around and wondering what the hell I'm going to do for the rest of the night. Even though his apartment, or whatever you call it, is beautifully decorated and ridiculous in size, I find it's missing something, especially when Dekker isn't here. I feel like this tiny mouse with way too much space, but yet, feeling closed in. There are no family photos. You can't open a window, except for the rooftop and the more I look around, I realize something else. It's just a house. Not a home.

Although my studio apartment is micro-small, I have family photos hanging on my walls, some greenery plants and it just feels lived in. Yeah, occasionally, I can be a messy person, leaving things lying around, but here, everything has a place with not a spec of dirt or dust. It's too organized, and it almost feels empty. I may feel differently if he had a balcony where you could sit outside and take in the scenery, but he doesn't. Yes, he has a rooftop patio that provides pretty much everything I described, but I still think a balcony with windows that can open on this level would help make this place feel a little more open, cozy, and maybe some plants.

I let out a sigh, turning the TV on for some background noise and head to the kitchen to find something to eat, but then I hear my cell phone ringing. I dash back into the living room, hoping it's Dekker calling, saying he's on his way home. I pick up my phone, and I smile.

"Hey, Mom."

"Hello, darling. How's the new job going?"

"It's good. Getting into the swing of things. Although, the first week was a blur," I say with a snicker, and mom chuckles. "How are things back home?" I ask.

"Oh good. Your father has been quite busy these last two weeks, which is always good for the bank account, but I'm just afraid he's going to run himself down, especially with this heatwave we're going through."

My parents are still quite young, with my mom being forty-two, and my dad forty-six. They still have roughly fifteen to twenty years of work before they can think about retiring. It really is a depressing thought. You bust your ass for forty-plus years, and when you can finally retire, you don't have as much energy as you used to in your younger years. But, then you hear stories where you have good, hard working people who worked all their life, never missing a day per se, only to become ill or worse, terminally ill, and your time is limited. Really, what kind of quality of life do you have when you retire? I personally think the government should make it mandatory that you retire at fifty and that everything is free for the middle to poor class. *Okay, that's wishful thinking on my part.*

"The only good thing about him working all these extra hours, we'll have no problem coming to New York for a visit. We were thinking Christmas this time."

"Really!" I shout, and my mom laughs. "Oh my God, I think I'm going to cry. That would be so amazing." I haven't seen my parents since last fall. Usually, Christmas is off limits because it's too expensive to travel, and not to mention accommodations in New York are through the roof. I also haven't spent Christmas with them since moving. It's the worst time of year when I truly feel lonely and homesick.

"Yup. I'm going to look into hotels come September, and if you don't mind, we'll stay until New Years' day. Maybe you can find something for the four of us to do unless you, and that handsome billionaire of yours prefer to be alone, which is completely fine. Your mom does remember how exciting it was to share your first holidays together."

I smile, but then it quickly vanishes. I'll be alone once again, but I don't have the heart to tell my mom this. I told her Dekker and I are kind of seeing each other, nothing too serious and we're keeping it low key for obvious reasons. *It's kind of a big no-no to be sleeping with your boss.* But she also doesn't know it's temporary— two months, and soon, I'll be out of a job and left with a broken heart.

"Yeah, that sounds great, Mom. I'll just wait until it gets closer to start planning anything."

"So, how are things going with Eric? He's treating you well, I hope."

"He is. He's sweet and caring, contrary to how the public views him."

"Yes, the media does have lots to say about him, along with many women." I cringe. "Kinsley, are you sure dating him is a good idea? I'm just afraid you're going to get hurt. It appears he doesn't have a good track record with women. It's easy to tell he is a ladies' man."

I let out a sigh, understanding her concern, but it's too late. The water is up to my chin and all I'm trying to do is stay afloat.

"That's why we're taking it slow. I'll be fine, Mom."

"I hope so, darling. I know you haven't had very good luck in the men department, and I'm sure dating Eric feels like hitting the jackpot. I just think you shouldn't put too much into the relationship. Men like him are players, Kinsley. Not the settling down type." If I thought I was depressed before, I feel like I'm in the dumpsters now. "I'm sorry, honey. That was kind of heartless of me to say."

"It's fine, Mom. You aren't telling me anything I don't already know. I'll deal with that when the time comes."

"I'm sorry, Kinsley. I'll keep my fingers and toes crossed for you."

I think if the entire world crossed their fingers and toes, I still wouldn't have a chance.

We talk for a bit longer until I hear Dad's voice in the background, and soon the phone is passed to him. We chat for another ten minutes, catching up before saying goodbye. Mittens jumps up on my lap a second later, wanting snuggles. I think he knows I'm feeling sad. I look around Dekker's place. It's going to be a long night, and I have no desire to sit here by myself.

If Dekker can go out, why can't I?

I open Google on my phone and search for nearby clubs. After scrolling for a few minutes, I come across a lounge bar that has live music nightly. Friday nights is classical music with a twist of today's favorites. The Google Map says it's a thirty-minute walk from here, but I don't think my feet are up to walking that distance, so I'll just flag down a taxi. After reading the reviews, I can tell it's a trendy club. I decide to call them to see if I need a reservation or if there's a waiting list. You never know with New York, as there are so many clubs and restaurants where you need to book months in advance. I keep my fingers crossed as I dial their number, and when I ask the lady that answers the phone, she confirms yes, you need a reservation, but they just had two cancellations.

Technically she is supposed to call the next person in line, and was about to, but she's going to pretend one of them is me. I thank her half a dozen times and tell her I'd see her in forty-five minutes.

I rush to the bedroom closet and quickly glance over the clothing. My eye catches a black sequined embellished dress that literally sparkles with glitz and glamour. It's strapless, and I see it's quite short when I hold it up against myself. I shrug. At this point, I don't care. I need to hustle. I slip it on, not bothering with a bra, and it fits like a glove. It's short, but not slutty short. My butt is fully covered with a few inches to spare. I match it up with a pair of ankle strap high heels and grab a black clutch purse and a glittery black shawl to wrap around my shoulders.

I give myself the once over in the mirror. Even though I look white as a ghost, I think I look pretty damn good. I would almost say hot. After brushing my teeth and running a brush through my hair, I'm ready. I'm getting used to wearing my hair down because I know Dekker likes it that way. Although, he does like a good ponytail to pull on. I say goodbye to Mittens, and once I'm around the front of the building, I hail down a cab.

I'm looking forward to this evening out, and I don't care that I'm spending it alone. I'm not looking for a hookup. *Done that, never again.* I'm there for the music, to have supper, and have a couple of drinks. I've got money in my bank account because of my gracious and very gorgeous boss giving me a healthy salary, and dammit, I need a night out so I don't go bonkers, wondering if Dekker is cheating on me.

Although with two hot guys out for the night, I think I'm fighting a losing battle, but can I really say anything? Yes, we agreed to be exclusive, but if you think about it, our secret love affair isn't permanent. It has an end date that's five weeks away. Why bother being faithful?

After paying the cab driver, I step inside the swanky club and immediately notice the place is intimately set with low ambiance lighting. It's romantic and sophisticated, with a mid-size stage for a band and a good size dance floor. It would be perfect for date night.

After the hostess leads me to my table, I'm overjoyed with a clear view of the stage. It's a bar height round table along the back wall, and I set down my purse, moving the second chair closer to me, and then remove the shawl, draping it over the back of the chair. A male pianist is playing the piano and a beautiful woman dressed in a stunning silver gown is singing a soft melody song.

It's not long before a waiter appears at my table. He's young. I'm guessing around Dekker's age, cheerful and pleasant as we have a light conversation, and then he gives me recommendations on what's popular, seeing how it's my first time. I decide on a glass of Cabernet Sauvignon wine and the seafood risotto. After the waiter brings me the glass of wine, I sit back, taking a sip. I'm not much of a drinker, but this wine tastes incredible. It should since it's twenty-two dollars a glass. The glass of wine almost cost as much as my meal. I see the drinks are expensive, but the food is reasonably priced. I pull out my cell to see if Dekker has messaged me. I'm hopeful, but, of course, he hasn't. It's shortly after seven, and I decide against sending him a text message, letting him know I've gone out. I figure I'll only be a couple of hours and be home way before him.

That's if he even comes home, Kinsley. Ugh!

I slip my cell phone back in my purse with a sigh, deciding I'm not going to think about that right now. I'm here to have a good time and not dwell on the things I can't control. If he sleeps with another woman, I can only hope he'll be truthful and tell me, because I certainly won't have unprotected sex with him again. As far as I'm concerned, he can wear a condom even if his test comes back clean. I'm not taking the chance. And, if he doesn't like that, I guess our arrangement ends a lot earlier because I'll walk. It will kill me to do so, but I'm not catching any sexually transmitted diseases, even for him.

As I wait for my food, I turn my attention to the stage where the lady is now singing "Someone Like You" by Adele, but Dekker remains in the forefront of my mind. I wish he was here with me as I glance around the club seeing couples dancing close together, others laughing and chatting, and I watch another couple lean across their table to share an intimate kiss.

It makes me realize I've never been on a date. I see a few loner guys immaculately dressed, sitting at the bar sipping on a glass of whisky and watching me, along with another woman sitting in a booth, eating her dinner. She has her laptop out, completely absorbed in her work as she eats. She strikes me to be a lawyer. Even when you're off the clock, your job never ends. I'm so glad I didn't go into that field. I glance back at the guys again, and one gives me a nod with a slight raise of his glass. I roll my eyes, ignoring him, and turn my attention back to the stage. I hope to God he doesn't approach me because I don't care how good looking he is, I'm not interested.

CHAPTER NINETEEN

Dekker

I can tell Jonas is ready to blow his top. I told him I wasn't discussing anything at work, which led to guys' night out. I feel like an asshole leaving Kinsley, but I'm hoping to be home by eleven at the latest. She looked hot in her black pencil skirt and a cream colored blouse, and my dick has been daydreaming about her all day. I was looking forward to seeing her on her knees and those gorgeous plump lips wrapped around my cock. I love watching my cock disappear in her mouth and seeing those eyes sparkle with lust as she looks up into mine.

She doesn't wear a stitch of makeup and doesn't need to. She's beautiful without, but one of these days, I would love to see her paint her lips a juicy red and then take my length on her knees. That will be so fucking hot. I'll probably cum down her throat in a heartbeat. Her sexuality has been taking leaps and bounds these last few weeks. A little seductress in the bedroom or after hours in my office, but I've also learned she has a naughty streak.

That little stunt she pulled in my meeting almost two weeks ago had me practically creaming my fucking pants. It was the first for me. No woman has ever been bold enough to do that, and I almost made an ass out of myself in front of my client. Luckily for me, he was an old fart and completely oblivious. *But fuck me that was hot.* She is now my dirty little minx and Ms. Scarlett. And speaking of dirty, I'm ready to claim that virgin ass of hers this weekend. I gave her another week's reprieve, but enough waiting.

"All right, spill it. You've got your beer in front of you. I want all the juicy details on the lovely Ms. Redhead. Starting with, did you hit your head or something while I was on vacation? Now, I'm not complaining. It's finally nice to see you break the mold. She's hot and all. A little small in the tits department, but her heart shaped ass is to die for, along with those deliciously long legs. When do I get her?"

After reading Kinsley's text message for the fourth time, I set my phone down on the table. I'm still amazed that she told me to have fun and not to rush home. Most women, no correction, any other woman would have had a hairy conniption fit. But not Kinsley. She really is one in a million.

"Never," I state, finally looking up at Jonas.

"Never? What the hell is that supposed to mean?"

"Exactly what it means. She's off limits."

"Since when?"

"Since now. Besides, aren't you tired of having my leftover scraps?"

"Hell no. I don't have to worry about training them, and oh, by the way, I'm done with Monica. She's all yours. I broke it off with her before leaving for Costa Rica."

Jonas is my longest friend and truly a great guy. We've always shared women in the past, but never together. I'm a little possessive when it comes to women, and I don't accidentally want a dick in my face. But once I'm done with a woman, he takes his turn or vice versa, but usually, it's the other way around. It's never bothered me, and that's how we like it. But I'm finding I don't want to discuss Kinsley with him. I meant what I said, she is off limits. If he touches her, I might just have to rearrange his face.

Our wings and nachos arrive, and Mia, our waitress, offers us another round of beer. We both accept, and I wait until she returns, but when she does, she stalls, fluttering her eyelashes and leaning over the booth to show us her huge tits that are practically hanging out. I roll my eyes looking away.

"Now, Mia, you know I don't double dip. Be a doll, and scurry along before you embarrass yourself any further," Jonas speaks up first, which I'm glad because I have the urge to actually shove her away.

"Eric hasn't had his turn yet," she dares to say.

"And I never will," I state coldly.

"What? I'm not good enough for you," she snaps, getting her back up.

"I don't fuck dirty little whores."

"You're such an egotistical asshole, Eric."

"Tell me something I don't already know," I quip back, which earns me a lips snarl from her.

"We're done here, Mia. Go away before I have you physically removed," Jonas jumps in, and Mia storms off, huffing and puffing.

"Not sure what I ever saw in her. Sorry man."

"You were probably inebriated," I offer.

"Well, I honestly don't remember a thing. Only waking up the next day with her in my bed. Anyways, enough about her. Back to your hot new assistant."

"I'm not done with her, and besides, she's still off limits."

"Whoa, she must have one sweet tight ass if you're making her off limits."

"I wouldn't know," I say and instantly regret my words.

I watch Jonas's eyes protrude, and I grit my teeth, silently cursing.

"Are you seriously telling me you haven't fucked her ass? Haven't you two been together for three weeks now?"

"We have."

"All right, what gives? I'm assuming she has a virgin asshole, and I can see you working her up to that within a couple of days, not three weeks. How are you even cumming, or have you taken an oath of celibacy? She can definitely pass off as a hot Sunday School teacher," he says with a chuckle.

I glare at him. "No, dick head, I'm cumming plenty."

"How?" he questions, and then recognition sets in. "No fucking way! Did she have a virgin pussy too?"

"Keep your voice down," I sneer, looking around the bar. The music is loud enough, but I certainly don't want anyone knowing my business. "For all intents and purposes, she was. She had sex once, it was a disaster."

"Oh, that sucks, but seriously, you're actually cumming inside her pussy, or are you faking it?"

"You can't fake an orgasm like a woman can, you dipshit."

"True. So she must have one hell of a tight pussy then."

"I've fucked asses that are not as tight as her pussy."

Jonas whistles. "So why is she off limits then? Unless... unless you have feelings for her. Bloody hell! I leave for three weeks, and my boy goes and falls in love with a redhead of all women." He bellows out a laugh, slapping his hand on the table, and I'm two seconds away from knocking his block off when my cell phone dings.

"I don't have feelings for her, so shut your fucking pie hole before I do," I bite out, collecting my phone off the table.

He holds up his hands, still chuckling, and my teeth clench again, looking at the incoming text message from Chase.

Chase – *Thought you would like to know the Misses has gone out.*

I frown. *Kinsley went out?*

Dekker – *When?*

Chase – *A little over an hour ago.*

What the hell? I dial Chase.

"And, you're just telling me this now!" I bark on the other end as soon as he picks up. "Where?!"

He tells me she took a cab to TT's Lounge Club. She's been there since seven, ordered a seafood entrée and just finished her first glass of wine. I glance at the time, it's twenty after eight. Why didn't she tell me she was going out? I can only assume she probably thought I would be out all night, and she didn't want to sit alone. I don't blame her, but goddamn it, it pisses me off. I should have been the one taking her out. But, technically, I blew her off. At least TT's is a reputable club, but I'm not taking any chances.

"I'll call you back," I say, hanging up.

"You're ditching me, aren't you?" Jonas says as I reach for my wallet.

"Sorry, an emergency came up. We'll get together some other time," I say, tossing a hundred-dollar bill on the table, and Jonas laughs.

"She went out and didn't tell you. Oh man, you've got it bad."

"Fuck off!" I bark, making him laugh harder. *Asshole!*

I storm off and call Chase when I see he's waiting by the door of my SUV.

"Who's watching her?" I snap, ready to pull my hair out. I don't like her being alone, even if she's in a respectable club.

"Trey's there."

"Good. I'll want a visual."

Chase nods as I slip into the back.

"One more thing, boss." My eyes snap to his. "Another gentleman sent a glass of wine to her table, but she sent it back."

I don't know if I should be relieved or more pissed off. Of course other men are going to hit on her. But, at least she's wearing her skirt and blouse. It's simple and less revealing. Although, she may be a little underdressed. I know it's a distinguished club with a waiting list. I'm surprised she got in. I haven't been there myself in close to a year, but I know they have excellent live entertainment nightly. I call Trey, and he picks up on the first ring.

"I want a visual."

"Figured you would. One second." I hear some rustling and Trey coming back. "You can connect," he confirms. I hold out my phone, pressing the link, and a few seconds later, I've got a visual of her and almost have a coronary.

"What the fuck is she wearing?!" I bellow into my phone.

"I... ah..." Trey stutters.

My eyes roam every single inch of Kinsley. Christ, she's showing a boat load of bare skin. I watch the waiter come into view with another glass of wine. Trey tells me she did not order this. I clench my jaw, squeezing my phone. If I could reach through my phone and strangle someone, I would. I watch the waiter walk up to her table. I can't see her, because he's blocking the view, but a few seconds later, he's turning and walking away with the drink untouched. He's smiling, probably thinking it's funny, and in most cases, it would be, if it wasn't my woman they're trying to hit on. *MINE!*

"How much longer?" I continue to bark, but directed to Chase.

"Ten minutes," he says, unfazed by my little rant.

I curse, and for the next ten minutes, I stare at Kinsley. Fuck, she looks stunning in that strapless dress. We should be home, fucking our brains out. *I'm going to take her home and fuck her brains out!* As soon as I get there, I'm hauling her ass out. I just might even take my belt to her fine derriere for going out without me and not telling me. *Also, for looking that damn sexy.* I have a clear view of her, but obviously, she is attracting considerable attention.

The vehicle slows and I glance up to see we're here. Chase parks, and I fly out of the SUV, not waiting for him to open my door. The good thing about this place, I don't have to worry about the media or paparazzi lurking around. Instead, they'll be at the more prominent nightclubs, hoping to get a snapshot of a celebrity or people with boatloads of money, like me.

As I step inside, my eyes flicker to Kinsley and then to Trey. He signals for me to join him as I see a glass of whisky waiting. As much as I would like to storm over to

Kinsley and drag her out, I need to get a hold of myself, so I don't make a scene and embarrass both of us.

A short, pixie blonde hostess greets me immediately, asking if I have a reservation. I see the owner from the corner of my eye coming in our direction with alarm in her eyes.

"Oh, Eric, what a pleasant surprise. Cecilia, Mr. Dekker doesn't need a reservation. Please accept my apologies, and I have the perfect spot for you. Will you be dining in?"

The hostess's eyes snap wide as her cheeks turn crimson red in color. She screwed up, but it's kind of nice knowing not everyone knows me.

"It's quite all right, Heather. She was only doing her job," I say, more or less for the hostess' sake, and I see the young pixie relax a little. "Actually, I'll be joining my buddy at the bar."

"Oh, that's wonderful. If you need anything, please let me know."

I give Heather a nod. She's in her early forties and looks fabulous for her age. She's also done very well for herself. She's never married and prefers it that way, but I know she's in a relationship with a gentleman for probably close to five years now.

I stroll to Trey, keeping one eye on Kinsley. She doesn't notice me as she is too immersed in watching the lady on stage singing.

"Figured you could use a drink to calm your nerves a little," Trey says casually as I sit on the bar stool beside him.

"You figured right," I admit, taking a solid gulp of the whiskey. It's rich and smooth, leaving a warm, lingering feeling throughout my limbs. It's what I like the most about this place. They don't spare any expense on alcohol.

"She's stunning with exquisite eyes," he remarks, staring at her.

I suddenly want to gouge his eyes out for looking, but he's right. It's the first thing anyone will notice if you actually stop to look, but now that she's dresses stylishly, she's attracting attention at warp speed.

I've heard the rumors at work. The women that think they deserve me are insanely jealous of her, and there are a few men who want in her pants. If they don't watch their mouths or wandering eyes, they will find themselves out of a job and real soon.

I look over at Kinsley and close my eyes for a moment. She literally takes my breath away. Seeing her on a screen didn't do her justice. The body hugging dress she's wearing sparkles like her eyes. She's strikingly beautiful as I watch her gorgeous leg swing to the beat of the music. She has a smile on her face and not a care in the world. *And God dammit, she's mine!*

I finally take a moment to glance around the bar, and see Trey and I aren't the only ones watching her. Two other gentlemen are sitting at the bar with their eyes glued to her, along with two other single gentlemen sitting in booths near the back.

But I have to admit, another good thing about this club is that it's geared toward couples with a romantic setting and a much smaller gathering. So there aren't a lot of blood thirsty men preying on women.

I curse myself again. I should have taken her out, and I wonder if she's ever been on a date. Knowing what I know about Kinsley's past, I'm guessing not. But she also said she didn't want to be seen together, so that's a date blocker right there. But I could have taken her to a private club, I know plenty, or even out of the city. It's clear she's enjoying herself and the music. I don't think people here will talk. It's primarily a club for the middle class people wanting an intimate date night, but I do see a few high rollers here.

Feeling much calmer, I drain the last of my whiskey, ordering another and a glass of wine for Kinsley. I'm about to take the drinks to her table when Trey puts his arm out, blocking me. I look up to see Ryder Kensington approaching her table. *Ah, for the love of God.* I hadn't noticed him before, and I see a dark brunette beauty sitting at their table, watching him. Ryder is a sharpshooter with the ladies, preferring two on his arm at all times. I know why he's here. He's looking for his second fling to complete his trio and has his sights set on my girl. He's filthy rich like me and has the look no woman can say no to. Overall, he's a nice guy, and he does love his threesomes. I haven't had any problems with him, but it looks like we're about to. I'm about to intervene when Trey pushes back.

"Do you fucking mind," I snarl in a whisper.

"Watch. I think your girl might surprise you," he says confidently.

I growl, ready to rip his arm off, but on the other hand, he's got a point. I would never cheat on Kinsley while we are together. I promised we would be exclusive, and I meant it. I can't see her picking up another guy while we're together, but it doesn't mean she can't flirt and get his number for when our arrangement ends. *Ends.* Something that's coming way too bloody fast. Jonas's words ring in my head, '*you have feelings for her.*' Like fuck I do. I don't do love. It's her pussy I'm in love with, if anything.

Ryder approaches her table, and she looks up at him. I'm too far away to hear what they are saying, but the look on Kinsley's face says it all. She's not impressed. Words are exchanged, and the encounter is brief. She turns him down. *That's my girl.* Ryder doesn't seem fazed by it, but I watch him pull out a card from the breast of his pocket. He's giving her his number. He slides it in front of her and says, have a good evening, with a slight bow before walking away. I did catch that part. I watch Kinsley pick up the card and rip it into tiny little pieces. It makes me smile, and glance at Trey. He's got a smug look on his face. *Asshole.*

"You're dismissed," I tell him. He picks up his glass, draining it, and then goes to pay. "I've got it."

"Have a good night. Call me when you need me."

I give him a nod. Trey is another good buddy of mine and tech savvy. I've offered him a job at my company a few times, but he prefers working for the police. I don't blame him.

Before heading to Kinsley, I ask Heather if she happens to have a red rose. She smiles and tells me I'm in luck. A minute later, she returns with a single red rose with all the thorns removed. She glances at Kinsley.

"She's beautiful, but if I can be candid with you, Eric. You may not want to let this one go, or there will be someone else ready to snatch her up."

An icy chill runs down my spine. I already know that but hearing it from another woman makes it sound so final. The problem is, I don't think I can give Kinsley what she wants.

"I know," is all I say to Heather, and she gives me a pat on the back with a brief smile before walking away.

I shake off the cold feeling and head to Kinsley. She has her head down, looking at her cell phone, and as I draw closer, I see she's no longer smiling. She looks sad. I take a turn so I can come up behind her, and catch a glimpse of her phone. I see she's looking at the picture she took of us last week. My heart squeezes as I watch her run a fingertip over my face. *She can't be in love with me?* I hope to God, for her sake, she's not. I've devastated enough women over the years and not give two shits, but I truly don't want to hurt her. I'll admit she's unique, but I'm not the guy for her.

I step in further, enough to slide the drinks on the table. I hear Kinsley sigh as she closes her phone, and I reach around to hold the single rose for her. Before I know it, she is flying out of her seat, throwing her arms around my neck and crushing me in a bear hug. I'm stunned momentarily, wondering how the hell she knew it was me but as soon as her body is flush with mine, I close my eyes, inhaling her sweet scent, and squeezing her back. *Christ, I've missed her.* We've never been apart this long. We might not see each other for a few hours during the day, but I know she's always just outside my door.

The plethora of emotions swirling through me is making me dizzy. I don't know how to decipher them or what they are trying to tell me.

Kinsley sucks in a ragged breath, grabbing my attention, so I work my hand up to her silky strands, cupping the base of her neck.

"I'm here, sweetheart," I whisper. She sniffles, and I squeeze her again. "I'm sorry, Kinsley. I shouldn't have left you tonight."

"But, you're here now?" she questions softly.

I pull back, looking into her glassy eyes.

"I am, baby."

"But weren't you a having guy's night out?"

I bring her lips to mine, needing to taste her. She doesn't hold back, slipping her tongue into my mouth first, and I groan low in my throat. My cock is straining against my pants, begging to be released, but he'll have to be patient. I reluctantly break the kiss and her vibrant eyes never waver from mine.

"How did you know it was me?" I question.

"I know your scent," she smiles sweetly, picking up the rose and bringing it to her nose. "Smells delicious."

Her eyes glitter seductively as she swirls the rose underneath her nose and flutters her long eyelashes. She looks so innocent, but yet, a ball of fire at the same time, and she makes me excruciatingly hard.

"Are you flirting with me, Ms. Everett?"

"Maybe," she says as a light blush creeps up on her face.

I chuckle, kissing her nose. Freaking priceless!

"You look stunning." I seal my lips over hers one last time before taking her hand. "Come. Let's sit down."

She nods, moving her purse and cell phone out of the way. Her eyes now wander, seeing we are the main attraction. People are smiling, and I take her hand, giving it a squeeze.

"I don't think you'll need to worry about anyone talking here. This is a small club where you don't have your typical socialites ready to spread tabloid rumors that's none of their business."

This seems to appease Kinsley as she visibly relaxes, taking a sip of her wine. I glance at Ryder, and he gives me a nod of acceptance. If he only knew she'll be available in five weeks, I'm sure he would stop at nothing to make her his. The thought sickens me. I can't give her what she'll want, but the idea of her being with another man turns my stomach into a cluster of knots, and summons a possessive beast, where maybe I'll just keep her locked up so no one can have her.

"The singer has a beautiful voice," she comments, bringing me back to the present.

"Her name is Delia. She's a regular here, and yes, she does. But you should come when they have jazz night. It's a real festival in here."

"Oh, that sounds exciting. Maybe next time."

We stare at each other for a moment, and I can almost guess what's running through her head, *"will there be a next time?"* It's the same thought I'm having and the same thought that happened to both of us last weekend.

"How was your dinner?" I ask, breaking the slight tension.

"It was incredible. How was yours?"

"Not as good as yours. Wings and nachos."

"Mmm, sounds yummy. Can't remember the last time I had those."

For the next hour, we settle into an easy conversation, occasionally taking a break to listen to the music as I hold her hand. Kinsley got super excited when Delia brought her violin out but then teared up when she played "Only Time" by Enya. She's been quiet these last few minutes, and I notice she's no longer watching Delia on stage, but instead, she's watching the couples dance. I take that as my cue. I slip off my suit jacket, rolling up my sleeves, and standing.

"May I have this dance, Ms. Scarlett?" I hold out my hand.

Kinsley grins, slipping off the chair and placing her hand in mine. I lead her to the dance floor, pulling her into my arms and snug against my body. I see Heather smiling in the background as Delia starts in with another song, "Meant to Be" by Bebe Rexha.

We dance in silence as we harmoniously glide around the dance floor. Kinsley is as graceful as ever with fluid movements, elegant and flawless. The background fades away, and there is no one else but the two of us. When I lean back to look into her eyes, I know instantly she loves me, and I feel my stomach clench in knots. Delia eases into a new song, "You are the Reason" by Calum Scott, and I feel the lyrics hit too close to home. It's disturbing and I don't want to deal with this right now.

"Are you ready to go home?" I ask, coming to a stop and needing to get out of here.

Kinsley seems surprised for a moment, but then she smiles.

"I would love to go home."

I pay her bill, thanking Heather, and tell her we'll be back sometime for jazz night. Heather assures me she'll have a table waiting. Kinsley wraps her shawl around her shoulders and gulps down the last of her wine before we head out. As soon as we step foot outside, she shrieks, yanking her shawl over her head. It's literally down pouring. Chase sees us, looking momentarily horrified, before leaping out of the vehicle to get the door, but I holler for him to stay put. I should have texted him, telling him we were on our way, but I knew he would be parked nearby. But, I didn't realize it was piss pouring out. He ignores me, opening the back door as Kinsley and I make a mad dash. By the time we're sliding in, we're drenched. We take one look at each other, and crack up laughing.

I grab a handkerchief from the inside of my suit jacket, handing it over to Kinsley. She dries off her face as I shake my head, spraying more mist.

"You look a little bit like Shaggy," she says with a giggle.

"Says the drowned rat," I wink, chuckling myself, and then I run my fingers through my hair, taming it. Kinsley snickers again.

As soon as we're home, I lead Kinsley into the shower to warm up. Even though it's warm out, being wet somehow makes you feel cold.

"Feel like playing?" I ask Kinsley while drying her off. I'm finding one of my favorite pastimes after our vigorous session of morning sex, I get to savor washing and drying every inch of her off. I always love seeing her cheeks a nice rosy red, while she looks starry eyed and a little dopey. Although our five PM meet and greet is also at the top of my list.

"I'm always up for playing."

"How about getting a little dirty tonight?" I whisper low by her ear. She turns her head, eyes meeting mine, knowing what I'm referring to. Worry blankets her face. "How about we use your safe words. Red to stop, and yellow, if you need a few minutes or need me to slow down," I tell her.

"Okay," she whispers, and I close my eyes for a second as a thrill of excitement shoots down my spine. *She can't be anymore perfect.*

I trace the shell of her ear with my tongue, sending a skitter of goosebumps all over her body. "Good girl. Why don't you blow dry your hair? I need a few minutes to set up. I'll come and get you when you're done."

She nods and I grab her ass, squeezing. She does have a perfect little apple and I can't wait to be inside. Kinsley jolts, with a squeak of surprise and I give her a wink, heading out and closing the door behind me. I don't want her peeking. Moving to my dresser first, I take out the things I'll be needing. I did some online shopping a week and a half ago and had everything sent here. I could have taken her to my other place where I have all of this stuff already, but truthfully, I have no desire. Maybe because she isn't my usual type I feel the need to do things differently with her. Everything I've done with her has been out of my realm, starting with her moving in temporarily. I'm pretty sure I've lost my mind and some days I find myself questioning why her. But the answers never come. I'm sure when it does, it will be the biggest epiphany of my life.

After retrieving the items I need, I place them on the bed and wonder how I'm going to attach the long red sash to the bed. The only downside being here is my bed is a sleigh style. The place I have downtown is a four-poster style bed with rod iron bars through the headboard. Excellent design for tying up my subject.

I pull the bed away from the wall, kneeling down. My only option is to attach the sash to the bedframe, but at least I have the length. After tying a secure knot, I push it between the mattress and headboard. I move the bed back and then strip the comforter off and place down a thin waterproof mattress pad and cover it with a deep red velvet blanket. *We're going to get messy tonight.*

Leaving the bedroom, I retrieve my next items from the kitchen, setting them down on the night table. I light a bunch of candles, turning off the lights and I'm done. I step back, surveying the area and feeling pleased.

I think about the rumors I've read on social media from women calling me the Kink Master. I really don't know where that came from. Yeah, I'm dominant in the bedroom and in the office, but I don't have any weird fetishes, like fire or water play and I certainly don't have a kinky dungeon. I do like control, and my weapon of choice is my belt or hand, but that's as good as it gets. I've never used a whip and it's rare that I will use a paddle, riding crop, or flogger. I like it simple.

I hear the blow dryer shut off and I smile. *Time to collect my redheaded beauty.* I open the bathroom door and see Kinsley is running a brush through her gorgeous red locks. The sight of her completely naked, sitting at the dressing table, sets my body on fire as I stand in the doorway, admiring her. She is exceptionally beautiful. Her figure is petite with soft delicate curves, a sculpture spine, and a narrow waist. A natural feminine beauty with the perfect size tits. It still amazes me how hard my dick gets simply by looking at her.

Kinsley catches my reflection in the mirror as she puts the brush down. I move in, coming up behind her, cupping her chin and tilting her head back to press my lips against hers.

"Ready?" I whisper.

"Yes."

I reveal the red eye mask in my other hand, and confusion crosses her brow. Did she think I would take her to bed and fuck her ass without preparing her first? I can be a dick, but I'm not a monster. And, besides, I want this to be memorable for her seeing how it will be her first time, so I'm going to do something I don't normally do.

"Trust me," I say, not revealing the purpose of the mask.

She nods, not saying a word, and I feel my heart flutter with excitement. I slip the mask over her eyes and then take her hand, helping her to her feet. She grabs my arm, slightly digging her fingernails in and squeezing as if she's afraid I'll let go. I turn her, wrapping my body around her backside and circling my arm around her waist. She's in front of me, and I feel her grip loosen as she relaxes against me, even though my cock is probing her ass. One thing I've noticed over these last weeks with Kinsley, she feels a sense of safety in my arms, and I absolutely love it. I'll do anything to make her feel comfortable. I lead us, careful not to walk into the door and over to the bed until her knees touch the mattress.

"Climb up, sweetheart, and lie in the middle of the bed." For this, I take her hand, climbing up as well and guiding her to the middle. Next, I take her arms, moving them over her head, and I use the sash to tie her wrists together. I see her chest heave once, but other than that, she remains quiet. I leave enough length so she can bend her arms and pull down to about the height of her head, but no further.

"Is it too tight?"

She wiggles her wrists around with some mobility. I left enough space not to cut off the circulation, but she also can't just pull her hand out.

"It's fine."

"That's good," I say, trailing my fingers down her milky white torso. She looks positively stunning tied to my bed as her skin prickles with a layer of goosebumps and her pink rosebud nipples harden to stone. I would have spread her legs, binding her ankles, but for this, I want to be able to flip her over at any given moment. It's also why I didn't fasten her wrists to the corners of the bed.

I lean back, grabbing the flute glass off the night table that's topped with champagne. I take a swig of the bubbly bubbles, tasting a bit of tartness and the sweetness of strawberries. Satisfied, I ease my hand underneath Kinsley's head, lifting up and bringing the glass to her lips.

"Open."

She obliges, parting her lips, and I tip the flute up, letting her have a drink. Her throat works quickly, trying not to choke or spill. The sight reminds me of her swallowing my cock, and watching her throat work feverishly to take my length and swallow my load. It's beautiful, and the little fiery minx can consume my entire length. Given it's merely a few seconds, but it's fucking amazing.

I ease her head back down, removing my hand.

"Do you like?" I ask her.

"It's good. Kind of tastes like strawberries."

"I think you might be right, but I need a little more taste testing to know for sure," I say with a smile, tipping the flute and pouring the champagne directly between the valley of her breasts. Kinsley gasps with a jolt as it runs down her torso to her belly button, and over the sides. I lean down and lap the bubbly liquid up with my tongue, and she lets out a deep groan next. When I get to her cute little belly button, I dip my tongue in and drink the remaining. She laughs, twisting away. I think I found a ticklish spot.

"Someone a little ticklish?" I ask, chuckling myself.

"If you tickle me, then I can't be held accountable if my bladder lets go."

I chuckle again, shaking my head. I swear she's the only woman that can make me laugh, and in the middle of foreplay.

"Dually noted," I say, and she snickers. "Another taste?" I offer, and she nods eagerly.

I take a gulp of the champagne, lifting her head again and placing my lips over hers. I open my mouth with Kinsley following suit, letting the champagne pour into her mouth, and then I plunge my tongue down her throat. She moans as some of the liquid escapes and runs down the side of her chin. I withdraw, sliding my tongue down her chin, over to her throat, and sucking in her tender flesh, causing Kinsley to whimper.

I put the flute glass down, grabbing the bottle instead, and move between her legs. I pour the liquid directly onto her nipple, sucking the tight bud into my mouth and flicking my tongue feverishly. She cries out, bucking her hips, and I'm quick to do the same with the other nipple.

"You have such gorgeous tits, but now I'm ready for the main course."

She opens her legs wider, anticipating my next move, but she's not going to see this coming. I pour the champagne directly on her dark, auburn curls, letting it dribble down to her pussy lip, and I slip my tongue between her slick folds, tasting her for the first time. Kinsley freaks out in a flash. She screams, trying to scissor her legs close and twisting, but I block.

"Eric, no!" I'm stunned momentarily hearing my first name from her lips. She rarely calls me by my first name. "What are you doing?!"

"What do you think I'm doing? I'm going to eat this hot little pussy of yours."

"But you... I just—" she groans, cutting herself off.

"What? You thought I don't eat pussy?" I ask, and she nods, biting her bottom lip, and I can tell she's a bundle of nerves. Technically, she is right. I'm selfish, always putting my needs and wants first, but no woman has ever complained because I make them cum hard, one way or another. "I'll be honest with you, I don't usually, but if I'm going to claim that virgin ass of yours, I need you dripping wet for me."

"Or maybe we just skip both."

I frown, coming up beside her, removing the mask, and untying her wrists. She blinks several times before her eyes focus on me.

"What are you afraid of, Kinsley?"

CHAPTER TWENTY

Kinsley

What am I afraid of? Everything! Why? Because he will own every piece of me, including my heart and soul, which I'm trying desperately to protect. Claiming my virgin derriere is one thing, but him going down on me is entirely different. I know in my heart I love him. He's given and taught me so much. There is no amount of words I can say to show him how truly grateful I am. Yes, we have been intimate, and he has been more than patient with me, showing me he has a tender and compassionate side. But at least there's been that one piece of emotional detachment.

Lord knows I would give anything to know what it will feel like just once, but if I let Dekker take this last piece of me, it will be the final nail in my coffin. I'll be shattered beyond repair when this ends.

"Talk to me, sweetheart."

"I don't care if you claim my rear end, but I'm begging you not to do the other."

"What? Why?" His face shows pure shock, but I can't tell him the real reason why.

"I don't like it," I lie, and his brows pinch together in a frown.

"How can you say that when you've never had it done?"

"I have, many times, and I hate it. It's a complete turn off for me. I'll be your fuck toy, and you can use me however you want. But that is off the table. It's *red* for me."

Just like that, his expression turns from confusion to severe. I've obviously hit a nerve, but I had to make him believe I hate it.

"You've been lying to me?" he sneers, causing me to flinch, and I instantly regret my words, and clearly, I didn't think this all the way through. "I suppose the whole first time story was bullshit too? Of course, it was. You set me up the day of your interview, wearing your good girl outfit and making me believe you were all innocent and special. God, I'm such a fool! I can't believe I fell for your bullshit lies. You're just like every other woman wanting to sink your hooks into my money. But you did get one thing right."

Tears roll down my cheeks as I lay there paralyzed, unable to move or speak. I virtually feel like a deer caught in headlights, where your brain scrambles not knowing what to do. He leans over, getting in my face, and I feel nothing but disgust and animosity rolling off of him. "You are nothing to me but a fuck toy, and that's all you'll ever be."

He gets off the bed, storming out of the bedroom and slamming the door behind him. I lay there speechless, trembling and trying to process his cruel words and wondering how everything went horribly wrong.

My heart beats erratically as I glance around the bedroom, taking everything in. Candles are lit, and on the night table, there are two flute glasses, one empty and one full of champagne, along with the bottle and a bowl of red strawberries. Glancing down, I run my hand through the deep red velvet blanket I'm lying on. It's so ultra soft, and near the foot of the bed I spot various sex toys. I shuffle down, taking a closer look, and see two different butt plug sizes, a bottle of lube, and a red vibrator. Tears run down my face harder, knowing I've just screwed everything up.

This was Dekker being romantic and taking every precaution to ensure this experience would be memorable for me. I have no doubt it would have been, starting with his face between my legs. I should have kept my mouth shut. Who cares if my pathetic heart shatters in the end? Isn't that what love is all about? To love deeply, then not at all. To feel your heartache when you miss someone, or the feeling you aren't complete until you're wrapped up in their strong arms.

I let out an ugly cry, burying my face in my hands, knowing that's me. He didn't have to go between my legs to prove that. I love him wholeheartedly. After bawling for too long, I get up and grab my housecoat. I need to fix this. Tell him everything I said was a lie and that I love him.

I race out of the bedroom, calling his name and searching every room, including the rooftop, but he's nowhere to be found. *His office!* I sprint to the elevator in my bare feet, pressing the button feverishly. I dash inside as soon as the door opens, pressing the floor below us. When they open a second time, I know instantly he isn't here. It's pitch black with only a dim light above the elevator. *Where did he go?* I can only assume he's gone out. I head back upstairs, glancing at the kitchen microwave for the time. It's quarter after ten.

My heart sinks, knowing he's out there thinking terrible things about me and probably looking for a distraction. *A blonde with big boobs distraction.* Another sob erupts from my chest as I blindly head back to the bedroom through blurry eyes. I'm sticky from the champagne, so I force myself to take a shower. For the next ten minutes, I sit on the bench listening to my teeth chatter and tears run down my face. The water is too hot, turning my skin a pinky-red, but I can't stop shivering. I'm chilled to the bone.

When the tears finally stop, I dry off and rush out, hoping by some miracle he has come home, but the place remains in darkness with dead silence. I face the bed, with my eyes brimming with tears picturing Dekker making love to me like he has countless times. He discovered a secret I never knew existed within myself, and showed me that dark desires and fantasies are nothing to be ashamed of.

I strip off the velvet blanket and thin mattress, pulling the comforter back up, and crawling into bed. Mittens joins me, curling up by my hip, as I stare at the bedroom door, hoping and praying he'll walk through any second. One hour ticks by, then two, then three. My eyes are dry and scratchy as I feel them droop for the tenth time, but I can't sleep until I know he's home, lying beside me. I need to feel his arms around me. We'll talk in the morning, and I'll be sure to set everything straight. Another sob erupts from my chest feeling my thoughts will be wishful thinking on my part. *I blew it.*

I pick up my cell phone, wondering if I should call him. It's one-thirty in the morning, and I just want him to come home. I dial his number, and it goes straight to voice message.

"Eric, it's me. Please pick up. I'm worried about you, and we need to talk."

I end the call, staring at my phone and waiting, but of course he doesn't call back. I send him a text message.

Kinsley – *Eric, please call me. I screwed up and I'm sorry. I need to set things straight. Please come home. I miss you.*

The flood gates open as I continue to stare at my phone, willing him to call me, but the minutes tick by, and as much as I fight to stay awake, my mind is exhausted along with my body. My eyes close on their own accord, and I'm out a second later.

CHAPTER TWENTY-ONE

Dekker

I slam back my fourth drink, still feeling on edge. My mind keeps replaying everything, and how Kinsley played me for a fool. Damn her for making me feel shit I never wanted to feel.

I'm at one of New York's lucrative underground sex clubs, trying to drown this aching feeling in my chest, but so far, I'm failing miserably. I thought she was different, and as much as I try to deny, I care for her. Too much, in fact. *Damn her!*

I stare aimlessly at the strippers baring it all, in hopes that some rich kinky bastard will take interest in one of them. If you are chosen, you are taken to one of the vacant rooms in the back for a bondage session. I signal for Sangeeta, and she rushes to my table. She's been watching me since I arrived.

"Yes, Mr. Dekker. Have you chosen a lady for this evening?" she asks expectantly.

"Do you have anyone that can slip into subspace?"

"I would suggest Mindy. She has an extremely high pain tolerance," she tells me, meaning she doesn't. Kinsley is the only woman I know that can do that. I feel another twinge of pain ripple through my chest.

"Which one?" I question.

Sangeeta points out a curvy, sandy blonde woman with big, round boobs. You can clearly tell they are fake, just like her. *She's perfect.* I give her a nod, and Sangeeta grins.

"I'll set up room number ten for you. Face up, face down or suspension?" she asks, handing me a key.

"Face down," I say and swipe my phone to log into my bank, and I transfer twenty grand to her account. I see I have a voice and a text message from Kinsley.

"Excellent, Mr. Dekker. Give me five minutes."

I nod, and she moves to fetch Mindy off the stage. I glance at the ladies to find Mindy ecstatic as she lets out a squeal when Sangeeta fills her in. I watch them rush to the back, all giggles, and suddenly guilt washes over me as if I'll be cheating on Kinsley. I read her text message, not bothering with the other.

Kinsley – *Eric, please call me. I screwed up and I'm sorry. I need to set things straight. Please come home. I miss you.*

I feel my throat tighten, re-reading her last part, *please come home, I miss you.* I haven't decided if I'm going to end our arrangement. Part of me wants to, furious that she lied to me, but the other part is unwilling to let her go. Maybe I just need to fuck this other woman to get her out of my head. The waitress brings me another glass of whiskey, and I tip it back, draining the bronze liquid in one shot. I don't bother listening to her voice message as I pick up my cell phone, tucking it in my pocket, and grab the key.

I reach the back getting a nod from two security guards. It's been a while since I've been here, but everyone knows me. I unlock the door, stepping inside, and I see Mindy has been tied to the bed, face down. Perfect. Our eyes meet and I see she has a glint of excitement in her pale blue eyes. I move to the bed, carefully setting my phone and key down, and start undressing. I watch her eyes dilate as they travel the length of my body, and when I remove my boxers, she sucks in a subtle gasp.

My cock lays heavy against my thigh, not even remotely interested. I close my eyes, trying to picture my cock buried in her ass, but all I see is Kinsley's beautiful face.

Christ, what the hell am I thinking?!

"Please come home. I miss you." It's like I can hear her voice ringing through my ears, sounding like an angel. I suddenly feel lightheaded and nauseous as guilt washes through me. I need to get the hell out of here. I dress in record speed, throwing a wad of cash on the night table for Mindy.

"For your time," I say, not bothering to untie her or make an excuse.

I head out the door, telling the security guards I've changed my mind. They nod, and one of the guards speaks into his earpiece. I don't stay long enough to hear, but I assume he's advising Sangeeta. I climb into my black Maserati, hitting the ignition, and I sit there, staring out the windshield for the longest time. I don't know how to deal with this situation. She lied to me, and I need time to think this through before making any rash decisions. I rub my face with my hands. I'm tired as hell, and I know I shouldn't be driving. I call Chase.

He picks me up without saying a word as he drops me off at home. I take the elevator up, and it seems the alcohol decided to kick in. I stumble out, tossing my keys on the counter and removing my shoes. I make my way to the bedroom, stripping off my clothes as I go. When I reach the bed, Kinsley is lying on her side with her cell phone in her hand. The candles are still lit, being battery operated, and I can tell she's been crying. Her face is blotchy, eyes are puffy, and her cheeks are stained with dry tears. The sight crushes my heart. *What have I done? Does it really matter that she lied to me?* It does, because I thought she was different, and I trusted her, but she played me for a fool. If someone crosses me in the business world, I make them pay. This is no different and I should wake her up, take my belt to her ass and then kick her out. That thought only sets my blood on fire, because I know she'll slip into subspace and it's fucking beautiful. And when I claim her pussy, I cum so hard, it's epic, seeing stars dance before my eyes.

I grit my teeth, squeezing my cock as anger surfaces again, and trying to decide what the right move I should take. I let out a sigh, taking her cell phone, instead and plugging it in. I switch off all the candles, before walking away and leaving her be. I'll deal with her later.

CHAPTER TWENTY-TWO

Kinsley

I let out a groan, reaching my hand out for Dekker, but the spot beside me is cold. My eyes flash open as I jackknife up in bed. Mittens meows at me for waking him, but I ignore him, glancing around the room for Dekker, but I'm alone. *Did he even come home?* I look at the clock, seeing it's eleven, and that's when I notice my cell phone is plugged in. I'm positive I fell asleep with it in my hand. I snatch it up, checking to see if there is a message from him. There is. I open it, and my heart breaks open all over again.

Dekker – *I need some time to think. Please don't contact me. I won't answer.*

I try his cell phone anyways, and it goes straight to voicemail.

"Dekker, I know you said not to call you, but I have to try. I desperately need to speak with you. If you just give me five minutes, I can explain."

I hang up and stare at my phone for the next five minutes, willing him to call me, but it stays silent. I call again.

"I'm sorry for hurting you, Eric. I know you think I've lied to you, but I haven't. At least not the part you're thinking. I really don't want to discuss this over a voice message. Please call me."

I end the call and wait in bed for the next hour, but he still doesn't call. I send him a text message in one final attempt.

Kinsley – *I'll be here when you're ready to talk. I miss you.*

For the rest of the day, I try to keep myself busy, but fail miserably, as I end up spending most of the day in bed having my phone glued to my hand. Dekker doesn't call or message, and the hours tick by at a snail's pace.

I imagine he'll at least come home for dinner, so I decide to surprise him, making a lasagna and a garden salad. I set the table, lighting some candles, and pour two glasses of wine. I then quickly dress in a sexy provocative red dress that feels heavenly against my skin, paint my lips a deep red, and even apply a coat of mascara. I forfeit the bra and panties for good measure, but when six, seven, and then eight o'clock rolls by, it's evident he isn't coming home. I break down at the dinner table, crying until my eyes feel like sandpaper and are almost swollen shut.

By nine o'clock, I blow out the candles, shuffling back to his bedroom and standing in the door, staring at the bed. I can't sleep in here anymore. Not without him. I remove my contact lenses, glancing in the mirror. I have raccoon eyes with dark circles, and my skin is a blotchy red. I look and feel like hell.

I change into a pair of sweat pants and a t-shirt, grabbing a pillow off the bed and find an extra blanket in the closet. Shutting off all the lights, I make my way out to the living room and curl up on the couch. Mittens joins me, laying across my hip and all I can do is cry until exhaustion consumes and I can no longer keep my eyes open. But unlike the night before where somehow I slept like the dead, tonight, I toss and turn with my mind constantly swirling, thinking of him and wondering where he is.

His face will come to me in my dreams, flashes of deceit and anger carved in his expression as I lay there frozen, unable to speak and his harsh words lacerating my poor heart. Other vivid images will cross my mind seeing Dekker's smug smile just before he goes down on another woman. Two will ping back and forth like a painful rerun until finally I wake up in a cold sweat. I gasp for air as if my lungs can't suck in a breath fast enough and the memories of my dreams come flooding back. My eyes glass over with tears spilling down my cheeks. This empty void in my chest only seems to be getting bigger.

I glance around the place seeing it's morning with the sunlight shining in. It's almost nine-thirty and I wonder if he even came home last night. I hear nothing but silence and if he did come home, I can almost bet he's already gone. I don't know if I have this sixth sense with him, but my brain seems to know when he's not around. The place feels cold and vacant. I'm not sure how much more I'll be able to take. The longer he stays away, the more I hate this place.

I pull myself up into a sitting position and Mittens jumps down wandering over to his cat tree to do his morning stretches and paw at the scratching post. My body feels slightly stiff, not used to sleeping on a couch, so I take a moment to stretch myself. I pick up my cell phone to see if he messaged during the night. I have one, but it's from my mom and when I read it, it only causes me breakdown again.

Mom – *Hi, sweetheart. I know we just talked a couple of days ago, but are you all right? I've been getting this strange vibe that you're feeling sad or something is wrong. I know you're probably thinking your mom has lost her marbles, but humor me, okay? Please text me.*

I text her back, telling her I'm fine, and there's nothing wrong and wonder if the sixth sense runs in our family. Another message comes in seconds later from her, saying she's glad to hear and reminding me I'm only a phone call away. I cry again wishing I could tell her what's going on, but I'm too embarrassed or I'm afraid she'll say, "*Told you so.*" Deep down I know she would never say that, but I'm not ready for the fifth degree and a hundred questions. Maybe I'm still holding onto hope that Dekker and I will work through this but as I make my way to his bedroom, again, I feel nothing but coldness. He didn't come home and I get the feeling this is the end.

I glance at the phone in my hand, wondering if I should try calling him. Clearly he's avoiding me, and I'm thinking the only way to get through to him, is to leave him a voice message explaining my side. Once he listens, he'll know I only lied about one thing, because I was afraid of falling more in love with him than I already am. It's a confession I'm willing to take because I have nothing else to lose.

I sit on the bed and take a few deep breaths before pressing his number.

"The person you are calling is unavailable. Please try again later."

I frown, hearing the automated message. I look at the number I'm calling, and it says Dekker. I try again and get the same message. There is no option to leave a voice message.

"How is that even possible?" I say out loud, and then it dawns on me.

Dekker has blocked me. That's a tough pill to swallow, knowing I've hurt him that badly, and I have no way to make this right. Not until he comes home, at least. He said he needed time to think so now I have no choice but to wait it out. It's a maddening thought. I want to scream and shout at the world, but I did this to myself. All I can hope is Monday will bring a new day, and I'll finally get my chance. He won't be able to avoid me all day.

The day turns into night, and come ten o'clock, I wrap a blanket around myself and sleep on the couch. I'm feeling a little hopeful because tomorrow is just around the corner. I hold onto that thought and close my eyes for the third time without Dekker.

CHAPTER TWENTY-THREE

Kinsley

His scent fills my nostrils. It's a clean, earthy fragrance that has my heart fluttering. It's a smell I've memorized and love. It's invasive, but a good invasive as it rushes through my bloodstream, making my body feel warm and tingly. I cling to his scent, not wanting to let go as I inhale deeply and savor every second. I feel like my brain is trying to tell me something, but I don't want to wake up. It's all I have of him. *'It's all you'll ever have, Kinsley,'* rings in my ears.

I wake up with a jolt, immediately rubbing my eyes to clear the fog. I reach for my glasses on the coffee table and look around frantically. He's here, and I realize it wasn't a dream. I leap off the couch when I hear the elevator ping. I sprint to the door to see the number descending down one. *Shit!* I just missed him. I glance at the clock and see I have thirty minutes to get ready. *Bloody hell!* I slept in, and now I have to rush.

I run to the bathroom, wondering why he didn't wake me. I can only assume he's still upset, which slightly pisses me off. He's a stubborn-ass man and obviously doesn't like getting lied to. I get that. He told me never to lie to him, but I had my reason. If he would just give me five minutes, I can fix this.

I get ready at record speed, and soon the elevator doors are opening on the ninetieth floor. I see Dekker instantly, heading to his office with a black folder open in his hands as he reads it.

"Dekker!" I shout, wanting to catch him before he disappears again.

He glances at me for a second, and it's hard not to miss the distaste on his face before he turns away and continues on. *Shit!*

"Please, Dekker," I say again as he steps through his door.

"Do not call me that, Ms. Everett. Now, if you'll excuse me, I have business to attend to. In case you have forgotten, it's the board of directors meeting today."

His words are cold as ice as I try to swallow the thick lump at the back of my throat, and my heart beats wildly in my chest.

"No, I haven't forgotten. My sincerest apologies, Sir, and it won't happen again."

He doesn't acknowledge me as he closes the door, and it takes everything in me not to break down. For the rest of the day, I wait on pins and needles, trying to gauge when the best time to approach him again. Every time I see him, he's aloof, keeping his distance, and I feel the wedge between us continue to grow in size.

At five o'clock, I wait at my desk for another ten minutes for him to open the door, but it's apparent he's going to continue to ignore me. I take a chance and knock on his door.

"Come in," his voice booms, and I take a deep breath before opening the door. I take one step inside, and again, he doesn't acknowledge my presence.

"Umm... Mr. Dekker, do you have a couple of minutes to talk?"

"No, Ms. Everett. I have an endless stack of papers to go through, and I need to focus on the Las Vegas contract. I'll be working all night."

It's evident his words are final, and his tone is not to be questioned. This time, I feel the pain in my chest.

"I understand. Sorry to have bothered you," I say dejectedly and close the door.

I pack up my stuff with tears trickling down my cheeks, and slide my sunglasses on before entering the elevator. People stare at me like they always do, and I consciously try to hold my head high as I leave the building. I feel like they are all laughing at me, even though they're not and have no idea what's going on between Dekker and me, but I feel like it's written across my forehead in flashing neon lighting.

I'm the stupid redhead who screwed my boss and actually thought we could have a happily ever after.

As soon as I get home, I change into my sweats and curl up on the couch with Mittens by my side. Tears continue to slowly trickle down my cheeks as I stare at my phone for the longest time. I desperately wish I could talk to my mom, but when my finger hovers over the call button, I chicken out.

My stomach growls for the seventh time, demanding food until I finally break down eating a bowl of fruit. I glance out the windows seeing the city lights come to life as the sun vanishes. I sit alone in the dark, trying to remain optimistic, but that little voice at the back of my mind keeps telling me it's over. Even if I tell him the truth, he won't believe me. I'm sure of it. He's too angry to see the truth in front of his nose. Maybe he doesn't want to, or perhaps this was his way out, having grown bored of me.

All these maybes and what ifs run through my head until I can no longer think straight and I've got a pounding headache. I'll give it another couple of days, and if by Wednesday, he still can't look at me, or give me five minutes of his time, I'll walk away. There's no sense in prolonging the inevitable. He's leaving for Las Vegas Thursday afternoon, and I refuse to sit around waiting like a love sick puppy. I'm already doing that and making myself miserable. Might as well be miserable at my own place.

The next couple of days drag by, and my attempts to reach Dekker are to no avail. He shoots me down every time I try to speak, and I feel his abrasive tone bone deep. He barely glances at me and has excluded me from all business meetings.

It's five o'clock Wednesday when I shut down the laptop. I place the work cell phone beside it, along with my swipe card. I glance at Dekker's closed door with tears streaking down my face. *It's over.* I've been a complete wreck these last few days, not eating, bursting into tears at any given moment, and waiting on pins and needles. I'm done because my heart has officially cracked wide open. I feel nauseous frequently, with anxiety increasing.

Something I've never had before, and I can't keep doing this to myself anymore. I need to put distance between us, so I can start healing.

I grab my backpack from underneath my desk, pulling out a card I made for Dekker, along with the money I owe him. I promised to pay him back for the contact lenses and glasses he bought, and I meant it. I had packed up all my personal belongings this morning and took nothing else other than what I initially brought with me. The only outfit I took is the one I'm wearing, and if he wants it back, I'll return it after cleaning.

I take a second to reread it before placing the card in the middle of the laptop. It's a simple card with the words Thank You handwritten on the outside along with the handcrafted red rose I made last night. I kept my message short and sweet but it broke my heart writing it.

I dry my eyes for the hundredth time and sling the backpack over my shoulder, along with my purse.

"Goodbye, Dekker. I love you," I whisper to nobody and then head to the elevator for the last time.

CHAPTER TWENTY-FOUR

Dekker

It's five minutes after five when I feel an icy chill run down my spine. My hands stop typing as I strain my ears to listen. It's quiet, but that's nothing new. This building is virtually soundproof, but for some reason, it feels more definitive today. I close up my laptop, glancing at my door. I had expected Kinsley to knock on my door at five like she always does, but nothing. I glance at my watch. It's now six minutes after five.

I look at the card she made for me when she first started. I keep it on my desk and read it almost daily. She's the first woman to ever give me a card, and what's even more special, it's homemade. The red rose is beautifully crafted, making me think of her every time. She's very much like a rose. Stunningly beautiful when flourished.

These last few days have been pure hell. I've been short and abrupt with her, constantly pushing her away, and it's been wreaking havoc on both of us. But it's apparent Kinsley is taking it the hardest. I can't keep doing this to her. She cries all the time. The bloodshot red eyes are a dead giveaway, along with the dark circles, but I'm still angry at her for lying to me, but I know I can't keep punishing her. I can tell she's remorseful, and either I put this behind me so we can move on, or I need to let her go.

Christ, I can't let her go!

I miss her so goddamn much, it physically hurts not to be able to touch her. I miss her smile, laughter, exquisite scent, her fiery red hair, and the little minx's friskiness, and I can't forget the sex. It's the best sex I've ever had, and that speaks volumes.

Damn her for lying to me!

I had one fucking rule, and she had to ruin everything, but we can't keep going like this. I know deep down I want to fix it. I'm leaving for Vegas tomorrow, and then we only have a month left. Time is ticking, and I can't keep denying she doesn't mean anything to me. When our time is up, I've been thinking about extending the offer, and we can go from there if Kinsley is interested. And if she isn't, then I'll move on like I always do.

I push away from my desk, standing up, and head to my door.

"Kinsley, we need—" I stop mid-sentence, seeing she's not at her desk.

I move closer, and feel my throat start to close with my heart rate spiking. My eyes latch onto the handwritten thank you card with another custom made red rose. I pull her chair out, sinking down, and stare at the card for a good minute. I don't want to read it. You don't have to tell me that it's a goodbye letter. That's the icy chill I felt earlier. She was leaving me.

I glance at the laptop, cell phone, and swipe card, along with some cash. I run my hand over the money, knowing she's paying me back for the glasses and contact lenses I bought. She didn't have to. I already told her it wasn't necessary, but it doesn't surprise me that she did it anyways.

My eyes move to the card again. As much as I don't want to read it, I reluctantly pick up the card, needing to know what she wrote.

My Dearest Dekker,

I have so much to say, but I'll keep this short and sweet.

Thank you for being you.

You are a kind, generous man with a heart of gold.

These last few weeks have been unbelievably incredible for me.

You've given me a lifetime of memories, I can't express my gratitude.

I'll cherish them forever and never forget you.

I wish you nothing but the best.

Be happy, my love.

P.S. Try to smile more often. It's blinding and beautiful, just like you.

Yours Truly,

Kinsley Everett (aka, Ms. Scarlett)

I reread her note several times, digesting every word, but one line captures my attention the most. *"Be happy, my love."* She doesn't come out and actually say the words, I love you, but I can read between the lines, but not only that, I feel it in her letter.

I sit back in my seat, feeling mixed emotions. I care for her, but do I love her? I never wanted to get tangled up in love, and perhaps I have my dad to blame for this. The last time I heard from him, he was gallivanting around Europe with another woman on his arm, and I believe she's only a few years older than me.

Some people would say good for him, but when his wife, my mom, lives in a twenty-four hour homecare center, it pisses me off. I get what's happened to her is no one's fault, and I wouldn't want to be in my dad's position, but do I agree with him moving on while they are still married? No. I realize there is no simple answer to their situation, but he has completely cut her out of his life like she didn't even exist, and that infuriates me. They have been married for thirty-one years, but in the last ten years, our lives slowly started to change.

At first, my dad and I thought it was funny when mom would forget something that just happened or maybe a few days ago. We would tease her, asking if she was having a blonde moment or if old-timers were kicking in already until it became a pattern. Something that happened once in a blue moon, turned into forgetting something almost daily. My dad finally took her to the hospital, where they did a series of tests, and that's when we were informed she was in the early stages of Alzheimer's. The doctors did various treatments, experimenting with numerous drugs, but nothing seemed to help, or if it did, it was short term gain. Her Alzheimer's progressed year after year until the day came we both were dreading. My mom looked at us and had no idea who we were. It only lasted a minute or so, but it freaked all of us out, and that's when my dad decided it was no longer safe for her to be home alone. It was heartbreaking and the end of our happy family.

My mom has now been in a medical care facility for over a year, where she's considered to have stage five with moderate Alzheimer's. I visit her at least once a month, and the last time I saw her, she was delusional, hallucinating that someone was trying to steal her blankets. Sometimes her memory is sharp as a knife, but I find it comes and goes on a flip of a dime, and sometimes, it's like you're talking to a stranger.

My dad didn't know how to deal with that, and I understand it's not easy. But cutting your wife out altogether isn't the answer either.

I read Kinsley's card once again. Maybe seeing what my parents have gone through is the reason why I'm avoiding relationships. Although, I like having sex with whomever I want, whenever I want, no strings attached.

I close up her card with my heart feeling heavy in my chest. Maybe it's best I let her go. I'm still upset with her lying to me. I feel like she played me for a fool, whether she did it intentionally or not. Either way, I think I'll only break her heart when I can't commit, and that's something I don't want hanging over my head.

It's time for me to find my next play toy, and forget about Ms. Scarlett.

CHAPTER TWENTY-FIVE

Kinsley

I never expected this ache in my heart to last this long. A month has passed by, and sometimes it feels a bit like purgatory, where I wish the gates would open and swallow me whole. There are days where I'll lay in bed for hours, thinking of him and crying my heart out. I miss his touch. His scent. Everything about him and sometimes the pain in my chest is unbearable, I struggle to breathe.

Some days I force myself to get motivated, go for a walk, or make a homemade card that someone has requested, but I know I'm only going through the motions. I'm not living, I'm surviving.

I haven't heard from Dekker, but that doesn't surprise me. I hurt him pretty badly, even though everything was a huge misunderstanding. What's done is done, and maybe it was God's way of telling me, it's for the best. *All good things must come to an end, right?* My good fortune ended all right, and sometimes, I wish I could turn back the clock and erase Dekker. Accepting his job offer and then making our ridiculous agreement was the biggest mistake of my life. I should have known I would have fallen in love, and it be one-sided. Dekker doesn't do love. But then, I wouldn't have all these incredible memories. Memories that will haunt me for the rest of my life, but I wouldn't trade them for all the money in the world. I guess that's what you call a double edged sword. You can't have it both ways.

I pull myself out of bed and pad my bare feet to the kitchen, looking for something to eat. My stomach has been grumbling far too often, and for some reason, it's like my body can't get enough food lately. It's annoying because the last thing on my mind is food. I open the fridge and stare at the empty shelves. I miss the rich, decadent food I ate daily when living with Dekker. Food that was ninety percent fresh and not processed. I ate like a queen when I was with Dekker. He always made sure my belly was full.

For the last month, I've been living off canned soup, cereal, or peanut butter and jam sandwiches. I'm sick of it. If I never eat those foods again, I wouldn't be too disappointed. I slam the fridge door shut, muttering under my breath. Today was supposed to be "*I'm depressed, now grouchy, and lay in bed all day,*" but I have no choice but to get my butt in the shower and go grocery shopping. I don't even have any bread or milk left.

After showering and still complaining under my breath, I'm dressed and riding the bus to the closest grocery store. I could have cabbed it. I had forty-five hundred in my bank account since I didn't have to pay July's rent, courtesy of Dekker, but I need to start saving money where I can. Who knows how long it will take me to find another job, and considering I haven't even started looking, I need to pinch pennies wherever I can.

I walk down each aisle, aimlessly filling my shopping cart with things I don't usually buy. I just want to get the hell out of here. I come to the last aisle, glancing down. It's your typical junk food, which I try to avoid, but I'm craving something salty today. I pick up two bags of dill pickle chips, almost tempted to crack one open and start eating. I'm starving, and my stomach growls, letting everyone around know as well. I feel my cheeks heat with embarrassment as I quickly head to the checkout counter with a couple people staring at me.

Thirty minutes later, I'm hauling four bags of groceries up three flights of stairs. To say I am a little winded would be a lie. I unlock my door, huffing, and puffing when a dizzy spell hits. I close my eyes, hearing a high pitch ringing in my ears and suddenly feeling nauseous. I reach for the counter to steady myself, but what happens next is a blur. The ground shifts below my feet as my vision fades to black, and then I feel nothing. Maybe purgatory decided to answer my invitation and swallow me whole.

CHAPTER TWENTY-SIX

Kinsley

"**K**insley, sweetheart, please wake up." I hear my mom's plead, and I frown.

What's Mom doing here? Am I dreaming?

I try to open my eyes, but I can't. It feels like someone has glued them shut.

"My sweet baby girl, please come back to us." My mom sniffles, squeezing my hand, and now I'm completely baffled.

I squeeze her hand back, and I hear her gasp.

"Kinsley? Dear, get the nurse. She's waking up!" Mom shouts, and I wonder if she's talking to Dad.

I hear a bit of commotion, and then someone is squeezing my wrist.

All right, this isn't funny anymore. Can someone tell me what's going on?

"Ms. Everett, I'm nurse Camila. Can you hear me?"

Nurse?

I feel fingers peel my eyelid open and a flashlight shining in. It's blinding, and I try to squint. She does it again with my left eye.

"Her pupils are dilating. She's coming around," the lady confirms.

"That's it, Kinsley. Try to open your eyes or squeeze my hand," Mom encourages me.

I squeeze her hand feeling like I have zero strength, but I hear my mom half laugh, half cry.

"She squeezed my hand."

"That's it, pumpkin. You're doing great. Can you open your eyes for Dad?"

Hearing my dad's voice brings tears to my eyes. It makes me realize I miss my parents so much. I give it all my energy, concentrating and willing my eyes to open. It takes me a good thirty seconds before I feel my eyelids cooperating and the outside world appear.

"Here, sweetie, here's your glasses," Mom says, sliding them on my face.

I blink several times, clearing the fog, and finally, my sight comes into focus. My parents smile down at me with tears running down my mom's face. Seeing both of them makes me cry, and Mom is quick to wrap her arms around me, breaking down herself.

"I've missed you," I whisper as my voice cracks.

"We're here, sweetheart. Both of us," Mom whispers back, and I feel my dad squeeze my hand.

Mom lets go of me, and the nurse hands her a cup of water with a straw. She helps me take a sip, and the cool water running down my throat feels amazing. I feel like I could drink a gallon of water right now.

"Are you in any pain?" Dad asks, and I glance at the nurse as she puts a cuff around my arm to take my blood pressure.

"Umm... I feel sore and achy all over, but I guess not too bad. What happened? Why am I in the hospital?" I ask, seeing an IV hooked up to me. "Wait a minute. Am I in New York or San Diego?"

"New York, pumpkin. You fainted, and your landlord, Selma, found you. She called an ambulance and then called us because we are your emergency contact," Dad informs me.

I frown for a moment, trying to recall, but everything is a little fuzzy. I remember getting groceries and lugging my bags upstairs, but after that, my mind is drawing a complete blank.

"How did you get here so fast?" I question.

"Kinsley, you've been unconscious for four days now. You hit your head on the kitchen counter when you fainted and knocked yourself out."

I feel my eyes shoot wide. *I did what?!* I slowly lift my hand to my forehead, feeling a square bandage on the left side of my forehead along with a goose egg. As soon as I touch it, I wince with pain.

"Careful, sweetheart, it's still healing," Mom says.

"I'll let the doctor know she's awake," the nurse speaks up and then leaves us be.

"Kinsley, do you remember anything before fainting?" Mom asks.

"No, not really?" My parents share a worried look which only increases my anxiety. "What's going on? Am I sick or something?"

"No, no, it's nothing like that," Mom assures me. I look between the two of them, and it doesn't ease my worry. I can tell they are hiding something.

"What's going on? Why are you looking at me like that?"

"Kinsley, sweetheart, what happened between you and Eric?"

I look away, rolling over to my side with tears brimming my eyes, hearing his name. I guess the good thing about being unconscious is that it gave my punctured heart a few days of reprievement.

"We're no longer together," I whisper.

The guilt and shame of what I did weighs heavily on me. I can't imagine what my parents will think of me if they know what I did. Mom rubs my back as silence fills the room, and a moment later, a man in blue scrubs walks through the door.

"Good afternoon, everyone. I hear someone is awake. I'm Doctor Benoit. How are you feeling, Ms. Everett?" he asks, coming around to the side of my bed to speak directly to me, and I quickly wipe my tears away. He looks young as I glance up at him. Around my age and if I wasn't pining over Dekker, I would go as far to say he's a good looking man.

"Fine," I say, keeping my answer short and sweet.

"That's good to hear. I'm going to ask you a few questions, and then I'll listen to your heart rate, okay?"

I nod, and he asks a series of questions, like what's my full name, date of birth, what city I live in, phone number, etc. I realize he's checking to see if I've suffered any brain damage. I answer all his questions without hesitation, and then he puts a stethoscope to my heart, listening.

"Sounds good. We did a CT scan on Tuesday, and everything is normal, but I think it will be best if we keep you here for one more night. If nothing arises, you should be able to go home tomorrow," he tells me, and I nod again. "The gash on your forehead is healing nicely, but you might be more prone to headaches. You can take Tylenol. It won't hurt your baby, but if you find they are persistent, please come back to the hospital and we will run more tests."

White noise hums in the background as everything fades, and the word "*baby*" rings in my ears. The doctor is still talking. I can see his lips moving, but I hear nothing as my body goes into shock. My mom takes my hand, giving it a gentle squeeze, and the reality that I just royally screwed up my life comes crashing down. I'm pregnant with Dekker's baby. A man that can't stand the sight of me and will probably go ballistic if he finds out.

"Ms. Everett, are you okay? You're looking rather pale," the doctor observes.

"She didn't know about the baby. We hadn't had a chance to tell her," my mom speaks in a whisper.

"My apologies. Why don't I give you folks some privacy, and I'll be back later. Please ring for the nurse if you need anything, Ms. Everett."

I lie there emotionless, staring at him like he's the devil that has just delivered my punishment for getting involved with the world's most coveted bachelor, who is filthy rich and made it abundantly clear he never wants to be tied down.

My parents thank him, and I watch the devil leave. I stare at the door, hearing my parents whisper behind me. I can't imagine how disappointed they are with me and knowing only half the story.

"Kinsley, are you all right?" Mom asks when the silence stretches to awkwardness.

I nod, feeling tears well up. I'm pregnant with no form of stability in my life. I'm jobless and soon to be a single parent in a micro-small apartment. This is my sentence for acting like an adolescent and making irresponsible decisions, and clearly, I'm way too fertile.

"Kinsley, you're father and I have discussed your... umm, wellbeing, and we would love for you to move back home." Feeling shocked, I glance over my shoulder at them to see my parents giving me a kind smile. "I know this is a lot to take in, and you're hurting, but your dad and I are very much looking forward to being grandparents. We want to help and will be here for as long as you need." Mom pauses to take my hand. "Just know you're not alone in this, sweetheart. You still have your old bedroom, and the third bedroom can be made into a nursery. Your father even suggested installing sliding doors between your rooms to give you easy access. And you'll have your own bathroom. You know we have plenty of space," Mom says with so much love and sincerity, it breaks my heart for other reasons.

"I'm sorry," I cry, sobbing into my pillow, feeling like a failure.

"Pumpkin, no need to feel ashamed. Accidents happen, and I know this one is a life altering one, but we'll get through this. We always do. And like your mom said, we'll be there every step of the way," my dad reiterates, coming around the other side of the bed to face me, and he kneels down to be at eye level. Seeing him only makes me cry more. "Pumpkin, think of this baby as a gift, and a new beginning. You have lots of love to give and will make a wonderful mother, and your mom and I are looking forward to being full-time grandparents."

"Are you sure?" I manage to mumble.

"Of course, we're sure, pumpkin."

I love this city, but the reality is, I have nothing other than some unforgettable, but painful memories. I know I can't do this alone, and there is no way I'm telling Dekker. At least not right now. He deserves to know, but the last thing I want him to feel is obligated and resent me more. He'll probably think I got pregnant on purpose to trap him or something like that. We should have been more careful, and I know I was a day late on taking my birth control pill the first time we slept together, but I didn't think anything of it. Obviously, it didn't take much to get me pregnant, or his sperm had other ideas.

"How far along am I?" I ask, turning my head to look at mom.

"The doctor suspects eight weeks," she confirms, smiling. It had to have been one of the first times in the first week. "Are you sure you aren't going to mind a screaming baby at one or two in the morning? Or what if he or she turns out to be colicky?" I ask, needing to see their reaction to know for sure.

"We are a hundred and fifty percent sure. Besides, your father sleeps like the dead, and I was already thinking about cutting back my hours to part-time after the baby is born."

"What about finances?"

"Stop worrying, Kinsley. We will be just fine," Dad says with firmness in his tone.

I give in, feeling a little weight lifted off my shoulders that at least my parents will be there to help, and that they seem genuinely happy. I'm discharged the next morning with a clean bill of health, and my parents insist on paying the hospital bill. My dad also hired movers to transport my belongings from my apartment back to San Diego.

As soon as I step inside my place, I break down with vivid memories of Dekker taking me against the wall, and the bed and realizing that this is the end. I'll never see him again. My mom consoles me, telling me things will get easier within time, and even my dad gives me a hug. He doesn't say anything, and I'm sure this is out of his comfort zone, but just holding me helps.

The next twenty-four hours are somewhat of a blur, but soon I'm walking into my old bedroom. I drop my suitcase, feeling a little overwhelmed and surreal. The last place I ever thought I would end up is back at home, living with my parents for who knows how long and raising a baby. I feel like a huge disappointment to them, even though they've assured me they can't be happier.

I plop down on my bed as tears consume me. I'm a huge disappointment to myself, and now I'm a million miles away from Dekker. I wonder if he thinks about me. Does he miss me even a little? I pull my cell phone out of my pocket, and bring up the pictures I took of the two of us together and one by himself. He doesn't know I took the one. It's a side view of when he was looking across the ocean. He's standing in his swim shorts, looking as gorgeous as ever, but I remember thinking he seemed deep in thought. I never did ask him if something was wrong because as soon as I put my phone away and wrapped my arms around his waist from behind, he was quick to turn around, lifting me up in his arms and ravishing me again.

"Hey, sweetie, I brought you a couple slices of pizza before your father eats it all. I need to go grocery shopping tomorrow," Mom says, standing at my door with a plate in one hand and a bottle of water in the other.

I look up at her, tears streaming down my face, and she comes in, putting everything down and wrapping her arms around me.

"You want to talk about it?" she asks, once I stop blubbering all over her.

I pull away, and she hands me a Kleenex from her pocket. She's been keeping a stash for me. I dry my tears, blowing my nose.

"Maybe tomorrow. I'm tired, and I think I'm going to go to bed now."

My mom squeezes my hand, giving me a nod.

"I'll leave the pizza, just in case you get hungry."

"Thanks, Mom. For everything."

"I love you, Kinsley. You are my heart and soul, and if I could, I would move heaven and earth so my daughter can be happy again. We both would, and it will come someday. People make mistakes, or accidents happen. It's part of growing up, but just think of it this way. This baby growing in your belly is a gift, Kinsley. Every time you look at your baby, you will remember the good times you had with their father, and you'll treasure them even more."

I place my hand on my belly. Up until now, I haven't thought much of him or her growing inside me. My heart is still breaking with Dekker constantly on my mind, but maybe she's right. This baby will become my world, as will I to him or her. We will depend on each other, and maybe having this baby will fill this empty void in my heart. I know every time I look at our baby, I'll think of Dekker, but at least I'll have some small part of him.

"Thank you. I needed that," I tell my mom.

She squeezes my hand and then leaves me be. That night I lay in bed for hours staring at the ceiling, thinking of this baby and Dekker. It's the first night I don't cry myself to sleep. It's a start. I know I have a long way to go, but maybe if I focus on this baby, the hole in my heart will slowly heal.

CHAPTER TWENTY-SEVEN

Kinsley

The next day, Mom urges me to go grocery shopping with her. I'm reluctant, wanting to stay in bed all day and nurse my broken heart, but I know I'm only hurting myself and I have to start putting the baby I'm carrying first.

Before I was discharged from the hospital, they were kind enough to do an ultrasound for me. I stare at the black and white photo with a tiny little peanut in the center that's apparently my baby.

"You're going to be a boy, okay?" I whisper to the photo.

I secretly want a boy, hoping he'll look just like Dekker. It might be more painful, but honestly, I want the constant reminder that his father and I made this perfect little creation that's beautiful inside and out like his father is.

While grocery shopping, my mom snickers at me when I grab two bags of dill pickle chips and then a tub of rocky road ice cream.

"It's the baby's fault," I defend.

My mom starts laughing and I giggle along. It feels good to laugh, and I realize this is exactly what I need and where I should be.

"One stitch at a time," my mom whispers, and although tears burn my eyes, she is absolutely right. I nod as we link arms together and head to the checkout counter.

"Kinsley?"

I turn at the sound of my name and see Nina Corral, an old friend of mine from high school.

"Hi, Nina," I say with a smile.

"Oh my God, I haven't seen you in years. How are you doing?"

"Living. How about you?" I remark, keeping my answer brief.

"Yeah, about the same," she says with a heavy breath, and I note the sadness in her tone. I guess I'm not the only one with issues. "Do you live here, or are you just visiting?"

"I… umm," I fumble with my words for a moment, unsure what to say, but then I decide to be honest. "Well, actually, I just moved back home with my parents. I'm not sure if you remember my mom, but this is Karlie. Mom, this is Nina. An old friend from high school," I say of introductions.

They both say hello in greeting and vaguely recall each other. Nina and I weren't besties, but we did hang out occasionally. I was a bit of a loner and didn't have any super close friends to tell all my secrets. Not that I had any juicy secrets to reveal.

"Cool. Maybe we can get together sometime if you're not busy?" Nina suggests.

I snort-laugh. "I've got nothing but time," I remark with some sarcasm.

"Yeah, me too. We definitely need to catch up."

We exchange phone numbers, and my mom smiles as we walk away.

"One stitch at a time," she mouths.

An hour after getting home and putting the groceries away, I hear my cell phone ding. Of course, my heart leaps out of my chest, thinking it's Dekker, but when I open the text message, I see it's from Nina.

Nina – *Is now too soon?*

I laugh and text her back.

Kinsley – *Now is perfect.*

And that's how the next three weeks of my life goes. I'm either spending time with Nina or my parents, and they turn out to be a lifesaver. The days get easier, but the nights I struggle. That's when I think of Dekker the most. I miss him, and I dream of him constantly. All of the special times we spent together, or our naughty after hours office meet and greet or the several times we spent rolling around in his bed. I even dream of him taking his belt to my derriere. How screwed up is that? I hate it, but love it at the same time.

I finally told my mom everything, from start to finish, but I did leave out the belt incidences and X-rated sex scenes. But she does know they were incredibly intense and not your usual vanilla sex. She didn't judge or chastise me, and this is when I found out my parents had similar chemistry. They couldn't keep their hands off of each other, and once, they were almost caught for indecent exposure at a local park. It was one in the morning, and they were fooling around when a police officer was making his rounds, and his flashlight caught them with their pants down. This was the condensed version she gave me, and when she told me, I felt my mouth drop wide open. She burst out laughing. I never realized my parents were badasses, or perhaps rebel is a more fitting word. I told her I hope I can find love like theirs again someday. She patted my knee and told me he's out there. I just have to be patient. I can't help but feel not very optimistic. What man wants to be with a woman that had a baby with another man? I get the feeling I'm destined to be alone.

I love spending time with Nina. She's always upbeat but not the annoying or obnoxious type. The first day we got together, I discovered she is a photographer and owns her own studio. She takes some amazing pictures that are literally jaw dropping. Whether it's sunset beach photos, family or couple photos, weddings, birthdays, you name it, she does it all. And she even offers intimate sessions for women or couples wanting to explore their carnal side, posing in racy photos. They are exquisite, tastefully done, and I think they are some of her best work.

I also learned she has had some bad luck in the men department, finding out that her ex-boyfriend, who she thought was the one, cheated on her. The breakup happened over four months ago, but sometimes it feels like yesterday for her. I know exactly what she means.

I revealed my secret, with many tears, and the real reason why I'm back at home. She was sympathetic, and gave me lots of hugs but was super excited to hear about the baby. We then somehow tiptoed into the world of bondage, and with flaming red hot cheeks, I divulged my ability to slip into subspace. Nina was speechless at first, until she snapped out of it and shouted, "No fucking way, subspace!" for the entire world to hear. Luckily we were inside her apartment or I might have had a mini heart attack. She then revealed she likes it just as rough, but no subspace for her.

Saturday morning, I wake up with Mittens pressing his wet nose to my chin. I peek my eyes open and groan, staring at the little toad.

"Mittens, I appreciate the kiss, but don't you realize it's—" I glance over at the clock and my eyes shoot wide. Holy cow, it's quarter after eleven. He stretches again to give me another kiss, and I shake my head. I lay there scratching his cheeks and chin for a good five minutes until my bladder decides it's time to go.

After relieving myself, and taking a long shower, I get dressed, pulling on my jean shorts. *What the hell?* I went from being able to do up my jean shorts last week to not a chance in hell now.

I plop down on my bed, feeling overwhelmed. I place my hand on my protruding belly. This baby seems to be growing like a bad weed in the past week. I seriously look like I'm four or five months pregnant, not eleven weeks.

"Why are you growing so fast?" I ask, tears swimming in my eyes.

Knock, knock, knock

"Kinsley, may I come in?" Mom asks through the door.

"Yeah," I say, wiping my tears, and she comes in, closing the door behind her, giving me a tentative smile.

"Having a rough morning, sweetie?"

"You could say that. I can't do up my shorts anymore," I tell her as she sits down beside me, and takes my hand.

"I see that. Maybe you should lay off the chips for a while," she says with sarcasm and a wink. I shake my head with a *pfft* chuckle. "Well, look on the bright side, your boobs are probably getting bigger as well."

I place my hands on my breasts for a moment. I'm sitting in my bra as I hadn't put on a t-shirt on yet.

"Nope. Not yet," I say solemnly.

Mom and I virtually have the same exact body type. Tall and slender, small breasted with similar hair color. Her hair is more like a coppery shade, orangey-red, whereas mine is like mahogany, a dark reddish-brown. I get the combination from my parents with my dad having dark brown hair, although, in the last couple of years, it's more of a brown and grey mixture, and the same goes for my eye color. Mom's eyes are a bright blue, and Dad's are a dark green. If you didn't know we were mother and daughter, you would think we were sisters, which has happened a few times.

"You don't need bigger boobs, sweetheart. You're perfect the way you are."

"Dekker said he liked them," I divulge. "I miss him, mom. When is this ache in my chest going to stop hurting?" I rub my heart, feeling like I've lost a few stitches somewhere along the way, as tears spill over.

I just want to feel his arms around me. Make love to me. Tell me I'm beautiful, and then I think about our baby. Part of me dreads doing this alone, and honestly, I'm not looking forward to the delivery. It scares me. I know my mom will be there every step of the way, but I need Dekker and his strength.

"I know you do, sweetie, and I think he will always be in your heart, but it will get easier. I promise you that."

I give my head a bob. I know she's right. I just hope it's sooner, rather than later.

"You know, I think this little one growing inside of you is going to be a boy."

"Why do you say that?" I question.

"Because when I was pregnant with you, I didn't start showing until I was five or six months pregnant. He wants to make his presence known," she says with a smile.

"That doesn't surprise me. He'll probably turn out just like his father. Beautiful, and I'll be chasing all the women away," I remark, and Mom laughs.

"It's a gorgeous day out. Why don't you and Nina go to the beach? It will be good for you to get some fresh air."

"Will you come?"

"I would love to come. Why don't you borrow one of my sundresses and then come downstairs when you're ready? Your father has something to show you."

"What is it?" I ask, feeling my spirits lift a little.

"Get dressed, and you'll find out soon enough," she says with a smile.

"Okay. Maybe we can go shopping afterwards? It looks like I need to start buying bigger clothes."

"Sounds perfect."

CHAPTER TWENTY-EIGHT

Kinsley

I text Nina first, asking if she wants to come, and of course, it's a "*hell yeah.*" I then raid mom's closet, settling on a cream colored dress that sits a few inches above the knees. I braid my hair and brush my teeth before heading downstairs.

I find my parents sitting at the kitchen table, sipping their coffees and one waiting for me. After exchanging good mornings, and dad giving me a quick hug like he always does every morning, I take a seat beside him. I see a vanilla folder in front of him, and he pushes it towards me.

"What's this?"

"Open it and find out?"

I do and it only takes me a moment to realize what it is. It's a blueprint of the baby's room with sliding doors connecting our rooms.

"What do you think?" Dad asks when I haven't said anything.

"It's perfect," I whisper, tears slipping down my cheeks. One drops on the blueprint, with blue ink smudging instantly. I quickly wipe it away, only to smear it some more. "I'm sorry!" I cry out, my hormones running wild, and my parents are out of their seats in a flash, wrapping their arms around me.

"Don't worry, pumpkin. It can be reprinted, and I can change whatever you want," Dad assures me.

"No, it's perfect the way it is. Well, minus the smudges," I say, causing all of us to chuckle.

"I have one more thing to show you and again, if you don't like it, you can pick something different," Dad says, and then leaves the room. The next thing I hear is something rolling across the floor, and when I turn around, and it comes into view, I start crying all over again. He parks a white and grey bassinette beside me, all smiles. "I know it's a little early, but I couldn't resist. And look, it has this built in crying detection. It will play soothing sounds and vibrations when he or she cries."

"And, this," I ask, pointing to a tiny little onesie that says, "Grandpa is my favorite."

My dad chuckles, and Mom shakes her head.

"I'll get you a new one that says, "Grandma rules, and Grandpa drools."

"I drool all the time when I see you naked."

I can't help but snicker and shake my head at the same time. This is going to be interesting, but there's no doubt my parents will love this little one to pieces, and he or she will be spoiled.

"It's beautiful, Dad. I love it. Thank you so much."

"You're welcome, pumpkin."

After more hugs, I pack a bag for the beach, and Mom packs some drinks and snacks.

"Don't forget the chips!" I shout to Mom, and I hear Dad laugh from the TV room.

We pick up Nina first and then head to our favorite beach. It's blazing hot out, but at least there's a breeze coming off the ocean. After picking out a spot that's not too populated, I lay out a blanket while Mom sets up an oversized beach umbrella to provide shade.

"All right, ladies, don't forget the sunscreen," Mom says as she slips off her shorts and t-shirt.

She looks incredible for her age. Her body is toned as she sports a one-piece black and white bathing suit with a deep plunging neckline. I swear she looks better than me, and the way the men are turning their heads to gawk at her, they probably would agree.

I pull my dress off, and so does Nina. Nina is a knock-out too. She's shorter than me, probably five foot six, with sandy blonde hair. She has a full figure being a size twelve, but I know she despises her hips. Yes, she's a little thicker in that area, but I think it adds to her attraction. She is what I would call a classical beauty, and at least she has full-size breasts that catch men's attention, especially now as she reveals a bright pink, skimpy bikini.

I own one bathing suit, and it's your standard black, one-piece. There's nothing remotely sexy about mine, and as I glance down, you would think I'm sporting a miniature pot belly.

"Maybe I'll just leave my dress on. I don't want to get a sunburn," I say, reaching for my dress again.

"Kinsley Maria Everett, stop worrying what people will think. You are a beautiful pregnant woman, and fuck everyone that thinks otherwise," she glares at me with her hands on her hips.

Whoa! It's not too often I hear my mom swear. I think I'm in trouble.

I feel my cheeks blaze red hot as Nina laughs, and if things can't get any worse, two gorgeous men make their way over to us, carrying surfboards. They are both built like a brick shithouse, fully tanned, and one has shaggy shoulder length hair and the other is sporting a buzz-cut on the sides, but longer on the top. Both are dark haired.

"Ladies, anyone interested in doing some surfing?"

Mom snort-laughs as my cheeks flame hotter. Nina is too busy eyeing them up like they are her next meal.

"I'm too old for surfing, gentlemen. I'll pass, but maybe my daughter and her friend will be interested."

Both guys raise their brows in shock.

"Talk about hot milf."

My mouth drops open hearing their blunt comment, and if I didn't know any better, I would say they are both more interested in my mom than Nina or me.

"I'm a happily married milf, so back off before I—"

"Before I rearrange your face," I hear my dad's voice, and my head whips back, seeing him a few feet away.

The guys finally retreat, but not without having a glaring competition first. You can feel the tension in the air as mom goes to dad, and he tucks her into his side, holding her tightly. I realize he's being possessive. I can see it in his stance, the way his eyes look dangerous, and you can feel the electricity buzzing around them. He's protecting what's his.

For the first time ever, I see my dad in a different light. He reminds me of Dekker. Possessive, domineering and will protect what's his at all cost. I never did tell Mom about the bar incident, but I did tell Nina. I realize now Dekker, and my dad have similar character traits. It's sweet, romantic, and it makes me miss Dekker even more.

The drama fades away, and my parents share a shameless kiss with too much public ass grabbing.

"All right, enough smooching. Don't you know you're in front of young children? You're hurting my eyes," I state, making Nina burst out laughing.

My parents chuckle, splitting apart.

"Okay, we'll keep it PG for now, and save the rated-R version until later," Dad whispers to mom.

Oh, good Lord!

"What are you doing here?" Mom finally asks.

"I'm here for the show."

"What show?" Nina pipes up first.

"You'll see," Dad says with a smirk.

"When does it start?" Mom asks.

"Oh, in about thirty minutes."

"All right, on that note, I'm starving. I haven't had breakfast or lunch. I need some fries, and maybe a hotdog. Anyone else hungry?" I ask.

Everyone grins at me, nodding yes, and my parents offer to get everything.

"Don't forget to get extra ketchup!" I shout as they're walking away, and Nina giggles.

"Your parents are cool and so in love. And well, your dad is totally—"

"Don't you dare say my dad is hot, or I'll kick your butt," I warn, cutting her off, and she laughs.

"My lips are sealed."

I roll my eyes, shaking my head. My dad is a good looking man, I will admit. He has taken care of himself, and it shows. I guess some ladies would consider him hot. Just don't say that in front of me. It's too weird, and kind of gross.

"You know, I've been meaning to ask you, I would love to do a mommy and baby photoshoot after you've given birth."

"Really?" I state, surprised.

"Yeah, really, and it would be on me, but you know what would be really hot. Doing a session where you're almost ready to pop. They always turn out so gorgeous."

"Yeah, maybe," I shrug my shoulders, feeling depressed, and Nina takes my hand.

"Don't worry, Kinsley. Your mom and I will be there every step of the way. You won't be alone.

"I know, and I appreciate that. It's just—" Nina squeezes my hand when I can't finish my sentence. No one will ever be able to replace Dekker.

My parents come back twenty minutes later with a tray of food, and as soon as it's within smelling distance, my mouth starts to water.

"All right, who's hungry?" Mom asks, grinning at me.

"Me! Me!" Everyone laughs, but I don't care. I'm ready to chew my arm off.

Mom hands me a hotdog, and fries with a ton of ketchup packages. By the time everyone else is eating, I'm almost done my hotdog, but I've been eyeing that chocolate milkshake sitting by Dad.

"Who's that for?" I finally brave asking, and Dad chuckles.

"For my one and only pumpkin."

"Oh, thank God, or I might have had to wrestle you for it."

Everyone cracks up laughing, and even I snicker. I think I'm turning into this starved crazed pregnant woman.

I take a few slurps and moan. *Soooo freaking good!* I start on my fries after emptying a dozen packages of ketchup on them when I realize something strange is going on. People are getting to their feet, standing and gathering in groups. Some are pointing behind us, others are whispering, and well, everyone is staring.

I'm about to turn around to see what everyone is looking at, when a guy dressed in a black tuxedo appears on my right side. I watch him come around and stand in front of me. He's holding a single red rose in his hand, and then kneels down, holding it out for me.

I glance at Nina. Her eyes are big as saucers and then my parents. They are both smiling. I look back at the man who looks ready for a wedding.

"Is this for me?" I question.

"Yes, ma'am."

I take the rose, and the guy stands, giving me a slight bow before walking away on my left side. When I turn my head back to glance at the red rose, another guy appears on the right, wearing the same tuxedo, and holding another single red rose. He kneels down, handing it to me and is gone a moment later when another guy appears. After the sixth rose, my heart rate starts to accelerate, and I reach for my mom, needing her.

"Breathe, sweetie, breathe," she whispers, hugging my back as tears stream down my face. The beach has gone eerily silent, except for the rolling waves you hear for background noise, and everyone watches in awe. One by one, I'm handed twenty-three single roses until the man I love more than life, stands before me.

CHAPTER TWENTY-NINE

Dekker

Twenty-four hours earlier.

I sit in my office chair, staring at the two cards Kinsley has made for me. They stand on my desk, collecting dust but if anyone dares to touch them, I'll break their fingers. I've even told the cleaning staff that if they move them, they can look for a new job.

I sip my whiskey. I'm on my third glass, and by the time I'm done, the bottle will be half gone. I drink to numb this fucking ache in my chest that won't go away.

The only light turned on is the one sitting on the corner of my desk. It's faint, but it's enough to see her cards. I look at them at least a dozen times a day. Occasionally, I'll bring the card up to my nose to take a sniff. It smells like roses. Just like her.

Christ, I'm losing my mind! Who goes around sniffing fucking cards?

I chug the rest of my whiskey, slamming the crystal glass down on the solid desk. The rest of the office remains in darkness, and that's how I feel. Like I'm in some kind of dark, murky pit with no light.

Someone raps on my door, and I grit my teeth, glancing at my watch. It's quarter to eleven. *Who the hell is in my building at this time of night?*

"Fuck off. My office doesn't need cleaning," I bark, not even attempting to be civil.

The door opens, and I'm ready to rip someone a new asshole. Jonas steps inside.

"What the hell are you doing here?" I snap.

"Seeing if my best friend is still a grumpy son of a bitch."

"I am, so fuck off."

He laughs and parks his ass across from me.

"What's this?"

He goes to pick up Kinsley's card and I lose it. I bare my teeth, flying out of my seat and snatching them up before he touches them.

"Whoa, dude. You need to get laid or something. Seriously, what's your deal? You have been a miserable prick ever since a certain redhead left."

"Don't talk about her!"

"All right, Eric, because I'm your friend and probably your only one at this moment, I'm going to pretend you're not being a grade-A asshole to me. Spill it. What happened between the two of you, and I'm not leaving until you tell me."

Fuck, I am an asshole.

Maybe if I tell him, it will help. You know, the whole closure thing. I pour two fresh glasses of whiskey before reciting the night I left him at the bar to meet up with Kinsley. My plans for that night, and how everything went from great to the shits after her confession. When I'm done, I sit back in my seat, waiting to hear what he thinks. What I get in return makes me see red. Jonas slaps his knee, doubling over, and laughing his ass off.

"I'm glad I can amuse you. Want to tell me what's so fucking funny?!"

"My God I can't believe you're that gullible, and how did you get to be the CEO of this company?"

"Watch it, Jonas. You're skating on thin ice," I bite out.

"Dude. Did you actually buy that bullshit lie?" I grit my teeth, ready to spring out of my seat. Friend or not. He disrespects me one more time and I'll throw his ass out the door. "All right, all right, cool your jets. I can see you want to kick my ass, but seriously, Eric. Tell me, what woman doesn't like her pussy eaten? Come on, man, she lied to you, but not for the reason you think."

"Why would she do that?"

"To hell if I know. I'm not a woman."

"Okay, let's say you're right—"

"I am right," Jonas cuts me off, and I clench my jaw.

"All right, Mr. Know It All. Help me figure this out and stop pissing me off!"

Jonas laughs, and I pick my glass up, downing it before I blow a gasket.

"Okay, start from the beginning. Maybe that will help."

I rub my face, feeling mentally drained. Honestly, I haven't been sleeping well since Kinsley left, and it's taking its toll. I have been a miserable prick, short and abrupt with everyone since she left. Jonas pours me another glass and waits. I know he won't go until I physically throw him out. I never would. He's a good friend, and I appreciate his loyalty.

I start from the beginning, he doesn't interrupt, and half an hour later, I'm done.

"She's in love with you," he blurts, not holding back.

"I kind of already suspected that. But it still doesn't explain why she lied."

We're both silent for a couple of minutes, and I put my head down, rubbing my temples, and trying to make sense of it all.

"I think I've got it," Jonas says, and my head snaps up, all ears. "She was basically a virgin when the two of you came together, and if you think about it, you were her first real experience. The first time for a woman can hold a lot of sentiment. She is emotionally connected to you, and going down on a woman for her first time will most likely seal the deal. I suspect she was trying to keep you at arm's length—"

"To protect her heart when our deal ended," I finish his sentence, now seeing the bigger picture.

"But I think it was too late for her. The question is, do you love her?"

"Is that why my goddamn chest hurts?" Jonas laughs at my question. "Yes, I love her," I finally admit out loud, and I swear I feel a weight lift off my chest. This must be the big epiphany I couldn't decipher. God, I am a complete moron! I can finally admit without her, I am nothing. She shattered everything I stood for and ruined me for all other women. She showed me that true love does exist, and I just stood by and let my fucking soulmate walk out of my life. Christ, I'm the biggest loser of all, and I certainly don't deserve her. But, goddamn it, she's mine!

Jonas sits back in his seat, stretching his legs out with a smug look of arrogance on his face. *Asshole.* I pull out my cell phone and text Chase, telling him I'll be down in a minute.

"You get that redhead beauty and get your dick ridden all night. Don't come back until you have a permanent grin on your face."

I stand, laughing.

"Thanks, buddy. I owe you one."

"I would like five weeks of holiday time and a fifteen percent salary increase."

"Done. Now get out."

"Dammit! I knew I should have asked for more."

We both laugh as I walk him to the door. We share a quick hug, and I thank him again. Two minutes later, Chase is driving me to Kinsley's place. I hope she hasn't changed the security code, but worst case scenario, I'll have to call her to let me in. I want it to be a surprise, and hopefully, she doesn't kick me to the curb when she opens her door. I was an ass to her, and realize now that all the times she tried to talk to me she probably wanted to tell me the truth. She loves me, but I was a heartless bastard, slamming the door in her face every time.

Chase pulls up to her apartment building forty-five minutes later, and I'm out of the vehicle before he even has a chance to open my door. I punch in her code at the gate, and it unlocks with a click.

"I'll text you when you can leave," I tell him, already heading inside. The hallway lights are on as I race up the three flights of stairs. The only sound I hear is coming from the second floor with a TV on low volume. Other than that, the building is quiet. I get to Kinsley's door and knock loud enough for her to hopefully hear if she's sleeping, but not wake up the entire building. I wait five to ten seconds, getting impatient, so I do it again.

"Kinsley, it's Dekker. Open up," I say this time, hoping that will get her attention, but what I hear next sets my blood on fire.

"Christ, hold your horses," a deep voice responds, and the door opens a second later. "Who the hell are you?"

"Where is she?!"

"Where is who?" he asks, looking dumbfounded, but he's not fooling me.

I barge inside, pushing this overgrown douchebag aside.

"Kinsley!"

"Are you for real?! Get the fuck out of my apartment before I call the cops."

I glance inside her bathroom, and that's when I notice male belongings, not female. I step out, looking around the place. None of her stuff is here.

"Where did she go?" I ask.

"Who?"

"The girl that lived here before you."

"I don't know, man. This place became available three weeks ago. I'd say your girl moved out."

I rub my face with my hands, feeling exhausted and like this is my worst nightmare coming true. Where the hell did she go? I pull out my wallet and count out two grand. The guy watches me like a hawk.

"Sorry for disturbing you." I place the money on the counter, not giving him a second glance. As soon as I'm in the SUV, I dial Trey's number.

"You're lucky I'm working the night shift. What's up, Dekker?"

"I need a favor."

"One that will cost me my job?"

"I need you to run a check on Kinsley Everett. I want to know every credit card or debit transaction she's made in the last two months and anything else you can give me."

"All right, that's simple enough. I'll call you back in ten." He hangs up, and Chase asks me where to.

"Start heading home for now."

Ten minutes pass by, and I'm itching to call Trey, but I restrain myself. Five minutes later my phone buzzes.

"All right, are you sitting down?"

"Why? Did she move to a different country?" I ask, feeling irritated.

"No, not exactly, but she did move back home three weeks ago. She hasn't made any credit card transactions that are questionable, but her parents have."

"Like what?"

"Are you sitting down?"

"Just tell me for God sakes!" I bellow, losing my patience.

"Okay. Don't say I didn't warn you."

The next thing I hear from Trey has my body turning ice cold, and suddenly, I feel lightheaded. I'm sure if I had been standing, I would be on the floor.

"Are you sure?"

"I saw the papers with my own eyes."

"Thanks." I disconnect the call, feeling numb.

I tell Chase to go home and stare out the window. Reeling with emotions, I don't know which to process first. It's one thing to finally admit I love Kinsley, but to find out she's pregnant with our baby is another. I'm going to be a father, and the woman I love is on the opposite side of this country.

Was it to get away from me? Was she going to tell me about the baby?

Chase pulls into the underground parking lot and opens my door.

"Will that be all, Sir?"

"For tonight, yes. I have some things to do, and then I'll be leaving for California tomorrow. I'll call you when I need you."

He nods, and as soon as I'm upstairs, I spend a few hours clearing my work schedule, and I also fill Jonas in.

"Wow, talk about killing two birds with one stone. How are you taking the news?"

"I'm flying out to California tomorrow."

"And?"

"I've got a plan. I'll fill you in later."

"I better be your best man."

"Deal."

"Hot dammit! My boy is growing up."

I shake my head, smiling and disconnect the call.

CHAPTER THIRTY

Kinsley

My lungs seize as I forget how to breathe, but yet, my heart feels like it's going to explode from my chest, beating too fast. This is a hallucination my brain tries to tell me, but I know it's not.

"Ms. Everett, I believe we have some unfinished business to deal with, but I've decided to terminate our original agreement because I have a new offer I'd like to make you. One I hope you will say yes to."

I watch Dekker ease down onto one knee, and my eyes burst with tears as he holds out a single red rose, but it's not just any rose. In the center, holds an exquisite diamond ring.

"Kinsley Maria Everett, I don't want just two months with you. I'm a greedy guy, and I want a lifetime with you, and even then, that won't be enough. I love you. I don't want to spend another minute without you. Will you do me the honors and marry me, Ms. Scarlett?"

I let out a half cry, half laugh, hearing my nickname. I never realized I missed it as well. I glance at my mom and tears are running down her cheeks. I look back at Dekker, and he smiles his brilliant smile, and I'm about to say yes when I remember he doesn't know about the baby.

"I... I have something to tell you first," I whisper.

"I already know, my love," he glances down at my belly, and I'm completely shocked.

"What? How?"

"Haven't you learned you can't keep secrets from me?" he whispers, and I feel my cheeks burn red hot. "We'll discuss that one later," he says with a wink, and I know what he's referring to. That feeling of "*I'm in trouble*," floods me, and Dekker chuckles, being able to read me like a book.

"Well, beautiful, what do you say?"

I'm well aware we have an audience and not just a small one, but I have one more question I need to ask.

"You aren't asking because you feel—"

He cuts me off immediately. "I promise you it wouldn't have made a difference. Let's just say the pot has been sweetened, and it makes me the luckiest man alive."

"Are you sure?" I question.

"Kinsley," he growls.

"Yes! My answer is yes."

A few people chuckle with everyone cheering as Dekker plucks the ring from the rose and lifts my left hand, sliding the ring on my fourth finger. I stare at it for a good thirty seconds. It's beyond stunning. I know it's platinum white gold with a square top holding the most prominent diamond, and around the band contains a smaller scale of diamonds. I'm probably wearing six figures on one finger.

"It's beautiful, Dekker," I say, looking into his eyes. "I've missed you so much," I whisper, tears still flowing down my face.

He holds his arms out, and I lift up, launching myself into his arms. He falls on his butt with my force, but a second later, we are devouring each other in a fiery kiss, I swear we could burst into flames.

A deep rumble erupts from Dekker's chest as he grabs my ass, squeezing harshly and digging his cock into my pelvis. It feels like granite, the hardest I've ever felt, and it wouldn't surprise me if he's on the verge of exploding.

"Excuse me love birds. I hate to break up this reunion, but there are young children around, and I really don't need to see a man groping my daughter. Fiancé or not," Dad says behind us, and I break the kiss, burning red hot.

Dekker smiles, pressing his lips to the side of my temple.

"To be continued, my love," he whispers low by my ear and then stands, lifting me at the same time and placing me on my feet.

I'm so mortified for giving my parents an indecent view that I can't look at them, but a moment later, Mom comes in, giving me a hug.

"I guess you don't need any more stitches," she whispers. I laugh, and she hugs me tighter. "I'm so happy for you, sweetheart. You deserve it."

"Thank you, Mom," I whisper, tears threatening to spill. My heart is whole again and bursting with love.

Dad comes in next, wrapping his arms around me.

"Well, I guess you won't be needing that sliding door or nursery after all."

I cave, breaking down, realizing my parents were over the moon excited and genuinely looking forward to the new baby. Especially my dad.

"I'm sorry," I cry, hugging him tighter, and he shushes me, telling me everything is fine.

"What's going on?" Dekker steps in, putting his hand on my lower back with a worried tone.

"It's nothing. I was just telling my daughter how super proud I am of her, and how Karlie and I are happy for the two of you."

"I'm sorry. I forgot to introduce everyone," I say, wiping my tears for the hundredth time. "Dekker, I mean Eric, these are my parents, Karlie and Graham. Mom, Dad, this is Eric, but I call him Dekker. Don't ask me why," I say of introductions, and then I see Nina peek her head out from behind my parents. "Nina!" I step around my parents, taking her hand and pulling her beside me. "Dekker, this is my good friend Nina. Nina, this is Eric or Dekker or whatever you want to call him."

Everyone exchanges pleasantries, shaking hands, and I glance around, still seeing people watching, mostly women eyeing Dekker, but at least the majority of the crowd has dispersed.

"How did you know where to find me?" I ask, realizing Dekker must have had this all planned.

"I received a tip," Dekker smirks, looking at my dad, and everything falls into place. I was the show Dad was referring to. That's why he showed up, and I can almost bet he filled in Mom when they left to get food.

"If you don't mind, Mr. and Mrs. Everett, Nina. I would like to steal my fiancée away. We have some catching up to do."

My cheeks warm, feeling a little embarrassed, knowing what catching up entails. Mom and Nina grin, but my Dad looks a little stone-faced as he stares at Dekker. Although, Dekker doesn't seem to be fazed by it.

"Will you two come for dinner tomorrow?" Mom asks and I glance at Dekker, unsure what his plans are.

"We would love to," he answers.

"Great. Is five too early?"

"That will be perfect," he assures her.

"Nina, you're welcome to come to," Mom invites, and she says to count her in.

I pack up my stuff, throwing my dress over top, and stuffing a few cold French fries in my mouth before we leave. Nina laughs.

"What? I'm still hungry," I remark, eyeing the bag of chips, and everyone chuckles.

"Have I been replaced already?" Dekker jokes behind me.

"Let's just say her appetite has been expanding," Mom tells him.

Dekker looks at the food sitting on the blanket, and suddenly I feel like a pig.

"Salty?" I nod, and I'm sure my cheeks are bright red. "May I?" he asks, kneeling down to pick up the bag of chips.

"Of course," Mom answers first.

"All right, my love, ready?"

I nod, and everyone gives me a hug, congratulating us, and Mom reminds us again to remember dinner tomorrow.

"Take care of my daughter. She's my one and only pumpkin, and if you break her heart again, I will break your face."

My mouth drops wide open, hearing Dad's bold statement. Even Mom and Nina have shocked expressions.

"I wouldn't dream of it, Mr. Everett, and I appreciate your direct approach."

He juts his chin out in a nod, and Dekker bows slightly, before pushing me along. I wave goodbye, and soon a black limo comes into view.

"You rented a limo?"

"I did."

"Wow. You really went all out."

"You deserve nothing but the best. I'm sorry it took me this long to come to my senses."

"Am I in trouble?"

He laughs. "Just a little, but don't worry about that now, Ms. Scarlett. Right now, I'm going to fuck you in the limo, hard and fast, because I can't wait another second to be inside you."

As we approach the limo, I can't help but wonder if he was with another woman while we were separated.

"The answer is no," he says, causing me to frown, and not understand. "No, I haven't been with another woman since you," he elaborates.

"Did I say that out loud?" I question, and he chuckles.

I shake my head as we come up to the limo, and a man holds the door open, giving us a nod, all decked out in a driver's uniform. I climb inside with Dekker behind me, and he immediately closes up the partition between the driver's seat and us. As soon as his hands are free, he pulls me onto his lap, gathering my dress and removing it. My bathing suit is shoved down to my waist seconds later, and his mouth latches on to my nipple as his hands squeeze my breasts. He's so fast, I barely have time to breathe, little alone suck in a gasp.

"Christ, I've missed you so much," he says in his deep raspy voice, it only soothes my soul, but when I think about the word missed, it doesn't even come close to what I've felt these last couple of months.

I never knew you could feel so much for one person. I truly felt incomplete. The hole in my heart has been mended, and I hope to God, I never have to feel that again. Dekker lifts his head, looking into my eyes.

"I'm so sorry, Kinsley. I can tell you're millions of miles away," he says, and I realize he's right. "I'm the stupidest man in the world. I'm sorry for how I treated you, or for not giving you a chance to explain yourself. I'm sorry for everything."

"I'm sorry for lying in the first place."

"We'll talk about that later. Right now, I need to see all of you." He lifts me up, placing me down on the seat beside him. "Take off your bathing suit." His voice is full of authority, and suddenly I feel shy.

It feels like forever since I've been naked in front of him, and now I have a small pouch showing, and well, it doesn't help that he's still dressed. He gets down in front of me when I haven't moved. His hands come up, grabbing my bathing suit that's around my waist.

"Up," he whispers.

I lift my hips, and he removes my suit, not taking his dark eyes off me. I lift my leg one by one, until he's tossing it aside. Only then does he allow his eyes to roam, settling on my belly. He lifts up, leaning in, and places a soft kiss on my belly.

"Hello, little one. I'm your daddy. Sorry for being a little late, but I promise I'll be here for you and your mom every day for the rest of my life." His words bring tears to my eyes, and he stretches up, placing his lips on mine. "I mean every word, Kinsley. You own my heart. I love you so much and I can't wait to meet this little one."

"Mom thinks he's going to be a boy, because it looks like I'm already five months along. Apparently, when she was carrying me, she didn't show until she was around five or six months."

Dekker smiles. "You're beautiful, Kinsley, and I can't wait to go through all the stages with you."

"I'm so happy you're here. I have to tell you, I've been dreading the delivery. It scares me," I tell him honestly.

"Don't worry, babe. I'll be by your side every second. I'm not going anywhere."

I give him a nod, and he grins.

"Can I get to the good part now?"

I laugh. "And what's the good part?"

He hooks his arms underneath my legs, bringing my butt closer to the edge, and then spreads them wide.

"Whoa, whoa, whoa, we're doing this now?" I say, covering my pussy with my hands.

"No more talking there, Ms. Scarlett. I should have done this from day one, but I already admitted I'm a stupid man. I have some catching up to do, and it starts now." I groan, flopping my head back on the headrest. "Focus on me and only me, Kinsley, and I promise you, you'll love it."

"No one's ever been down there. It just feels weird or wrong. I don't know."

"It's never wrong, so get that out of your head. And do you know how that makes me feel knowing I'll be your first?" I shake my head no. "So fucking proud. I'll be your first and your last. You're mine, Kinsley. You've always been mine, and I'm going to eat this pussy for the rest of my life because I own it. I own every inch of you, and soon I'll make it legal."

"How soon?" I ask with a brow raise, and he chuckles.

"Real soon, but enough stalling. Remove your hands, or I'll bind your arms behind your back. Last warning."

"Mr. Bossy Pants," I grumble, removing my hands.

"Damn straight, and don't you forget it," he says with a smug smile. Before he can move away, I reach for his face, cupping his cheeks.

"Kiss me first," I whisper, He moves up, and before his lips land on mine, I whisper. "I love you, Eric."

"I love you too, baby."

He kisses me deeply. The kind of kiss that has your heart thumping in your chest, your insides gushing, and leaves you breathless. And my head... it's still in the clouds, trying to digest the last thirty minutes. I know this isn't a dream I've conjured, but it's still hard to believe I get to spend the rest of my life with this man. A man that is technically out of my league, but somehow I've managed to steal his heart.

He releases the kiss only to nip my bottom lip before sliding his lips down, and smothering my neck with fiery kisses. His eyes burn with lust, an intensity that has my nipples pebbling, and moisture collecting between my legs. His hot breath feathers along my skin, making it hypersensitive and he sucks in a bit of flesh by my collarbone. I gasp, feeling a blast of heat surging through me. He makes his way down my front, leaving open mouthed kisses, nipping my nipples, and sucking in each one with added finesse. I moan instantly. My body becomes greedy, absorbing every single touch, and starving for his affection. It's been too long, and my pussy clenches around nothing, desperate for him to fill me. It's pulsating with such force, I swear I'm going to cum any moment.

"Please, Dekker," I beg, chest heaving.

He places kisses on my belly, spreading my legs further, and a moment later his mouth latches on to my pussy as he buries his face.

"Oh God!" I shout, hands flying to his hair as my body jolts, and goosebumps flay my skin.

Dekker grips my hips, digging his fingers in as he plunges his tongue deep inside me and lets out a fierce groan, pulling back.

"Stupid fucking man. I can't believe I waited this long," he mumbles, kissing my inner thighs, and then dips his tongue back inside, swirling around before giving me a long lick up to my clit.

I gasp, feeling a rush of heat spread through my limbs, into my lower abdomen, and between my legs. My brain scrambles, not knowing how to process these new powerful sensations. I'm not sure if I want to run away, or grind my pussy into his face harder. They're overwhelming, and I squirm, unable to sit still, the pleasure building at lightning speed. I always knew Dekker had a skillful tongue, but he brings the meaning to a new level.

"Jesus, you taste exquisite."

He teases me, blowing on my clit and changing it to quick lashes of his tongue, from different angles, adding pressure and various speeds. I can't keep up. My breathing turns choppy as I struggle to stay afloat, the pleasure is extremely intoxicating. There's not one part of my body that isn't throbbing, and soon my muscles are tensing, ready for a release.

Dekker picks up on my body language, stiffening his tongue, and flicking obsessively. I reef on his hair harshly, giving into the tsunami of pleasure that has me detonating. I scream his name as waves of ecstasy all but consume me and I shake violently. It's blinding, seeing white spots dance before my eyes, my climax is that intense.

"Breathe, Kinsley," I hear Dekker say and I suck in air, not realizing I was holding my breath.

My heart rate starts to slow, and I peek my eyes open. A beautiful grin greets me and my body flushes with warmth. His hair is messy, having a tousled look, and I can't help but giggle.

"I suppose my hair is standing on end?" I snicker again as he runs his fingers through, taming it. "Yeah, you yanked on my hair pretty good. Next time I'll restrain you, or at this rate, I'll have no hair left." I laugh again, and he chuckles.

"All right, my naughty little minx. I suspect we'll be at the hotel in five minutes, but I'm an impatient man. I need your hot, tight pussy wrapped around my cock now."

He unbuckles his belt, zipping down his zipper and lifting up to pull his pants and boxers down mid-thigh. I see somewhere along the lines he lost his tuxedo jacket.

"Turn around, beautiful."

He reaches for me, turning me around so I'm facing the seat with my knees on the ground, straddling his legs. It's basically the reverse cowgirl style as he lowers me down onto his cock, and my body quivers, feeling every solid groove as my pussy gets stretched to the max, accommodating his size.

We both let out a lengthy groan when he's rooted deep inside, holding our position.

"Christ, how the hell did I get so lucky?" he rasps.

As my body immerses with tingling sensations from head to toe, I find myself asking the same question. He lifts my hips, signaling it's time to move and sets a pace that has me a little surprised.

"That's it, baby, nice and slow."

I figure he would have preferred hard and fast, but that's one of the things I love about Dekker. He's unpredictable. His hands wander, letting me take over, and they first land on my protruding belly.

"You're so beautiful," he murmurs softly, causing a shiver to skitter down my back. He continues upwards, cupping my breasts with gentle squeezes until he tweaks my nipples. I whimper, loving the feeling he creates with each touch. I only crave more with the intensity rising. "So incredibly sexy." He moves up until his hand is wrapping around my throat, adding a bit of pressure. It only heightens my endorphins as he leans in, so his chest is against my back.

"Mine," he snarls at my ear with authority that sounds dangerously hot, I almost cum again. "Fuck my dick like you own it, Ms. Scarlett."

He urges me to move faster, and I do. His possessiveness is highly erotic as I clench around him, and he hits my g-spot every time, but I'm barely hanging on by a thread.

"Please," I beg, needing to cum, but I know better. He's in control now.

"Not yet," he growls, and I almost weep, desperate for a release, but thankfully, he doesn't make me wait much longer. "Now," he commands seconds later, driving his hips upwards, and adding more pressure around my throat.

I cry out, instantly letting go and seeing those white spots flash before my eyes.

"Fuck!" Dekker booms, releasing his grip around my throat as his voice echoes off the walls of the limo, and I continue to convulse, my climax completely annihilating me.

I finally slump over, laying my head against the cool leather seat, trying to catch my breath and slow my heart rate down. *So good.*

"You still with me, beautiful?" he asks, rubbing my back.

"Always," I remark, not moving.

"Good answer, my love, but we need to get dressed. We're here, and I'm not showing the world how sexy my soon-to-be wife is naked."

Hearing him say, soon-to-be wife, heats my skin all over again. It still feels like I'm in a dream-like fantasy. Dekker slides on my dress, not worrying about my bathing suit, and moments later, the passenger door opens. I look up, seeing the Ritz Carlton hotel. Of course, I've never been here. It's for the first class, and it's hard to believe I'll be a part of that life. I'm marrying a billionaire. That in itself is difficult to wrap my head around.

Doesn't that kind of fairy tale only happen in movies or books?

But that is my life. A fairy tale filled with love, affection, and devotion from New York's most coveted bachelor, Eric Dekker.

A man that's dangerously gorgeous, a master in the bedroom, and he is all *mine.*

EPILOGUE

Dekker

A year and a half later

I'm startled awake hearing a loud screech, and I bolt upright. Kinsley groans beside me, rolling away to lay on her belly. *Always a belly sleeper.* I glance at the clock that's glowing green numbers in the darkness, seeing it's shortly after one. I rub my face, wondering if I'm hearing things until I hear some gurgling sounds coming from the baby monitor on the night table.

I smile, shaking my head. I turn off the monitor so it doesn't wake Kinsley, and slip my boxers on. I pad next door to the culprit making all this noise, and as soon as I open the door, Gavin squeals, seeing me, bouncing up and down on his bum. I chuckle softly, my heart bursting with love as I move in to pick him up.

"What are you doing awake, you little turkey?" I whisper softly.

He coos, all smiles with his chubby little legs and arms moving a mile a minute while his vibrant green eyes shine, bright as ever, and clearly determined not to sleep. I think he ate too much cake and is still on a sugar high.

I take a seat in the rocking chair, rocking back and forth and patting his little bum. Our boy turned one today, and we had a small gathering to celebrate his first birthday. We all helped blow out his first candle, and Kinsley got all teary-eyed, realizing our baby boy is growing up too fast, and I can't disagree.

This last year and a half have flown by with two life-altering changes, I'll never forget. First, marrying the love of my life, and second, watching my baby being born. Both days were unbelievably incredible, and I'll admit, both times brought tears to my eyes.

After surprising Kinsley in California and proposing, I swept her away to Fiji the following weekend to get married. Initially, she wanted to wait until after the baby was born to get married because she was showing already but I wasn't having any of it.

I told her we're not waiting, to me she's barely showing, but if it helps, she can wear a burlap sack for all I care. I'll marry her a million times over. She huffed, rolling her eyes, knowing she didn't have a say, and then she called me a control freak. I told her she loved it and to stop complaining. She proceeded to stick her tongue out, like the little she-devil she can be, and then dares runs away, knowing she was in trouble. She didn't get very far as I pounced on her, bending her over the couch's arm and slapping her ass with my hand until it was flaming red and my hand was stinging. She was so damn wet afterwards, that I nearly blew my load as soon as I slammed into her.

This woman was made for me.

The following weekend, I flew her parents, Nina, Jonas, Trey and even Chase, to meet us for our wedding ceremony. I would have liked to have spent at least a couple of weeks here for our honeymoon before returning to reality, but unfortunately, I could only free up a few weeks in a short amount of time.

Kinsley cried, seeing our lavish suite where I spared no expense, having our own private pool off our bedroom, overlooking the ocean. She spent the whole week picking out her wedding dress. The next day we were to be married, Nina was Kinsley's matron of honor and Jonas was my best man. I stood by the rose-embedded archway on the beach, waiting on pins and needles and when Graham walked out with Kinsley on her arm, I almost dropped to my knees, overwhelmed with emotions and choked up with tears.

Kinsley wasn't dressed in a traditional white dress. No. She surprised me in a stunning A-line wedding gown with a sweetheart neckline, handcrafted red roses sewn along the bottom of the train, intricate red lace trim and embroidered beading sequins. She looked like the Queen of Hearts, my fiery red goddess. And what made Kinsley happy, she didn't look pregnant. I wouldn't have cared if she was nine months pregnant. She's stunning.

The wedding day was more than perfect, and I chose "You Are The Reason" by Calum Scott and Leona Lewis, the duet version, as our wedding song, and when we danced to our first song as husband and wife, I knew my life was complete.

That night, I finally claimed Kinsley's gorgeous derriere— starting off with a bit of a rewind, one bottle of champagne and a bowl of strawberries. Kinsley flushed crimson red when I finally got to insert the strawberry into her pussy and then feast on the berry afterwards. Always so deliciously juicy. After much needed foreplay, and priming her as much as possible, I inched forward until my length was buried in her ass. Although it was incredible for both of us, I realized very quickly I preferred her pussy. Something I never thought would have been possible, but I should have known. My redhead beauty shattered everything I knew and stood for right from day one.

After finding out what Graham's plans were for Kinsley, the nursery and what he already bought, it was more than evident her parents were excited about this baby, and I knew something had to be done. After having a lengthy conversation with Kinsley's parents, they finally agreed to move to New York. I found Graham a job in construction as he was adamant he still wanted to work, and Karlie decided she was interested in doing some voluntary work at the children's hospital. I even offered to move Nina here. She was more than agreeable and super ecstatic, because the girls had developed a tight friendship over the last few months, and I knew having her parents and Nina here meant the world to Kinsley. I even bought Nina her own studio shop, and sent a few clients her way to get her business up and running.

Upon returning home to New York, the media went berserk with my marriage to Kinsley. The news was leaked to the press even before we made it back home and the leeches even discovered this was my permanent residence. It was a little touch and go for the first couple of weeks with the media and paparazzi camping outside my building, front and back, to catch a glimpse of one of us. It was so bad that I had to hire extra security, and Kinsley didn't leave my place for four days straight, but eventually, we became old news and things calmed down.

I finally told Kinsley about my parents, and asked her if she was interested in meeting my mom. Of course she was, and the next day we went for a visit. I would have loved for my mom to be at our wedding, but with her medical condition, the doctors advised it was unsafe as you never know when she'll have an episode or how long it will last. Instead, we brought tons of pictures, hoping today would be a good day. But when we got there, my spirits instantly dropped. She remembered me as the boy who brings her beautiful flowers occasionally, but not her son. I introduced Kinsley as my wife and that we were expecting a baby boy in March. My mom, Lucinda, congratulated us, saying babies are precious and a gift from God.

Kinsley squeezed my hand and made an awkward situation comfortable. She suggested we take a walk outside and enjoy some fresh air. My mom was more than thrilled, and she sat in her wheelchair as I wheeled her around because she's too weak to walk on her own. We didn't get very far when my mom said something, making me stop dead in my tracks.

"Let's just hope he isn't a little hellraiser like you were, Eric. You always loved scaring the bejesus out of me."

And just like that, her memory was back. I teared up and was quick to tell her I love her so much, and I miss her terribly, but she reminded me she's always with me, here in my heart, even when it appears she's not.

We spent the next two hours touring around the immaculate sculpture gardens this facility has to offer, and in many ways, this place feels like a resort with a twenty-foot tall water fountain as the main attraction. We talked a lot, catching up, and we showed her dozens of wedding pictures. My mom cried softly, staring at one of our photos, and it suddenly occurred to me that this is probably hard for her, considering she's still married, but has a husband that abandoned her.

"I'm sorry, mom. I wasn't thinking."

"No, no. It isn't that at all. I'm just so very proud of you, Eric. You're a dashing young man with a level head on your shoulders, a heart of gold, and you couldn't have picked a better woman to spend the rest of your life with."

Upon returning to her room, Kinsley showed her how to make a homemade card from scratch. I watched the two of them bond together, and Kinsley made her a card with a sunflower in the center, and writing, "forever in our hearts."

From then on, we made a point of visiting my mom every other week. When she didn't remember us, Kinsley was amazing, keeping her occupied with some type of craft, and Mom even taught her how to knit a quilt. She even made us a baby blanket with grey elephants with blue ears and colorful butterflies.

Kinsley returned to work as my personal assistant, and our five o'clock meetings resumed. There have been dozens of times where I bent her over my desk or took her against the glass pane wall, mid-day, unable to keep my hands off her. My appetite for her continues to grow to this day. Her pussy is like the Holy Grail that I covet twenty-four, seven.

My dirty little minx does like to surprise me occasionally, and once, when I returned to the office with one of my clients after a lunch meeting, I was surprised to find Kinsley wasn't at her desk. Figuring she was in the ladies' room, I directed Mr. Quail to my office, gesturing for him to take a seat in front of my desk. As he did, I pull out my chair, sitting down myself, and when I moved in, I end up kicking something very large underneath my desk. Kinsley let's out the tiniest squeak as my heart thudded in my chest. Mr. Quail knitted his brows together, and I didn't dare move, knowing she would be mortified if I revealed her.

Instead, I cleared my throat, thumping my desk as a distraction for Mr. Quail. It works, and we continue our business conversation from the restaurant. Ten minutes into the discussion, I feel delicate fingers reaching up, undoing my pants, and freeing my swollen erection. I freeze, not knowing what to do as Mr. Quail continues to chat away, and when Kinsley pushes my legs further apart and lifts up to wrap her mouth around my cock, I inhale abruptly, with my body jerking. Mr. Quail stops, asking if I'm okay.

"Hell yes, continue on," I blurt out like a complete moron, and Kinsley takes that as her cue to suck me hard. "Fuck!" I shout, and Mr. Quail stills, eyes shooting wide. "Actually, I apologize, Mr. Quail, but I'm not feeling very well. Perhaps we can continue this tomorrow?"

"Oh yes, certainly. Unfortunately, there is a nasty flu bug flying around. You take care of yourself."

I give him a nod, and thankfully, he sees himself out, closing the door behind me. I push back from my desk, causing my dick to pop out of her mouth, and I watch Kinsley's cheeks flare Scarlett red.

"I'm sorry. I didn't know you and your lunch date were coming back here?"

I can't help but chuckle. My naughty little minx is a force to be reckoned with, and Christ, I love her so goddamn much.

"You know you'll be punished later, but right now, I need to fuck my wife before I cream myself."

At eight months pregnant, bending Kinsley over the desk isn't an option, but she is able to get on all fours. I reef up her skirt, exposing her wet pussy, and slam into her sweet heat. Kinsley bites back a scream with her back bowing and knowing better than to keep quiet. I buck my hips, pounding into her ruthlessly, knowing full well, she's getting rug burn on her knees. But I know my wife loves it rough. Her pussy is tight as ever, and it's not long before she reaches her peak, clenching all around me, and stealing my orgasm like she always does. I'm finding I have very little control when she squeezes the shit out of my cock.

But I can't forget the little stunt she pulled a few months ago. I went to work early that morning because I was closing a huge acquisition deal that's had me on edge for the last week. Kinsley sent me a text message, telling me her zipper was stuck. She needed help. I frowned, looking at the time. It was seven-thirty in the morning. I knew she was getting ready to take Gavin clothes shopping this morning with Nina because he's growing like a bad weed. I shrug it off and I told her to come. I continued reading and scrutinizing the legal document before me when the elevator dings two minutes later. The door slides open as I take a gulp of my coffee. Kinsley steps out, and I nearly have a mini heart attack.

I choke on my coffee instantly, pushing away from my desk so I don't spray it all over the document I've been working on for months.

"Fucking hell, Kinsley, you made me choke on my coffee!"

The dirty little minx smiles, swaying her hips as she draws closer. She's sporting a red and black lacy teddy with cups that barely cover her tits, and black, thigh-high stockings with a garter belt. She even painted her lips a deep red.

Christ, I will never tire looking at my wife. She is smoking hot!

"Well, I was hoping you can choke me on your big fat cock," she purrs out seductively, and I nearly cream my pants.

I hiss, pouncing on her and in a flash, I have her bent over my desk. At this point, I don't fucking care if my legal documents get destroyed. I remove my belt, and Kinsley shivers, anticipating what's coming. I don't hold back as I whip her ass, giving her four bright red stripes, and she screams each time, gripping my desk with white knuckles.

"Get on your knees. Make me cum, Mrs. Dekker."

Instead of whining or protesting, she gracefully lowers herself to the floor with a devilish grin. *Bloody hell!* I swear my fiery red minx has a dual personality. One that's sweet and innocent, and the other that's a seductive temptress.

She sucks me into oblivion until I can't see straight, and I take a trip to paradise like I always do, and only

Kinsley can send me there. *Christ, I needed that.* Somehow she always knows when I'm stressed, and she can't be any more perfect for me.

We did a minor house renovation when Kinsley finally admitted that she found my place a little cold, especially when I'm not home. I told her I would buy her a house with a wraparound porch and a white picket fence if that's what she wanted. She laughed and said no, but windows that could open with a balcony that's a hundred and fifty percent childproof and maybe some greenery would be nice. She liked being here because I was a minute away, and I couldn't disagree.

So with the help of some engineers and contractors, we added in a balcony that was twenty feet long and six feet deep with sliding patio doors and mesh screening to have the doors open on a nice day, and I also converted a few of the floor-to-ceiling windows, into regular style with the ability to open and close. Kinsley decorated the balcony, adding lounge furniture, some potted plants, and a rose bush that would grow up a ten-foot lattice. She also added some greenery inside, hung photos from our wedding, and pictures of my mom and the three of us together.

I didn't realize my place was missing all this stuff, until it finally all came together, and I realized it doesn't matter how big your house is or if you own top of the line furniture pieces. If you don't have someone you love to share it with, it's only a house, not a home.

I gaze down at my sleeping boy in my arms and smile, remembering the second greatest day of my life. The day he was born.

It was Monday, the board of directors meeting, and Kinsley was due within a week. She had put on a healthy forty-five pounds and was virtually carrying a turkey around. She only became more beautiful the bigger her belly grew, but I also knew she was having a tremendous amount of back pain these last few weeks, and her feet were swollen so bad, she had to wear flip flops or slippers every day. But she continued to work against my wishes, being a stubborn redhead. I understood though. I know she didn't want to be bedridden and preferred to be by my side at all times, and in a way, I also preferred it so I could keep an eye on her.

Everyone was seated around the boardroom table, having lunch before we started the meeting, and I excused myself, walking out to find Kinsley.

"Hey, did I forget something?" she asks, seeing me.

Lately, she's been having baby mush brain. I smile, handing her bottle of water to her.

"What's going on?"

"You're coming with me."

"But you have a meeting," she remarks, reaching for her desk to help her stand, but I stop her immediately.

"Sit, and don't move."

She frowns, and I start to wheel the chair towards the boardroom.

"Eric, what are you doing?" she starts to panic.

She doesn't sit in on these meetings because, quite frankly, they are boring, but today she is.

"You're sitting in. No more talking," I tell her, opening the door and not giving her a chance to argue.

Her cheeks flame red as everyone turns to look at us.

"You all know my beautiful wife, Kinsley, that's due any day now, and because of that, she'll be joining us."

Everyone says good afternoon or hello, with big smiles on their faces, and more than understanding. Kinsley, on the other hand, isn't too happy, and I'm sure if she could shoot daggers at me, she would. Call me an overprotective, possessive A-hole, but I don't care.

I park her chair right beside me and put my hand on her knee, needing to touch her at all times. Kinsley softens, putting her hand over mine, and we link our fingers together. I start the meeting, discussing the usual stuff, and soon two hours have passed by. Refreshments are brought in with a tray of goodies along with fruits and veggies.

Kinsley lifts up from her seat to grab a chocolate chip cookie, when I hear the strangest sound. I frown, looking around. I swear it sounds like someone is taking a piss. The room goes deathly silent as the sound trails off. I glance at Kinsley that's still in mid-air with a horrified look on her face. I push back from the table, glancing at the floor to see a huge wet spot on the carpet.

"Fuck!" I shout, leaping out of my chair, and gently ease Kinsley back down in her seat.

"Umm... my—"

"I know, sweetheart. Time to go to the hospital," I cut her off. "Jonas!" I bark, looking for my buddy and thankful he attends these meetings.

"On it. I'll be right behind you."

"Okay, beautiful, time to have this baby of ours. Arms and legs in at all times," I say, wheeling her out the door and towards the elevator.

Everyone wishes us luck, and I tell Andy he's in charge. He's second in command as I recently promoted him several months ago to alleviate my workload.

"My purse!" Kinsley shouts and I curse, racing back to her desk and reefing the drawer out of its spot where she keeps it. I dump all the contents, grabbing her purse off the floor.

A few people stick around, holding the doors open or either ushering people out of the way. Chase is outside waiting with the door open when Kinsley has her first contraction.

"Ahh! Fuck!" she yells, trying to double over, holding her belly and her breath.

"Breathe, baby, breathe."

She pants through her contraction, and Chase tells me to climb into the SUV. I frown at first. I was going to pick her up and climb up myself, but I realize it would be too awkward to balance her in my arms. I nod, taking a seat, and hold out my arms. Chase eases her into his and walks her sideways, close enough to make the exchange. As soon as I have her, she lets out a whine, and I quickly manoeuvre her between my legs so she's laying an angle, and I hold her belly, coaching her through the contraction. She has another one before we reach the hospital, and this one causes her to cry out with big plops of tears sliding down her cheeks. Seeing her like this slices my heart wide open, knowing she's in so much pain, and there isn't a damn thing I can do about it.

We arrive at the hospital, and she's wheeled into a delivery room right away. I'm suited up in scrubs, and the nurse confirms she's doing well at six centimeters dilated. Kinsley then asks if it's too late to have an epidural and the nurse smiles, telling her no. She'll get the doctor.

The epidural helps immensely when it finally kicks in, and I see Kinsley visibly relax. The contractions still come every couple of minutes, but they are less intense. Thank God for drugs, and three hours later, she's fully dilated. I would like to say the delivery was easy peasy, but unfortunately, Kinsley cooked a turkey at nine pounds, four ounces, and because Gavin was so big, she tore. I never heard an ear piercing scream like the sound that came from Kinsley. It literally shoved a knife right through my heart, and twisted for good measure. I never felt so helpless as I kissed her forehead, telling her I loved her so goddamn much. The room went silent and moments later, another cry was to be heard. I looked up, seeing our baby boy for the first time, and I choked up instantly. He was wrapped in a blanket and then the nurse handed him to me for the first time.

Kinsley, unfortunately, passed out from pure exhaustion, and the nurse pressed cooling compresses to her forehead and face while the doctor stitched her up.

I sat there completely humble as I counted ten fingers, ten toes, and saw dark blue eyes staring up at me. Once the doctor congratulated us and we were semi-alone, I leaned over kissing Kinsley's lips.

"Wake up, beautiful. Someone wants to meet you."

It took her a full minute to open her eyes, but then she cried a second later as I placed Gavin in her arms.

"You did a phenomenal job, baby. He's perfect."

"We did," she corrects me.

"We certainly did, didn't we?" I whisper to the perfect little boy sleeping in my arms as Kinsley peeks her head in Gavin's bedroom.

"Does he need a bottle?" she whispers.

I shake my head no, standing and placing Gavin back in his crib, tucking him in. Kinsley joins me, and we both take a moment to admire our son.

"He keeps getting more handsome every day. He's definitely taking after his father."

I have to admit, Gavin is eighty percent me with his dark hair and similar facial features, but I see Kinsley in him as well. I take her hand, leading us out and back to our bedroom. Once in bed, I pull her naked body close.

"I think it's time we make a girl version of you," I whisper low in her ear.

"Really?"

"Mmmhmm. But only if you think you're ready."

"I was born ready."

"Then spread those gorgeous legs of yours, wife of mine. I need **a taste of red.**"

The End

Thank you so much for taking the time to read 'A Taste of Red'.
I really hope you all enjoyed this book as much I enjoyed writing it.

If you loved this book, please consider leaving me a review on Amazon or Goodreads, and spread the word. It truly does help me immensely.

You can find Christine online through the following social media platforms.

Acknowledgments

Thank you to all the readers and friends for taking a chance on me and reading this book. Your support is always appreciated. To my beta readers, your guidance and enthusiasm on this novel were greatly valued. Thank you!

Dedications

I would like to dedicate this book to all the people that have constantly supported me through my writing career, and my husband, Dwayne. You've been with me through every step and always my biggest fan. Thank you, and I love you. Cheers!

Inspiring You

True passion is doing what you love and making that dream come true. Dedication and Patience will make all your dreams come true.

About the Author

Christine Axford Christine Axford is a fictional writer in the Contemporary Romance genre with a dab of humor, a sprinkle of spice, along with some naughty smut.

She's a certified Payroll Compliance Practitioner by day, a writer by night.

She has spent the last seven years reading, writing, and editing her romance novels, giving her characters a tangible spark!

If you haven't checked out her other books, 'His Angel' trilogy series, is currently available on Amazon worldwide, Kobo & Goodreads.

Christine lives and works out of her home in Ontario, Canada, with her husband, son and two rescue cats.

Printed in Great Britain
by Amazon

10334886R00196